KT-426-969

WHO NEEDS MR DARCY?

30130502344019

WHO NEEDS MR DARCY

JEAN BURNETT

ISIS
LARGE PRINT
Oxford

Copyright © Jean Burnett, 2012

First published in Great Britain 2012
by
Sphere
An imprint of Little, Brown Book Group

Published in Large Print 2013 by ISIS Publishing Ltd.,
7 Centremead, Osney Mead, Oxford OX2 0ES
by arrangement with
Little, Brown Book Group
An Hachette UK Company

All rights reserved

The moral right of the author has been asserted

British Library Cataloguing in Publication Data
Burnett, Jean.
Who needs Mr Darcy?.
1. Large type books.
I. Title
823.9'2–dc23

SLOUGH LIBRARIES
AND INFORMATION

ISBN 978–0–7531–9164–4 (hb)
ISBN 978–0–7531–9165–1 (pb)

Printed and bound in Great Britain by
T. J. International Ltd., Padstow, Cornwall

To Jane for giving me the spark.

Acknowledgements

I am indebted to the Bristol Women's Writing Group for their continuous support and criticism. Caroline Hogg, editor, read the manuscript and ran with it. Jane Buchanan, local studies librarian in Bath gave invaluable help with research into Regency Bath. Thanks also to my family and friends for their encouragement.

The adventures
and exploits of the bad
Miss Bennet

CHAPTER
ONE

Pemberley, September 1815

Black does not become me: I am convinced it deprives my complexion of all life. I am one of those pale-skinned, chestnut-haired females given to freckling if I venture out in the sun. I suggested to Lizzie that I might wear something in pale grey, perhaps a frilled muslin threaded with a purple velvet ribbon, at dinner this evening. The look of horror on her face rapidly put an end to that idea. Marriage to Mr Darcy has transformed my once outspoken sister into a model of propriety and mysteriously removed her sense of humour.

"How can you think of going into half-mourning so soon?" she gasped. "Think of the scandal it would cause." I lowered my eyes so that she could not see the gleam in them at the prospect of a little scandal, anything that would lighten the atmosphere here at Pemberley. Spirits were higher on the battlefield at Waterloo.

"I only thought . . . my black dress is so drab. I would not want to embarrass you." I am, naturally, regarded as an embarrassment to the entire family. Miss Georgiana Darcy looks down her long, aristocratic nose at me. I am not fooled by her reputation for sweetness.

"Are you *quite* comfortable in your rooms, Mrs Wickham? We all feel *deeply* for your loss, Mrs Wickham." She sneers elegantly at my poor apparel, as if I did not know of her previous entanglement with my late, unlamented spouse. If only Wickham had successfully enticed her away and married her. I would not then have attached myself to him. I might have set my cap at a wealthier and less indifferent officer.

I loved him once. He was my handsome hero for a while, until I realised that money was the only thing he cared about. I can hear his voice still.

"I bought you, my dear. Ten thousand pounds if I would make an honest woman of you." Except that I am no longer honest. Wickham saw to that. These thoughts tumbled through my brain as Lizzie patted my arm awkwardly.

"You need not worry about anything, Lydia dear, while you are under this roof — least of all your wardrobe." I smiled gratefully as she left the room. Peering out of the window, I saw my brother-in-law riding up to the house. I must contrive to meet him alone so that I may persuade him to make me a small allowance. Then I might retire to the continent and begin to live. Paris! Paris is calling to me like a siren song. If I could live in the city of amour and splendour among all the nations gathered there, what opportunities might I find? The number of officers gathered in that wonderful place is unimaginable.

Naturally, I shall suggest Calais to Darcy. I hope that the prospect of being rid of me will be an inducement. I need only a little time to work my feminine wiles upon him, although he is not an easy subject. His eyes bulge slightly when he looks at me, but this may be due to exasperation rather than to any other sentiment.

Now I must go to the salon to admire my infant nephew, Charles Fitzwilliam, the heir and pride of Pemberley. Yesterday, when I held the child for a moment the little wretch spewed all over my black dyed tussore, the only respectable mourning gown I possess. I shall prevail upon Lizzie to lend me her black silk with the lace trim and the treble flounce. It is the least she can do in the circumstances. I swear the housekeeper is better dressed than my poor self.

I have been sorely tried since I arrived here a mere seven days ago. I had barely settled before I was being quizzed by Darcy as to the whereabouts of my husband's corpse, his final resting place.

"Where have you buried him?" he demanded. His eyes bulged on that occasion too. Perhaps it is a family trait.

"I will be happy to give you a full account of my grievous trials and the whereabouts of my poor husband's body," I replied. With hindsight, the dazzling smile I bestowed on him was not wise in the circumstances, but at least I had the forethought to bury Wickham in Brussels, saving the family additional expense and inconvenience.

Thus I find myself in this predicament: homeless, lacking in personal possessions, and with nothing but an army pension scarcely sufficient to keep a mouse in cheese. Of course, I told everyone that my husband died a hero's death. My brother-in-law looked unconvinced, as far as one can detect any expression on his face.

In fact, my husband was ingloriously trampled upon by his own horse, its reins having become entangled around his scabbard. These details were given to me by an eyewitness. I am only surprised that he had not gambled the beast away before the battle.

Ah, Waterloo — or rather, the eve of Waterloo. The glory, the dancing, the excitement! Of course, I know the loss of life was dreadful, and we were all in the most appalling state of fear and shock afterwards, but it was all so . . . *thrilling*.

The Duchess of Richmond's Grand Ball was the most marvellous and magical event of my life thus far. I cannot imagine anything greater happening to me unless I can contrive to be presented at court. I know the Prince Regent always has an eye for a pretty woman and now that he has grown tired of Mrs Fitzherbert, that other widow, I might have a chance. But I digress.

The first thrill was in actually obtaining a ticket for the ball. In the normal way we would never have been invited, but during that week Wickham was experiencing one of his rare runs of luck at the card tables. The invitation was accepted from another officer in the 5th Inniskillen Dragoon Guards who could not pay his gambling debt to my husband.

It was extraordinary, I recollect, because I had also been modestly successful at cards so that I was able to purchase the lilac silk gauze gown with deep lace border, and dark blue velvet cape, that were so much admired at the ball. Wellington himself was heard to remark, "Who is that pretty little thing?" before returning to the arms of silly Lady Frances Wedderburn-Webster. Men say she is alluring but I cannot see it myself.

I am aware that we should have spent the money on clearing some of our debts but such an opportunity occurs only once in a lifetime.

It is true that the gowns of the ladies were completely overshadowed by the red coats and magnificence of the men in uniform, but I was very satisfied with my appearance, despite the excessive heat in the ballroom.

How wonderful, how glittering were the surroundings and the company on that night. When I think of the occasions when we danced cotillions at the assemblies in Meryton, I am filled with shame that I ever thought them elegant, or the company anything other than dreary clod-hoppers of the most parochial kind.

My dance card was filled all evening and I barely saw Wickham who was occupied with gaming in one of the ante rooms, to our mutual satisfaction. The Prince of Orange actually asked me to dance. I cannot describe my feelings at that moment. I was quite transported with joy. He had mistaken me for the wife of a General. Nevertheless, he was most gracious.

Entertainment was provided by Scottish dancers from the Highland regiments dancing merry reels to the sound of the pipes. The atmosphere of gaiety was, I suppose, tinged with desperation. So many of those gallant officers would be lost in a few hours or days. However, I had only Wickham to lose and that would be a blessing to both of us. I think my husband was ill at ease with himself and bitter with lost hopes and thwarted desires. For myself, I had spent three years learning the truth of the old adage, "Marry in haste, repent at leisure."

Despite the splendour of the evening it ended all too soon as groups of officers departed to take up their battle positions and the duke himself left the ballroom.

When we emerged into the splendid Grand Place in Brussels just before dawn the anticipation was almost tangible. The shouts of the soldiers and the beat of the drums mingled with the sound of trumpets and the wailing of the Scottish pipes. Women cried out from nearby houses as the men prepared to leave, news having come of Napoleon's advance. I bade farewell to Wickham who was in a strange mood, defiant and resigned simultaneously. He was even prevailed upon to give me what remained of his winnings.

"It's all up with us, my dear," he told me. "The little emperor is nearby with a huge force." He kissed my cheek and rode away to Quatre Bras. I, however, had every faith in Wellington. He would see us through.

And so, after the bloodshed and dust of battle, the burying of the dead and the final farewells, I returned to Pemberley trailing widow's weeds and anticipating Paris. You must not think me hard and unfeeling, dear reader. I mourned the loss of life at Waterloo as we all did. I would not have wished Wickham dead. But I could not help being glad that we would not meet again.

Naturally, my family disagreed with my plans.

"My husband will never allow it, Lydia, you may be sure. France, indeed! How will you manage there? You do not speak a word of the language. Now if you had applied yourself when our father was instructing us . . ."

I interrupted at this point, not wishing to hear another lecture on my intellectual deficiencies from my bluestocking sister. I am very fond of dear Lizzie but I am amazed that someone of only average looks, and overly fond of reading, should have snared one of the richest and most eligible men in the country. One cannot help feeling a few pangs of jealousy.

"Never fear, dear sister, I shall manage very well. I plan to live quietly in Calais where I understand there is a small colony of the English. My living costs will be greatly reduced in France, and of course I shall apply myself to the language. You will be surprised at my determination when it is necessary."

"I shall indeed," she replied with heavy sarcasm. Ignoring this unfilial display I begged her to speak to Darcy on my behalf, but I intended to snaffle him first. Tactics were required here and I had not spent the last three years among soldiers without learning the basics.

I well remember the occasion when Wickham was almost cashiered for stealing a horse belonging to one of Wellington's Generals who was at the time inspecting the regiment. Wickham managed to hire out the horse for a few hours for a large sum before returning it.

When questioned about the animal's abduction, Wickham had claimed — the effrontery! — that his wife was at death's door and he had seized the nearest animal in order to ride for a doctor. The general chose to overlook the matter on compassionate grounds and I was forced to remain indoors for many days before being allowed out. Even then he obliged me to whiten my face in order to keep up the pretence.

I decided to approach my brother-in-law after lunch. Never ask a favour of a man who has not eaten recently. I dressed with care — I am in mourning, after all. I wore the gown borrowed from Lizzie, which was most becoming. I did not think Darcy would recognise it. He has a better eye for a horse these days. Some discreet jewellery, my deep red garnets, and a soft but tantalising perfume — a spray of essence of lily and clove — completed the ensemble. I prevailed upon Lizzie's French maid to arrange my hair. I do believe that my chestnut curls are my crowning glory. Oh, to have the luxury of a French maid. It is so unfair — Lizzie cares very little for her appearance. She still takes long, muddy walks despite being mistress of this great estate. Wealth is wasted on some people.

After enjoying an excellent jugged hare and a glass of claret I followed Darcy in the direction of the orangery where he invited me to inspect a fine specimen of tiger lily lately arrived from India. I made the appropriate noises of admiration before heaving a deep sigh, fluttering my bosom as much as possible. The triple frills moved most satisfactorily. Darcy looked puzzled.

"Are you unwell, Lydia?" I looked up at him coyly and then fingered the red stones at my neck. I noticed that his eyes had fallen towards my bosom.

"I am greatly perturbed about my future, dear brother. I could never be a burden to you or the rest of my family, but my financial state is a parlous one. If I could manage to live quietly abroad on a reduced income I feel that would be the best solution."

"Abroad?" Darcy yelped. He had a horror of all the foreign parts for which *les rosbifs* are noted. (I am already acquiring a smattering of the French language.)

"Oh, yes," I continued. "The cost of living is so much lower on the continent. I might offer English lessons to some genteel French families in order to supplement my paltry income. Do you not agree dear brother?"

At this point I contrived to lift my skirt discreetly so that a glimpse of a trim ankle in white silk hose flashed before my brother-in-law's eyes. This ruse has been known to send men mad with desire. In Darcy's case his eyes began to swivel alarmingly before bulging in the manner I have often remarked upon.

"That will not be necessary," he snapped. "I am prepared to make you an allowance that will enable you to live as a lady should, although not in any great luxury." Did I hear a note of satisfaction in his voice?

"Naturally," I murmured *sotto voce*.

"However," he added, "there is no question of my sister-in-law living alone on the continent, it is unthinkable. Arrangements can be made for you to live closer to your parents at Longbourn." I hope he did not catch the look of horror I could not suppress at this suggestion. Some quick thinking was required. Fortunately, I had been married to a master of devious behaviour for three years. My brother-in-law would be child's play in comparison. I heaved another sigh.

"I could not possibly live at Longbourn, dear brother. My father would not wish it and my mother would be mortified. If you were generous enough to make me an allowance I could not think of leaving Pemberley. I would stay here and make myself useful to my sister and yourself in any way possible. It would be my solemn duty."

I stared mournfully at his face watching the expressions of alarm and disgust passing over them at the prospect. This was my opportunity.

"Of course, I have been offered an invitation for an extended stay with the Caruthers in London, friends from my late husband's regiment. Captain Miles is now retired from the army and his wife, Selena, is a dear friend." My voice trailed away and I watched to see if he would clutch at this straw.

"Well, er, umph," he spluttered, "that is a possible solution." He turned away abruptly. "We can discuss the details later. I have an appointment." He strode off and I gazed after him, sorry that he could not see the face I made at his retreating back. Why must I be treated like a child solely because I am poor and female? If I had a reasonable pension my relatives might disapprove of my removal to France but they could not prevent it. I am a respectable widow — at least for the moment.

London: there could be worse fates for a single woman. It would certainly be an improvement on the army quarters in Newcastle, Longbourn or Pemberley — and it was considerably closer to the continent. Something could be contrived.

First of all I needed to contact the Caruthers and inveigle an invitation from them. We have not spoken for a while but Selena owes me a favour after I distracted her husband one evening to prevent him finding his wife accepting a *billet doux* from his commanding officer.

The next important matter was how much of an allowance Darcy could be persuaded to part with, followed by the question of where I would lodge in the capital. I could not remain forever with my friends and I absolutely refused to be placed under the watchful eye of any relatives. There was always the home of the Gardiners, my aunt and uncle. They are a benevolent couple, but they had disapproved of my marriage to Wickham, and they are far too close to Lizzie and Darcy for comfort. In addition they have no *entrée* into high society and I . . . *I* have danced with the Prince of Orange.

I needed pleasant rooms in a respectable house in a fashionable street, with an obliging but unobtrusive landlady who would act as a sheepdog on occasions when I needed a chaperone. Perhaps I might cross paths with my hero, the celebrated poet Lord Byron, the most infamous man in London. What a delicious thought.

Having thus arranged my immediate future satisfactorily in my mind I wandered towards my room, almost failing to notice Miss Georgiana Darcy emerging from the library, wearing an elegant forest green velvet gown trimmed with leaf green taffeta. I ground my teeth silently as she gave me an all-encompassing regard that took in the borrowed gown and the red necklace.

"Oh, Mrs Wickham, is that gown not excessively elegant? It looks so well on your sister — and on you too," she added, after a pause that could only be described as pregnant. I curled my lip in a semblance of a smile and pointed to the book she was carrying.

"I see you are reading Miss Clara Reeve's new novel, *The Old English Baron*. I was greatly diverted by it and I would be happy to explain some of the more difficult passages to you at any time convenient." I continued on my way with a gay wave of the hand leaving Georgiana with her mouth fallen open in a most unattractive manner.

CHAPTER
TWO

London

I would not wish to give the impression, dear reader, that my transference to London and the obtaining of suitable lodgings were easy tasks. There was a great deal of wheedling, pleading and what can only be described as horse-trading to be seen to before I was able to leave. I confided this to my journal — the only means of expressing my resentment. I pleased Lizzie by agreeing to stop at Longbourn en route for a short time. Very short if I can find a suitable excuse.

Fortunately, the Caruthers came to my rescue. Selena quickly extended an invitation. They have taken up residence in Curzon Street in St James's London. This is quite a fashionable street, I understand, and will serve as a starting point for my adventures. Naturally, I told my relatives that I can stay indefinitely. This met with Darcy's approval as he informed me that he would give me an allowance of three hundred and fifty pounds per year, more than a governess would earn but not exactly riches. What a soul of generosity he is! How many gowns will I be able to buy with that? However, I am not too downhearted. I have plans, stratagems, ambitions. If only they knew of my aspirations. These I confide to my journal where, no doubt, they will be read by posterity in due course.

A woman in my position must fend for herself or be resigned to a life of dull, dragging poverty and boredom as a poor relation, the suppliant in the corner. Such a life would be unbearable for someone of my temperament. Have I not suffered enough these last few years?

I finally made my escape from Pemberley on a bitter cold day in early December. Lizzie was kind enough to bequeath me some of her unwanted wardrobe which I shall alter and make tolerably modish. I was especially grateful for a long, worsted wool pelisse in dark green with fur trimming that would offer me protection from the elements on the long journey south. The green was so dark it was almost black and thus satisfies my sister's sense of propriety. My valise was loaded onto the mail coach by one of Pemberley's footmen, who was escorting me — the one with the shapely calves who has been most attentive to my needs.

After long hours in a public vehicle feeling every jolt in the abominable roads and suffering the companionship of dolts, hags and clergymen, I arrived at Longbourn more dead than alive. I was greeted by my mother with tiresome exclamations of misery and floods of tears at my widowed state. My father gave me a long, hard look and pronounced me "Somewhat improved with age" as if I was one of his precious bottles of claret.

Immediately, I fancied I was back in my childhood again with Kitty begging to share my bedroom and

16

Mary moralising about Napoleon. I was plagued incessantly to recount the details of my stay in Brussels, the ball, the battle at Waterloo and the ghoulish delights of widowhood so that the womenfolk in my family could exclaim and twitter to their hearts' content. My father merely remarked, after a slight pause, that he was glad to hear of my husband's courage on the battlefield. I suspected that, like Darcy, he was not convinced by my version of events.

My mother was predictably delighted to hear of my removal to London.

"What good fortune, my dear and such an opportunity to enjoy the delights of the capital. Your friends will, of course, escort you to the balls and assemblies?"

"She is still in mourning," remarked my father, but my mother was not discouraged. "That situation will not last forever. She is still young enough to marry again. What better place to find a husband, unless it be Brighton?"

I contrived to be on my way as soon as decency permitted with my father's solemn warnings and my mother's advice about bonnets ringing in my ears. Papa had reminded me again of my foolish marriage to Wickham and the potential disgrace it brought upon the family, only averted by the generosity of the noble Mr Darcy.

"You will need to marry again, Lydia. You are only nineteen. I trust you will choose a new spouse with greater care. You cannot expect your brother-in-law to rescue you a second time."

Indeed not, I told myself.

"Think of your sisters," he warned me. I thought it unlikely that my two very plain, portionless sisters would be affected by my behaviour. They were not prime marriage market material. *And neither are you!* rang a voice in my head.

My sister Jane and her husband were out of the district so there was no possibility of being conveyed to London in any style. The prospect of another journey by mail coach was not enticing and it was another reminder of my lowly status, but at least my companions were more agreeable this time.

As we drew near to London a handsome, well-dressed gentleman with dark eyes and a spirited manner conversed pleasantly with me for a while until he decided to "take a turn up top with the horses". Immediately our speed increased to a ridiculous rate and we were tossed about like corks.

Suddenly, we came to a shuddering halt on a quiet stretch of the Barnet Road and everything became very quiet except for the whinnying of the horses. A woman clutching a child began to whimper with fear and presently my spirited companion appeared at the window and, almost apologetically, asked us to get down from the coach.

We tumbled out stiff-legged and weary while the men demanded to know what was happening. Another complained about our reckless speed. The spirited man merely smiled and indicated a rider who had appeared from behind a tree. He wore a kerchief wound around the lower part of his face under his hat. He held a pistol pointed in our direction. I turned towards the spirited man only to find him pointing a pistol at our backs. Highwaymen! Are my misfortunes never to end?

"This is ridiculous!" exclaimed one of the braver male passengers. "The days of highwaymen are over. You are an anachronism, sir, you and your accomplice. Be off with you."

"Alas, my fine fellow, you are right, but we must scratch a living as best we may." With that he raised his pistol and blew the unfortunate man's hat into the trees leaving the poor fellow gibbering with fright.

Thus I arrived in London without my garnet necklace to which I had been so much attached. My pleas to the scoundrels that I was the penniless widow of a war hero fell on deaf ears. They would have our jewellery and would remove it by force if necessary. As I handed him the necklace, the spirited villain even had the effrontery to express a wish that we might meet again, telling me that his name was Jeremy Sartain — "known to my friends as Jerry". The rogue was evidently quite fearless, not caring who knew his identity. He courteously left me my wedding ring — the one object I would not have missed.

I sat fuming in a corner seat as we resumed our journey to London amid much weeping and wailing of women, and harrumphing of men bellowing on about what they would do if they caught the robbers. The prospect of a hanging always fills the English with a sense of well-being. The robbers had made quite a haul of gold coins but I was the only woman on board with any jewellery of value. My companions offered me their sympathy and assured me that the garnets would be trafficked at one of the many "flash" houses in the capital by nightfall. When I looked puzzled they explained that such places were inns where stolen goods were taken and exchanged for cash.

I finally arrived that evening at the Caruthers' house and fell into Selena's arms bewailing the loss of my jewels.

"Alas!" I cried, "I am quite done up . . . *frappé en morte!*" (My grasp of the French language is improving daily.) "What shall I do?" I sobbed, "I have only a few pearls and a small gold cross in which to go out and about in society. I shall cut a very poor figure." Selena laughed and told me not to fret.

"We are giving an intimate party here in a few days. There will be an opportunity for card games and plenty of flippant coxcombs and wealthy witlings to play with. I have chosen them with care. You will soon make good your losses." Thank heavens for good friends. Especially those who are in one's debt.

I was able to write in my journal that evening that Curzon Street has proved to be a delightful spot, at least from first impressions. The sight of rows of tall houses, the traffic of carriages, the cries of tradesmen and the general *life*, combine to lift my spirits. I love cities, the potential for living is so great compared to the empty wastes of rural England.

I am vastly content with Selena and Miles and I am accommodating myself to their small eccentricities. It is obvious that their financial state is almost as bad as my

20

own, but that does not prevent them from living life to the full — a philosophy I have always shared.

Selena was showing a greater fondness for gin and display than I previously remember, but no doubt that is due to her nerves. She takes full responsibility for the running of the household, Miles being amiable but useless for anything off the battlefield. He has been spending too much money on prints of a distracting nature (according to his wife), obtained from a certain Joseph Stockdale, bookseller and coal merchant, who keeps a shop at No. 24 Opera Colonnade which is frequented by most of the ton and lowlifes in the city. Yesterday, Miles showed me his most valued print depicting the Countess Godiva saving the city of Coventry. He was most put out when I burst into a fit of the giggles.

"And the price is . . .?" interrupted Selena. When Miles told her she became faint and went in search of the laudanum bottle.

We have been frantically preparing for the soirée to be held here on the day after tomorrow. It was essential for my hosts to obtain some relief from their many creditors and for me to make some useful contacts, I have agreed to pay a reasonable amount for my board and lodging but I am eager to blossom forth into my own establishment.

The guests have been selected with great care, mainly for their wealth and their bad luck at the card table. Selena gave me exact descriptions of the most likely fellows. I may need to cultivate one for money and another for influence. I am determined to gain entry to a *soirée* at Almack's in King Street, St James's, the acme of society, but I must first find a sponsor. The assemblies at this establishment are frequented by the *ton* and the highest in the land. Great opportunities might come my way if I could but be included in their company.

Selena thought this scheme entirely unnecessary.

"Surely you could like any good humoured man with a comfortable income?" Perhaps she was right and I was aiming too high but I have aspirations.

On the night of the party I decided to appear in half mourning.

"Nobody here will be aware of my circumstances," I told Selena. I wore a gown of pale grey gauze trimmed with violet velvet with a white lace fichu. I borrowed an Indian shawl of the finest work from my hostess. It glowed with deep, peacock blues and greens and purple.

"Arrange your hair a little higher than usual and adjust your bodice a little lower," my friend advised. Indeed, I may lose the bodice of my dress completely should I lean too far forward at the card table, but needs must as the saying goes and one always needs something to distract the other players. Indeed, I may add to the entertainment.

Selena had set off her blonde curls with a gown of white muslin banded with green and gold satin ribbons matching the gold thread binding her hair. My friend's fair, refined looks were much admired, although they concealed a will of iron.

22

I could barely contain my feelings of anticipation mixed with nerves as the hour approached. Miles offered me a little brandy to buck me up but I refused. I must keep a clear head. This could be the beginning of my new life. I am not generally a prey to nerves but I found that I was operating my fan so vigorously that he went in search of the mysterious draught.

The guests began to arrive at nine and we divided the company between two tables. Selena and I were the only females present. I sat at one table and she at the other. I would have enjoyed seeing the expression on Darcy's face at that moment, should he have been able to catch sight of us. Miles took up a commanding position near the window, striking a Napoleonic pose with his arm across his chest and his reddish hair *en brosse*. I think he disliked being out of uniform. Fortunately, he remembered that his task was to keep the faro bank and he quickly took up his position.

The men had already drunk liberally at other establishments and they continued in this way as the evening progressed. My neighbour at the table was a dwarfish, unremarkable fellow who introduced himself as Mr Getheridge. I noticed that he had enjoyed moderate success at the cards and I asked him why he did not continue. As he escorted me to the supper table he said with a slight smile that he was a banker and, therefore, cautious by nature.

"Losing money does not agree with me, madam. I prefer to stop while I am winning."

At the mention of the word banker I began to revise my former opinion of Mr Getheridge. He suddenly appeared less ordinary in my eyes. A lone female should always include a banker or two among her acquaintances.

He kept up a flow of conversation as he procured ices and champagne for me. As I had been required to contribute to the cost of the refreshments, I decided to enjoy them.

"Are you appreciating what London has to offer, madam?" He gave me what can only be described as a leer. Without waiting for a reply he began to sing a few bars of a popular song, "London Town's a dashing place, for ev'rything that's going on". I drew away from him, declaring that I preferred a good book. (This is not entirely untrue, dear reader.)

"I confess I am a lover of the Gothic, sir. A frisson of horror enlivens a tedious afternoon, I find." My companion positively twinkled.

"I find that there are many ways of enlivening a dull afternoon, my dear!" Miles signalled to me at this point and whispered that Mr Getheridge was not only a wealthy banker but also a great lover of women.

"He has a wife and family, but he keeps several mistresses at Brighton and London, in some splendour, I believe. They say he is a very devil between the sheets. You would not credit it from the look of him, would you?"

Miles returned to his duties and I returned to the tables, Mr Getheridge having gone outside for a little air. Selena and I paused to exchange notes behind our fans. Her winnings amounted to three hundred and fifty guineas and mine were two hundred guineas. As we also took a share of the house money we were quite content. We agreed to change tables at this point.

My new neighbour was a certain Lord Augustus Finchbrook, a young man with watery blue eyes, a thatch of pale blond hair and a weak head for wine and brandy. I hoped his credit was good. I was encouraged by his talk of the high perch phaeton he had just purchased, together with the two finest Arabs in the country. I gathered he was referring to horses.

"You must come for a spin in her, my dear Mrs Wickham," he said, slurring his words a little. He leaned perilously close to me as he spoke, peering down at my bosoms. The brandy fumes were almost visibly wafting from his pink ears.

I smiled winningly at him and said that nothing would give me greater pleasure but first I intended to win a large sum of money from him. He let out a neigh of a laugh and then muttered something that sounded like, "A demned fine little filly and pert as they come," before promptly nodding off for a moment.

I poked him in the ribs none too gently before I shuffled the cards. The rattle of dice from Selena's hazard table could be heard in the background. Milord woke with a start and to my surprise he gazed wistfully across the room to where Selena was holding court at the next table.

"That lady has a very purposeful walk," he announced. "Indeed she is so purposeful that I am terrified to approach her. She fills me with alarm." I could detect that my friend filled this young man with other emotions as well as fear. He showed a marked

25

lack of concentration on the game, not seeming to care where or how he played. Meanwhile he continued to gaze across at Selena and I prepared to move in for the kill.

"Will you play to win or lose, my lord?" I asked.

"Oh, I always lose against the house so I shall play to lose," he yawned, quite unconcerned. I proceeded to place the cards as the players made their bets, praying that the pagan gods of fortune would smile on me. I gave the gods some encouragement by using my special cards which were slightly doctored or sanded for the purpose. Wickham had shown me this trick soon after our marriage. Indeed, he knew so many ways of cheating that I cannot understand why he lost so often.

CHAPTER
THREE

"You are enjoying good fortune, my dear." Mr Getheridge suddenly appeared behind me and placed his hairy hand on my shoulder, squeezing it a little as he did so. "I admire a woman who is lucky with money. The gods smile upon you." If only he knew the truth — yes, I would tell him! I turned and gazed up at him, batting my eyelashes.

"Alas, sir, I am merely a poor soldier's widow. I cannot imagine why I have been so fortunate tonight. Those gods must indeed be smiling on me."

Getheridge laughed and indicated the almost comatose Finchbrook.

"I fancy you have found yourself a good mark, Mrs Wickham." I looked outraged and he quickly invited me to take some air in the garden. I refused with indignation but he insisted, whispering urgently into my ear, "You will get no further with this one. Take my advice, whatever you planned for him must wait until he is recovered a little."

I allowed my hirsute friend to conduct me to the garden where he continued to whisper in a conspiratorial manner. "If I do not mistake, you madam, you are in search of something that is my forte. I think I may be able to help you."

"Truly, sir?" I replied, "And what will be the cost?"

"We can speak of that later."

"I have heard that you are not impervious to female charms, Mr Getheridge." A strange expression swept over my companion's face and he seized my arm once more, propelling me back into the house.

"I must leave now, madam, but we must meet again. Come to my office at the bank. I believe we can discuss something to our mutual advantage." He wrote a few words on a card and pushed it into my hand before bowing and leaving rapidly. I saw him bidding farewell to Selena as a newly resuscitated Lord Finchbrook weaved his way unsteadily towards me.

"Oh my fair companion," he called out, "lovely despoiler of my finances! Have you deserted me?" He made me an elegant bow and then almost toppled sideways. I caught him by the arm and restored him to an upright position. Mindful of Mr Getheridge I decided to seize the moment.

"Do you ever grace the assemblies at Almack's, my lord?" I enquired casually. Finchbrook gathered his scattered wits and brushed an imaginary crumb from his cuff.

"I believe I have spent a tiresome hour or two at that establishment, madam. A tedious place full of simpering debutantes and their ghastly mothers — and no strong drink served, I recall." He gave me suddenly a clear-eyed glance and added, "I should not have thought it your kind of thing at all."

I clasped my hands together in a prayerful gesture and assured him that it was the place I most desired to be in all the world.

"But you have not been given the seal of approval by the bulldogs at the gate!" he guffawed, meaning Lady Jersey and the Countess Lieven, the dowagers who vetted young ladies for their suitability.

"Alas, no" I replied, "but perhaps your lordship could assist me in this matter?"

"It is the least I can do after allowing you to win so much money from me."

"Your lordship's logic is beyond reproach."

Unfortunately, at that moment Selena appeared and Finchbrook immediately forgot my very existence and began mooning over her in a quite revolting manner. She appeared not to notice as she whispered excitedly that she had just sold the Countess Godiva print for a third more than Miles had paid for it.

"But surely he will notice its absence?"

Selena brushed this aside. "He will forget about it when he realises that I can now pay his tailor's bill. At the moment he can scarcely leave the house without being molested by his creditors."

I persuaded his lordship back to the card table and proceeded to win a trifling amount from him before he made his farewells.

By this time most of our guests had begun to leave and my mood changed suddenly. Despite the money now stuffed into my reticule I felt curiously let down and chilled although the room was very warm. Perhaps

I had overindulged with ices and champagne or allowed my hopes and dreams to interfere with reality.

These speculations were so unlike my normal self that I feared I was lapsing into a fit of the dismals. I confided as much to Selena who was often a prey to such emotions herself, usually after an over indulgence in the ginevra. We counted our winnings which restored our spirits a little and allowed Miles to congratulate us. He, of course, had lost what little his wife had allowed him.

Later, as I prepared for bed, I found Mr Getheridge's card. Before falling asleep I pondered whether I would visit him at the bank as he had suggested. I also pondered whether I could afford *not* to keep the appointment. In my dreams I was waltzing at Almack's in the embrace, not of a belted earl or duke, but of a large, hairy ape with twinkling eyes.

"You are a beautiful stepper, dear lady," the ape assured me.

My first thought when I awoke next morning was of the dance. As we drank our morning chocolate I announced to Selena that we must take lessons in waltzing immediately.

"I had a dream about waltzing at Almack's last night," I told her. "Everyone swirled around the room in their partner's arms. It was beyond imagining."

"It is still considered somewhat improper in society," I understand," she demurred. My friend can be remarkably conservative sometimes.

"It is becoming more popular by the day," I assured her. Selena was not convinced.

"I have heard that Lord Byron disapproves of it," she said, cunningly referring to my great hero as a way of settling the matter.

The mention of his name subdued me for a moment. I knew that my wild, poetic, dream lover was disgraced in society and it was rumoured that he would soon leave the country for an indefinite stay on the continent. Byron had been ejected from society and I could not gain admission. Our mutual afflictions gave me a warm feeling in the pit of my stomach.

"Nevertheless, I am determined to learn this dance," I said. "The sensation is amazing and the rhythm exhilarating. We must find a teacher this very day." Selena gave in without a struggle and admitted that she knew of a certain Viennese dancing master, Herr Schiffenberger, who would serve admirably.

"We can visit his studio this morning if you wish."

While we were discussing these arrangements Miles was peering out of the window searching for the presence of bailiffs and creditors when he gave a cry of surprise and announced that Lord Finchbrook had arrived in his stylish new equipage.

His lordship burst into the room in a very effervescent manner showing remarkably few signs of the previous night's drinking.

"I beg you, Mrs Wickham, allow me to take you for a spin in the park." I knew he would have preferred to take my friend. He lingered over her hand, caressing it and touching it with his lips in the manner of a stoat savouring a rabbit.

I agreed to accompany him but insisted that we return in time for our dancing lesson. His lordship looked ecstatic, "The prospect of a dancing lesson with two such delightful ladies overwhelms me with joy. I must insist on offering myself as a partner." I glanced at Selena and gave a slight shrug. If the man wished to cling like a leech we should make use of him. After I had perfected the steps of the waltz I would remind Finchbrook of his promise to help me gain entry to Almack's. Selena was not impressed by my ambition.

"Anyone can gain admission anywhere in London if they have sufficient effrontery and a drunken lord to accompany them," she sniffed. "The Duke of Wellington presents his actress friends to the Prince Regent at Brighton." She can be quite hurtful at times.

I reminded her that I was not an actress and that certain of those women had married into the aristocracy. Selena sniffed again. "I have heard that the price of a mistress to the aristocracy is two thousand pounds per year and a down payment of eight hundred pounds — if you are an opera dancer." I thought of my meagre allowance from Darcy and wished that my thespian skills were worth such a fortune.

"You are forgetting, my dear, that my own sister married one of the richest men in England despite having no dowry." In reply she smacked me with her reticule and said that I was a stupid minx for not doing likewise.

Glancing across the room to where Miles was in animated conversation with Lord Finchbrook she smiled and said, "I think we have learned our lesson, have we not? Never be seduced by the glamour of a uniform unless the commander-in-chief is inside it."

When Lord Finchbrook handed me into his phaeton I observed that he was wearing a starched collar so high that it made turning his head an impossibility. As he was chiefly concerned with controlling the horses and staring straight ahead this was not a problem, but as far as conversation went it was disconcerting, if not ludicrous. He was forced to turn his upper body completely in order to look me in the face. It was like being interrogated by an amiable marionette. When I ventured to tease him about this he declared that his valet had taken lessons in the matter from Beau Brummell's valet.

"The only sin, dear lady, is to appear in the wrong clothing at any event."

Finchbrook insisted on referring to me as "the merry widow". He pointed out the various members of the *ton* sweeping by in their carriages. Selena followed in a hired barouche with her maid. His lordship shook his head — carefully — saying that such a carriage did not cut it at all.

Later, we presented ourselves at Herr Schiffenberger's studio for our lesson in waltzing. It was obvious that our escort intended to spend the entire day with us.

We turned our attention to mastering the dance aided by Schiffenberger's assistant who tinkled out a tune on the pianoforte. It proved to be harder than I had anticipated. Not as complex as the cotillion or the quadrille but the rhythm was difficult to catch causing us to jerk up and down as if we were posting on a horse.

"Von-two-tree, von-two-tree!" sang out Herr Schiffenberger waving his arms encouragingly. "Make your circle," he commanded as we shuffled around. After we had fallen over our own feet several times Lord Finchbrook was so giddy from twirling that he was forced to lie prone on the floor for a few moments. The dancing master surveyed us sorrowfully, no doubt he was comparing us unfavourably with the serene waltzers of Vienna.

"Svay into the rhythm, ladies," he implored. "Let us try again. Von-two-tree!" Finchbrook clasped Selena enthusiastically to his breast and I followed, making do with an acned youth who claimed to be Schiffenberger's nephew.

If I closed my eyes I could just imagine myself in a gilded ballroom with violins playing a yearning melody. I am wearing satin and diamonds and a dark face comes close to mine . . . I opened my eyes suddenly to find the spotty youth regarding me with alarm. In my mind I could hear Darcy saying, "So this is how you waste my money."

"Von-two-tree!" screamed Schiffenberger, sweating profusely. "Listen to ze music. You are off ze beat, madam." I was off ze beat in more ways than one.

We left the studio and returned home to recover our strength and change for our next engagement. "I declare my shins are quite black and blue," Selena complained, "Lord Finchbrook's boots found their mark several times."

"Never mind," I replied. "We will soon be able to grace any ball in town."

During the following weeks we occupied ourselves with daily chores, making expeditions to Soho to obtain cough medicine for Miles and triple distilled lavender water for Selena. Christmas and New Year passed and April approached but the weather continued as cold as ever with not the slightest sign of spring. I was forced to obtain more essence of mustard from Whitehead's. I am a martyr to chilblains.

The gloom was only lifted by an announcement in the *Times* that Millard's East India warehouse in Cheapside was holding a cheap day. Selena and I set off to buy muslins and silks before our money disappeared.

"I must spend before Miles has a chance to look for more etchings," she explained.

When I searched for coins in my reticule I found Mr Getheridge's card once more. This time I took a deep breath and vowed to visit the bank as he had suggested.

It was becoming more and more difficult to go about the city in safety. The disastrous state of the economy meant that the poor had become more desperate and dangerous than ever. The risk of being attacked in the streets of St James's was very real. To venture into other areas of the city without a suitable escort was madness.

Miles complained that he could not take a stroll through Piccadilly or a turn or two in Bond Street without being set upon by rogues, "Especially if one flashed a little rhino." His wife replied tartly that it was fortunate, then, that he had little rhino to flash.

I knew I could not go to Berners Street unescorted but I did not want Miles to know my business. Selena would keep my confidences but Miles would spread them all over town in days. Fortunately, my allowance from Darcy was paid into Mr Getheridge's bank. I told Selena that I needed to discuss my finances, begging her for the use of the carriage and her maid as chaperone. She winked and smiled and wished me well.

It was unusual but not unknown for a woman to visit a bank, but I was not surprised to see that I was the only female in sight. I left the maid in the foyer and told an obsequious clerk that I had an appointment with Mr Getheridge. I gave him the card on which I had scribbled my name. He showed me into an anteroom away from prying eyes and told me that Mr Getheridge would attend on me in a few minutes.

I sat staring at the impressive plaque on the wall emblazoned with the name of Marsh, Sibbald and Co. in gold letters, trying to decide what answer I would give to the question I knew I would be asked.

Eventually, the gentleman himself appeared looking more genial and ape-like than ever.

"My dear Mrs Wickham, what a splendid surprise. You will take a dish of tea in my office, I trust?" As he swept me into his office he whispered, "Is that dandiprat with you?"

I looked puzzled. "Do you mean Lord Finchbrook, sir? I can assure you —"

"No," he interrupted, "I mean that Miles fellow." I told him he was speaking ill of my friends who had offered me a roof over my head in the city. He laughed and said. "I am sure we can do better than that for you."

I swallowed hard and felt a shiver of apprehension. Darcy would surely cast me into the gutter if he could see me now. I looked up to find Getheridge smiling slyly at me as if he read my thoughts.

"In love and war there is all to play for, my dear," he said gleefully rubbing his hands together.

His office was very well appointed with an enormous mahogany wood desk laden with many gilt trimmed ledgers placed in rows upon it. Surprisingly, there was also a capacious chaise longue placed against one wall. Mr Getheridge led me to it and placed himself next to me patting my gloved hand reassuringly. I removed the gloves, the better to fiddle with them, and he immediately took two of my fingers and began stroking them.

I had been in a number of perilous situations during the past three years but nothing as equivocal as this one. I reminded myself that I was a hapless widow needing to make her way in the world and that way inevitably would be through the affections of a wealthy man.

I smiled in what I hoped was an alluring manner. "How reassuring to be in a banker's office," I remarked. Mr Getheridge toyed with my left hand.

"Lydia, Lydia." He rolled my name around on his tongue as if it were a delicate morsel. "What a charming name, my dear, and quite unusual these days."

"I believe I was named after Lydia Languish, an idealistic and wealthy character in Mr Sheridan's play *The Rivals*. My father is of a literary bent. She cared nothing for money, like most people who have plenty," I replied. "I have always thought the name was singularly inappropriate for me."

Mr Getheridge raised his eyebrows. "You and I know the real value of money, Mrs Wickham. I wish that some of my clients, especially the nobility, possessed the same acumen."

"Nevertheless," I sighed, "money does not stick to me with any degree of enthusiasm."

CHAPTER
FOUR

There was a knock at the door and a bank employee entered with the tea things, arranging them with the greatest servility and carefully avoiding my eyes. When we were alone together Mr Getheridge whispered in my ear that he would be delighted to lavish benefits upon me and direct certain people to me who enjoyed gambling and were seldom successful in that regard.

"Naturally, I would only select those clients I knew to be well in the funds," he added. "Of course," I murmured.

"You could enjoy a second income, my dear." His expression indicated that he expected something in return, possibly a great deal. It all sounded like hard work to me. I took a deep breath. "What exactly would those benefits include?" I asked. "I must tell you, sir, that my need is for a reliable, enhanced income, not nebulous gifts."

My companion gurgled a little through his tea. "Upon my word, Mrs Wickham, you come to the point in no uncertain terms." I gazed at him steadily as I sipped my tea assuring him that I knew the lie of the land very well as far as his lady companions were concerned — and the affairs of the bank. I exaggerated this last point of course. I knew very little about the workings of banks, but I suspected that it was highly irregular for the manager of such an establishment to be breaching his clients' confidentiality, or to be making immoral suggestions to young ladies in the bank's offices.

Mr Getheridge would not be drawn any further. "Let us talk at length in my box at Drury Lane," he insisted. "I shall call for you on Thursday evening, madam. And now I must return to business, pray allow me to show you out." Once in the foyer I approached a clerk who allowed me to withdraw a little cash from Darcy's parsimonious allowance.

When I arrived back at Curzon Street I found the mistress of the house eating a dish of fruit curds and reading *The Maid of Moscow*.

"This is no time to be eating slops and reading romantic trash," I admonished her. "I am in need of urgent advice. I may be on the brink of making my fortune or of ruining my life." Selena looked alarmed for a moment and then collected herself.

"I thought you had already done the latter by marrying Wickham."

"Yes, yes, in a manner of speaking, but at least I am still respectable." My friend's expression denoted a degree of disbelief but she understood my general drift.

I told her of my conversation with the banker and his dubious offer. Selena considered this for a moment, frowning horribly.

"You know of his reputation with women, I trust?" I nodded. "I believe he treats his mistresses lavishly. It is

40

only his first wife who has been overlooked. As long as you avoid the pitfalls of matrimony you should do well."

"There is little likelihood of that," I pointed out, "since he has acquired another wife and family." Selena shrugged and returned to spooning curds into her mouth.

"Then what is the problem?" I thought for a moment and then reminded her of Getheridge's offer to direct gaming clients my way. She put down her spoon and became more animated. "That could be a wonderful opportunity for us. We could operate the best syndicate in London."

"We?" I echoed. "I thought the offer was made to me."

"Yes, but you will need assistants and premises," she reminded me. I sank down in to a chair and tried to identify the thing that was niggling away somewhere at the back of my mind.

"Do you not think it was a strange offer to make to a woman . . . in the circumstances?"

Selena shrugged. "No doubt he has some ulterior motive of his own connected with his finances — or the bank's. The man is known to be an utter fraud and rogue but at least he is honest about it. He knows you will not betray him because you wish for a share of the golden goose." I could only agree with this assessment but I still had one other obstacle to overcome. "The man is so confoundedly hairy," I sighed. "I am not sure I can bring myself to . . ." She made a *tchk* sound.

"Think of the money and think of England."

At that moment another thought struck me with great force. "Almack's!" I cried. "How will I ever gain admission there? If a whiff of scandal attaches itself to me I will be lost; the guardians will not even interview me." Selena looked sceptical.

"I told you, effrontery is the only virtue needed in high society."

"Not at Almack's, they are more discriminating than the Prince Regent." Selena was growing impatient. She threw the curd spoon at the cat, which had cautiously entered the room. "Mistresses have great cachet these days. All the royal family have them and most of the aristocracy. Their children are often given titles."

"And the women themselves are often cast aside after a few years," I pointed out.

"At least they are well provided for."

"I do not intend to be cast aside by anyone again." At that moment Miles wandered in with a note delivered by hand and addressed to me. Getheridge had written a few lines.

Go to the jewellers Rundell and Bridge on Ludgate Hill. You will find some trinkets awaiting you. It would give me great pleasure if you would wear them on Thursday evening.

Rundell and Bridge were the most fashionable jewellers in London. The Prince Regent patronised them extensively. Selena raised an eyebrow. "Think of England, my dear."

The next morning we hot footed to Ludgate Hill where I was so mesmerised by the glittering display in the shop window that I had to be almost dragged inside. I was handed a satin lined box containing two identical diamond and amethyst bangles.

On Thursday evening I had leisure to admire my gift as I changed into a gold and white silk gown and drew the bangles over my long gloves. Selena and Miles had arranged to take a box at the theatre in order to chaperone me from afar, as it were.

"Just scream if you are in any distress, dear Lydia," said Miles puffing out his chest. "I am a military man after all. I was in the Fighting 52nd under Sir John Colborne you know."

"That will not be necessary," said his wife rolling her eyes and dragging him aside. "We are speaking of a trip to the theatre not another battle with Napoleon. Lydia is perfectly capable of looking after herself." I swallowed hard and agreed.

"It should be a capital evening," Miles continued oblivious of the undercurrents in the room. "*The Beggars' Opera* is a rollicking piece of work and it stars the luscious Vestris in a breeches part, I understand. A rollicking piece in a rollicking piece, eh?" He laughed heartily at his own wit while his wife sighed and urged him to ring for the carriage they had hired for the evening.

When Mr Getheridge handed me into his elegant dark barouche he eyed the bangles approvingly and told me how well they became me. I looked suitably gratified and said how much I was looking forward to the play.

"Oh, it has already started," he replied as if the play was the least important part of the evening. "We will have a little supper in my box, yes? There will be time to observe the play later."

I discovered that evening how little the society of London considered the wishes of the players. The audience preferred promenading, visiting each other in their boxes, eating, drinking and making as much noise as possible. When they had exhausted these pastimes they paid a little attention to the stage, often shouting disapproval at the piece or whistling at the female players. The young Italian actress known as Vestris was the idol of London, adored — by the men at least — for her beautiful legs.

When we reached Mr Getheridge's box I also discovered to my annoyance that it was almost impossible to see the stage unless one twisted one's body and head into unusual and agonising positions. Obviously my companion did not intend to spend much time watching the players.

"As it is an opera, my dear, you do not need to watch, you can listen."

I sat down and felt a long arm snaking around my waist. I fancied I could feel the hairs tickling my skin through the thin silk of my gown. Some women might find this erotic but I confess I did not. He placed his rather short legs upon a chair and relaxed. He began to lick my right ear lobe but was distracted by the servant arriving with our supper.

44

I was forgotten for a moment while he exclaimed over the lobster and champagne, the game pie and other delicacies. "A veritable feast, my dear, I trust we shall do it justice." The lobster suddenly appeared to be staring at me accusingly, bright pink and furious on its bed of ice. For a moment it metamorphosed into the face of my brother-in-law, bulging eyed and grim of mouth. I started and gave a little scream.

"I am afraid I could not eat a thing," I murmured faintly, searching in my reticule for the sal volatile. Mr Getheridge did not notice my discomfort.

"Come now, Mrs Wickham, a little lobster, a little champagne and *l'amour* while the singers serenade us on stage. What could be more delightful and romantic?" He nudged me playfully in the ribs and I almost collapsed. I refrained from telling him what I thought was romantic. It would not serve in the circumstances.

Eventually I composed myself and sipped a little champagne while my companion demolished most of the food, occasionally waving a chicken leg in my direction to emphasise a point. I realised I would have to make myself more agreeable to him. A man who has bestowed two diamond bracelets on a woman expects more than a token gesture in return.

I tensed as many muscles as I could place under my command, clenched my teeth for a moment, then turned and bestowed a dazzling smile upon my host and would-be benefactor. I leaned across the intervening space between our chairs and stroked his cheek languidly while he admired my *embonpoint*. (I

45

am still persevering with the French language, if only to spite Lizzie.)

Mr Getheridge gasped out, "Call me Tom," before clutching me to his person in a bear-like grip. On the stage the hero MacHeath was serenading us with *"How happy I could be with either, were t'other dear charmer away!"* I was bent backwards over the edge of the box in an alarming manner which at least enabled me to see part of the audience from an interesting, if dangerous angle. I could have sworn that I recognised a face in the crowd below. It was the highwayman's accomplice, the handsome one who had beguiled me on the coach to London. With him was a young woman of the streets, pretty enough, if somewhat highly coloured. She was decked out in feathers and lime green satin and around her neck she wore my garnet necklace.

I was overcome with excitement and fury at this discovery as well as being squeezed almost to death as "Tom" wreaked havoc upon my person while uttering guttural, incomprehensible sounds probably ape-like in origin. It was my misfortune to be wooed by an enthusiastic baboon.

"Stop!" I cried, imperiously, pushing away the baboon's hand that was creeping up my thigh. I wriggled away from him and tried to rearrange my dishevelled toilette. Mr Getheridge had fallen to his knees and was endeavouring to get up.

"What the devil is wrong now?" he exclaimed. "I had not thought you one of those demned minxes who like to tantalise a man and . . ."

"Quickly, sir," I interrupted him and seized his arm. I could see that he was miffed but I did not care. "We must return immediately to the salon. There is a villain in the audience who stole my jewellery. You must help me to apprehend him and his moll who is wearing my necklace." Mr Getheridge allowed me to drag him to the door while he exclaimed and moaned about interruptions, villainry and the need to call the watch.

We joined the *melée* in the salon where crowds were pouring out from the various parts of the theatre. Getheridge complained as we were buffeted about by a variety of people parading and strutting around in their finery like peacocks on a terrace. He frequently stopped to greet clients from the bank and I soon lost sight of him. Using my sharp elbows as weapons I managed to reach the far side of the salon where I was able to obtain a better view of the crowd. I soon spotted the highwayman and his companion. The woman's vivid emerald satin gown acted as a beacon and I immediately fought my way towards them becoming quite dishevelled in the process.

I looked around for Mr Getheridge but he was nowhere to be seen. As Selena always remarked, men are useless in a crisis. The highwayman recognised me when I was almost upon him. He gave a guilty start, seized his moll by the arm and hustled her towards the theatre's entrance. I rushed after them crying out "Stop thief!" as loudly as I could, but the general level of noise and animation was so great that my desperate appeals went unheard.

As the pair disappeared through the door I threw caution to the winds and rushed out into the street in hot pursuit. I cried out to the coachmen and linkboys waiting outside and a few tried to assist me. We all threw ourselves at the hansom cab in which the pair were making their escape. My helpers drew back as the vehicle began to move but my gown became caught in the door as it was slammed shut making an unmistakable rending sound.

I was dragged along the street for a few yards in the greatest peril until an arm appeared from the carriage window and yanked me firmly inside. I was thrown onto a seat in complete disarray, my gloves and indeed my face covered in dirt, my reticule left lying somewhere on the ground — fortunately with little money in it — and my dress badly torn.

I lay sprawled on the seat for a moment trying to catch my breath before finally looking up furiously at my companions. The highwayman smiled and gave a shrug while his moll giggled and pointed at me with her fan. Mr Getheridge would have described her as a highly finished piece, painted and curled and feathered to a tee but scarcely more than fifteen, I would guess.

Without a second thought I lunged towards her and tore the garnets from her throat. Immediately she screamed and threw herself on top of me attempting to tear out great clumps of my hair, which everyone knows to be my greatest asset. Heaven knows how we should have ended if the highwayman had not separated us and hurled the girl back onto her seat where she began snivelling and whining. He sat back in a corner and watched us both, silently with a cynical smirk on his handsome face.

The vehicle had picked up speed and I knew I could not attempt to leap without risking life and limb. Besides, the area through which we were travelling looked decidedly unwholesome. I clutched the necklace to my bosom.

"These are my jewels and I will not return them to that purloining slut. You will have to kill me first," I announced loudly with only a slight tremble in my voice. The highwayman shrugged again.

"As you wish, young lady. Killing is my trade." These words chilled me to the bone despite my overheated state but somehow I did not believe that he really meant them.

I swallowed hard and asked where he was taking me.

"We are bound for Seven Dials." He smiled broadly as he named one of the most notorious areas of the city. "I do not recall inviting you along but you seem to have invited yourself."

At that moment the moll giggled, snivelled, wiped her running nose on her satin skirt and stared truculently at me. She pointed with her fan at my tattered gloves and the bangles adorning them.

"If I can't 'ave the necklace I'll 'ave one of them!"

I stared down at my wrists while the highwayman gave a low whistle and seized my right arm in an iron grip.

"We must meet more often, madam. Whenever our paths cross you improve my fortunes considerably." Anyone could appreciate my feelings of mortification at this point. If only I had not been so hasty. If I had waited for Mr Getheridge ... I would have lost the garnets again but now I stood to lose all the jewellery — and who knew what other misfortunes awaited me at the hands of this brute? My thoughts were rudely interrupted when the moll suddenly threw her fan at my head and launched herself upon me once more trying to wrench one of the bangles from my wrist.

The highwayman batted her away viciously and banged on the roof of the carriage. As the vehicle came to an abrupt stop I was thrown into a corner while the door on the opposite side flew open and the moll was unceremoniously heaved onto the ground. The highwayman threw a few coins onto the screaming heap, shut the door and signalled to the driver to move off.

"There was no need for that," I spat at him. "You cannot treat a female in that manner, whomever she is." He sat down beside me and fondled one of the bangles on my arm. A slight but definite *frisson* passed through that limb. The man was so alarmingly handsome. I knew that he was aware of the effect he had. He smiled broadly and continued to hold on to my arm.

"She is just a whore, a Ratcliff Highway stroller before I brought her to Covent Garden. And I paid her well. She was beginning to annoy me. Do not fret, madam, our journey will soon be over. I do not believe we were properly introduced last time we met." He gave a slight bow. "Jerry Sartain at your service once more. And you are?"

"Mrs Lydia Wickham," I replied haughtily, "and what iniquities do you intend to inflict on me, sir? Assuredly, your neck will be stretched if you kill me. I have influential friends."

My companion did not seem unduly upset at this possibility. He moved closer and took my hand. "You are far too precious an asset for any harm to come to you, Mrs Wickham. I have a feeling that we could form a valuable partnership."

I recollected that I had heard something similar from Mr Getheridge. Men were anxious to form alliances with me providing they were of a dubious nature. And now a criminal whose name corresponded suspiciously with Old Nick or Satan, was making me an offer that I would be unable to refuse in the circumstances.

I must admit that I did not find Jerry Sartain's proximity altogether unpleasant. In fact I was quite overcome with emotions I had not experienced for some time. However, I did my best to affect severity in my looks and voice. He continued to watch me carefully with that same sardonic expression. He was dark haired and smooth skinned — quite Byronic in appearance. I could be undone if I did not take care.

The carriage came to a halt and I was told to hand over all my jewels. They promptly disappeared into Sartain's capacious pockets.

"It is for your own protection, madam," he assured me. "This is an unsavoury area." He was not exaggerating.

I got down onto a poorly lit street and was immediately pulled into a maze of narrow, black alleyways full of tenement houses. The stench was very bad and my slippers made contact with something I did not wish to identify. Bedraggled women appeared out of the shadows and made lewd suggestions to my companion, pulling at his sleeve and coyly asking, "On yer way 'ome love . . . lookin' for a good time?" When I stared at them they made aggressive gestures towards me and snarled, "Whachoo lookin' at?" Jerry batted them aside and tapped on the door of one of the hovels. It was quickly opened and I was dragged inside. I was aware of a hall barely wide enough for one body and an equally narrow staircase before we arrived in a meanly appointed chamber lit by two candles, containing a small table and two chairs and little else.

"Sit!" commanded Sartain, before striding to the door and calling for refreshments.

A slatternly woman eventually appeared with a jug of wine, beer, a loaf and a hunk of cheese. My captor ordered the smoking, tallow candles to be replaced with beeswax — a surprising addition to this mean hovel. I wondered if they were for my benefit. The woman gave me a curious and contemptuous look as she banged the items on the table and sidled out. Sartain emptied the jewels on to the table and invited me to share his supper. I declined although I had taken very little nourishment that evening. I felt sick to my stomach wondering if I would ever escape alive from this place.

Sartain, or Satan as I silently named him, decided to break the impasse. "I recall when we met in the forest that you described yourself as an impoverished war widow, Mrs Wickham. Am I correct?"

"Yes!" I said, teeth gritted. "You will gain nothing by keeping me here."

"I shall be the judge of that. Perhaps you could explain to me how an impoverished widow happens to be wearing diamond bracelets in company with that rogue Getheridge."

"I shall explain nothing," I cried, feeling more exhausted and vexed by the minute. "My private affairs are not your concern, sir. You are nothing but a common thief who will hang at Newgate." He nodded as if in agreement and smiled at me as he lifted a glass of wine.

"Come now, we have sparred long enough. If you wish to be released you must consider my proposition. It could be of great benefit to both parties. The alternative for you . . ." he paused, "will not be pleasant. You are unlikely to be rescued from this place."

I shivered, remembering how many young women disappeared without trace in London. "What is your proposition?"

"Why, simply to make myself richer with your assistance. I propose to offer you employment." I gaped at him in astonishment.

"Employment? You are mad, sir. I am a gentle-woman!" He nodded calmly.

"A gentlewoman who has fallen on hard times, I believe. My plan will relieve you of that problem. Unless, of course, you can earn more money as Getheridge's light o'love."

At this point I endeavoured to stand up, reach across the table, grab the jug and hurl it at him, but my knees betrayed me and I sank back onto the hard chair. Sartain waited patiently for me to compose myself and then repeated his offer. I surprised myself at this point by bursting into tears. It had been a difficult evening, as my readers will appreciate.

To my consternation my companion leaned across the table and slapped my face. I screamed and covered my face with my hands. After a few seconds I lifted my head and looked at him. "I shall have a fit of the megrims if you treat me in this despicable way."

"You will not," he replied, pushing bread and cheese towards me. I was forced to eat something and to swallow some wine. I admit that I felt restored afterwards and I decided to do whatever was necessary to escape from this place.

"It is quite simple, madam," said Jerry. "You will give me details of your wealthy acquaintances and their movements and I will give you a share in the money and valuables I extract from them. Your familiarity with Getheridge will prove invaluable. Theft is my speciality. I rob the rich to aid the poor." He smiled and pointed at his chest. "Specifically, me!"

"How do you know that I will not betray you to the authorities as soon as I am free of this place?"

"Because you wish to be rich, madam. I know the signs of covetousness very well. Believe me, my scheme is more certain than cheating at the card tables."

He picked up the diamond bangles and put them in his pocket, pushing the garnets towards me. "I will keep these as surety. I will send a message to you with further instructions in a few days."

I almost wept with frustration. "Please!" I begged. "Give me back the jewels. Getheridge will never forgive me. At least give me one of them." He leaned forward and placed his face close to mine, smiling and looking devilish and desirable at the same time. "Persuade me, madam."

I cannot readily describe, dear reader, how we came to be in the adjoining room lying on a skimpily covered bed with dusty curtains. I recall the dust in my nostrils but nothing else. We stepped out of our clothes and Jerry obligingly unlaced my bodice. We threw ourselves on to the bed where we were transported into a world of fleshly delights such as I had never experienced before and not often since. After Mr Wickham's perfunctory efforts in this department the pleasures offered by Jerry were a revelation to me. Despite his earlier threatening tone towards me, he was all consideration and passion when we were between the sheets. I knew I was lost from that moment. Whatever he wished me to do, whatever crime I might be called on to commit I would do it willingly if these delights were to be my reward.

Afterwards, I recall searching for my (deliciously decadent) pink silk stockings, attempting to calm my disordered appearance, and being sent back to Curzon Street in a cab in a dazed and delighted condition.

I found the household in an uproar with candles blazing everywhere although it was the middle of the night. There was general consternation over my tattered appearance.

"I feared the worst for you," cried Selena. "Do not attempt to describe your ordeal, my dear." I was given a hot posset and hurried to my bed where I fell instantly into a dreamless sleep.

CHAPTER
FIVE

I did not wake until the following midday and after a cup of chocolate I was soon luxuriating in a hot bath prepared for me by Selena and the maid. They hovered around me solicitously, urging me not to upset myself on any account. I realised that the entire household believed me to have been kidnapped and probably violated in a horrendous manner and that they were trying to show their sympathy in any way possible.

I toyed with the idea of allowing this misapprehension to continue but I knew they would soon tire of showing constant compassion and I might as well tell the truth. I was thinking how I might best explain this as I sat in my room after the bath nibbling a sweet roll. Selena for once was lost for words and was resorting to patting my hand constantly, which I found irritating. At this point there was a knock at the door and Miles begged leave to enter.

"How is the, er, victim . . . I mean, patient?" he stuttered as his wife glared at him. I waved a languid hand and gave him a wan smile. Miles hopped awkwardly from one foot to the other, not knowing what to say. "My sword is always at your service, dear madam," he continued, "should you wish me to call out the person who perpetrated this outrage!" I waved my hand again and said that I was unable to collect my thoughts adequately at that moment.

"There, there," said Selena patting my hand again. I resisted an impulse to lob a pellet of roll in her direction. She nodded sharply at the door and Miles began to retreat.

"In moments of crisis, dear madam, I always say thank heavens for the salts of Epsom," he burbled. "A purge of the whole system can work wonders." The door closed rapidly as his wife threw her shoe at him.

"Do *not* pat my hand again!" I cried out. "The situation is not as grim as you imagine."

"Do you mean . . . are you trying to tell me that you were not . . . that you have not been . . .? Well, I am dismayed at your impudence, Lydia. How can you play upon our sympathies in this way?"

"I *was* kidnapped," I retorted, "and treated abominably by a highwayman and attacked by his moll. Is that not enough to merit sympathy? Must I also have been cruelly violated?" At that moment a thought occurred to me. I looked around in dismay. "Where are my jewels?"

"They are in the cabinet under the window. We had to prise them from your fingers when we put you to bed. I see you retain your grasp upon life's priorities."

The next hour was spent in recounting my adventures and listening to my friend's outraged comments. The gist of her remarks was that I could not expect to advance myself in society if I entered into liaisons with highwaymen, however dashing.

"Only one," I reminded her. "There is no need for the plural. And he made me an interesting offer that I could not refuse at the time."

Selena fixed me with a beady eye. "There will be no question of Almack's if this little episode leaks out. You will, of course, hand him over to the authorities?"

"Of course," I replied, not meeting her eye. I changed the subject to the matter of Mr Getheridge and his reaction to the loss of one of the diamond bangles. Selena continued to regard me suspiciously.

Mr Getheridge himself put in an appearance soon after accompanied by a trio of Bow Street runners who were waiting to scour the area in search of the villain who had made off with me. They awaited only my direction as to the neighbourhood.

Chief among the three was a man called Townshend, a short, fat man wearing a flaxen wig, a blue coat and a broad brimmed white hat. This man was the most famous of the runners, recommended by the royal family for his daring and cunning.

I suppose I should have been flattered that my patron thought me worthy of the best, but my hand trembled a little as I waved it in the general direction of South London. Then I put my hand to my brow and said weakly that I had little recollection of the events but the words "Ratcliff Highway" came to mind. The men nodded in sympathy and set off for that district.

Mr Getheridge agreed to leave me in peace saying that he would return in a few days to escort me to Brighton where my spirits would soon be restored and a few furbelows could be purchased to aid my recovery.

Before he left he presented me with a small gold watch locket to be worn on the breast — a delicate, lovely thing for which I thanked him profusely. In view of the loss of the diamond bangle his generosity was most touching.

When I had dressed and ventured downstairs I found a letter awaiting me all the way from Derbyshire. Lizzie wrote peevishly that they had heard little from me since my arrival in London and they trusted that I was not entirely taken up in the social whirl. I was, after all, still in mourning. I screwed the letter into a ball and threw it away wondering uneasily whether any news of my escapades would reach them in their rural paradise.

I returned to my room and sat down to write a soothing reply to my sister. I needed to allay any suspicions in that quarter. Reviewing the events of the last few weeks I had to admit my stay in London had been full of incident but that I was no closer to achieving my ambitions, to wit, dancing at Almack's and getting to Paris. A great deal more money, subterfuge and pleasing men would be required before I realised these simple desires. The very thought made me fatigued and I looked longingly at the bed I had just vacated.

My encounter with Jerry Sartain had disordered my wits completely. I needed to calm myself and decide on a course of action. I wondered uneasily when I would receive the message he had spoken of. Would he know I was leaving for Brighton? I suspected that his spies were numerous.

Normally, such an excursion would fill me with joy but the complications in my life were causing me great anxiety. I am known for my carefree nature but life has a way of curing such tendencies.

When I went down to the dining room for lunch I was displeased to find yet another letter waiting for me. This time it was from my parents requesting a close account of my life in the capital. My vexations grow larger by the minute.

Selena was despondent, drooping over her soup after checking the family budget.

"I am afraid we will not be able to join you in Brighton, my dear," Miles remarked apologetically. "My beloved wife, who holds the purse strings, tells me we have not a penny to bless ourselves with — or at least, not many."

"We must pay some of our creditors," snapped his wife. "If you spent less on tobacco, gambling and strong drink, not to mention etchings, we might be in a less parlous condition." Miles looked suitably chastened and kissed her hand.

"I will endeavour to sell a few items, my dear. That will set us right. We have been in this situation before and we will pull through." His wife looked unconvinced.

"We must have another *soirée* with the cards when I return from Brighton," I declared.

"Has Mr Getheridge mentioned where you will stay when you are there?" my friend asked. "Shall you stay in a hotel or will he take rooms for you? You know he has a house there. His mistress, Maria somebody, resides there and she is a fearsome woman I have heard."

I told her he had not mentioned any details but he had promised that we would attend the Prince Regent at the Royal Pavilion amid scenes of unrivalled splendour and gaiety. Selena gave me a look that spoke volumes but I preferred to anticipate the pleasures awaiting me.

"The sea air will be most beneficial," said Miles with his beatific smile.

As for Sartain, all I had to do was supply him with a few details easily acquired. I struggled with my conscience, truly, dear reader, but the would-be victims were wealthy and could afford the loss. I knew I had a duty to hand the villainous Jerry over to the authorities but my desire to see him again overpowered my better nature.

The problem of Mr Getheridge remained. I fingered the gold watch at my bosom and decided to adopt a course of "wait and see" as far as that gentleman was concerned.

As we were getting up from the table Selena's maid rushed in with the news that Lord Byron was expected to leave his house in a nearby street within the hour prior to fleeing to the continent.

We were agog with excitement, throwing on our bonnets and rushing out of the house. Miles was obliged to follow unwillingly. I confess that I was overcome with joy at possibly seeing my hero in the flesh and desolated that it might be the first and last time.

London was afire with talk of his lordship's indiscretions with Lady Caroline Lamb and many other society women. There was also dark talk of a liaison with his half sister but I refused to believe such things. Hypocrisy and the narrow minds of the English had combined to ruin our greatest poet, the very embodiment of Romance and Passion. Now he was being forced to leave the country, leaving many a broken heart in his wake.

Selena and I tried to force a way through the crowd but it was impossible. I saw only a glimpse of a pale, set face and dark curls as he entered a carriage and was driven away. Later, we heard that many women had followed him to Dover to bid him farewell. How I longed to be one of them but I was obliged to review my wardrobe in preparation for the visit to Brighton. My heart was lightened by the thought that I also might one day reside on the continent and our paths might cross.

When we returned to the house Selena and I retreated to the music room where a cosy fire had been lit. We had barely settled ourselves when another caller was announced.

"Are we at home to Lord Finchbrook?" Selena asked.

"It is your choice," I replied. "You know he only comes to make sheep's eyes at you." When his lordship entered I was relieved to discover that he knew nothing of my adventures. He was delighted to hear of my departure for Brighton.

"Excellent, my dear, we will all take a jaunt down there. I shall have an opportunity to show the paces of my new pair." I assumed he was referring to horses. Miles burst into the room at this point exclaiming, "Turkey rhubarb and sulphuric acid!" Seeing our startled faces he explained that he had just heard from the cook that this combination was a sovereign cure for all ailments.

Finchbrook looked puzzled. "I thank you, sir, but I am quite well at the moment." I closed my eyes.

"Miles," said Selena, "do be quiet."

I had a great deal to add to my journal that night, although I was puzzled as to how to record the more intimate details without offending a gentle reader. I consulted Mrs Radcliffe's works but they offered nothing appropriate. After I had written letters of duty to my family I sent a note to my sister Kitty giving her a hint of my exciting new life in London, omitting the more scurrilous events, naturally. I knew she would enjoy the stories and could be trusted to keep her own counsel. We had always confided in each other.

CHAPTER
SIX

Brighton, January 1816

Two days later I departed for Brighton with Mr Getheridge. As I was handed into the carriage the footman contrived to press a note into my hand. I hid it in my reticule. My highwayman had not forgotten me.

It is said that the road to hell is paved with good intentions. Certainly, the road to Brighton provided some time for formulating intentions, good and otherwise. I tried to obtain details from Mr Getheridge about my lodgings but he would say only that they were conveniently situated near the centre of town, in George Street. I noticed that he would not meet my eye when he said this. Selena's words rang in my ears.

"Maria somebody, his mistress, is a fearsome woman." Not to mention his wife or wives. I resolved to avoid these ladies as far as possible. Selena had also voiced doubts about going to Brighton so early in the year. Would anyone of consequence be there? In between pleasing Mr Getheridge, fulfilling my promises to Jerry Sartain and avoiding fearsome women, I would have little time to please myself. Why and how had my life become so exhausting?

Mr Getheridge changed the subject, preferring to describe the delights of the Royal Pavilion, still under construction, with its curious oriental domes and exotic appearance. He promised me that we would attend one of the Prince Regent's assemblies. I closed my eyes, imagining the food, the music, the dancing and the opportunities for dalliance.

My companion droned on ceaselessly as the green and chilly countryside passed the windows.

"The opulence of the prince's apartments is unimaginable: the lights, the perfumed chambers, the finest music." I nodded and smiled, half asleep and worrying about fearsome women.

"The prince has a shower bath, a vapour bath, a douche bath and a plunge bath," he continued. I gathered that Prinny was fastidious in his bodily hygiene, if not in his morals.

"It is unfortunate that the weather will not permit any sea bathing," said my admirer with a provocative leer. "You would look charming in your swimming costume, my dear!" I struck him with my reticule at this point. "I was merely thinking of your health!" he protested. "Sea water is very beneficial. His Royal Highness rates it very highly." I closed my eyes for a moment imagining the corpulent Regent staggering into the waves. It was not a pretty picture.

Getheridge seemed as excited as a child about a trip to the seaside but there was a wild edge to his gaiety that unnerved me a little. He chattered like an old woman, only attempting an occasional embrace or knee squeeze.

Thankfully, at this point we stopped at Cuckfield to take lunch at the Prince of Wales Inn. We were three

66

quarters of the way through our journey, unmolested by highwaymen, and during the meal I attempted once more to extract information about my living arrangements.

Getheridge gnawed on a lamb bone like an anxious terrier and told me not to upset myself. I had engaged a maid to accompany me but I was well aware that if it became known that I was unchaperoned tongues would wag and my widowed status would not protect me.

The maid had been recommended by the cook at Curzon Street before she left in high dudgeon due to the late payment of her wages. The girl had duly presented herself, offering excellent references which I did not take up at the time and which in any case she later admitted were fakes. Her father was a printer and could supply her with any number of such things. Nevertheless, her manner was bright and intelligent and she proved to be adept at her duties, scurrying around like a perspicacious ant, her small, bright blue eyes agleam with curiosity, and her fair curls standing up around her head like a halo. Adelaide, however, was no angel.

She was sharp-eyed and quick-witted, able to judge a situation immediately and act accordingly. Most of the time she acted for my benefit, but there were times when she furthered her own ends. With hindsight I could scarcely blame her for that.

When I found a few moments in which to question her about her previous employment her account was quite startling.

"I worked for Lady Fortescue before I came to you, madam. I went to her household, but I didn't intend to be a slavey, did I?" I nodded and she continued.

"The house was but a few yards from the London home of that Lady Caroline Lamb. You know of her, don't you, madam?" Indeed I did. Everyone in London knew of that lady — Lord Byron's tempestuous former lover.

"Well, madam," Adelaide continued, "Life at Lady F's was all very fine but very quiet like. I was treated well enough. I was a housemaid, you see, not a kitchen wench." I felt puzzled.

"What exactly are you trying to tell me?" Her face twisted into an alarming rictus.

"I just wanted you to know what I did, madam."

"Which was?"

"I used to watch Lady Caroline's comings and goings. Up to all sorts she was, even though she was married. Sometimes she would soak her muslin gowns and wear them like that. The muslin would cling to her body showing everything.

"To be exact, I used to give titbits of gossip to one of the scandal sheets — the *Chronicle*, it was. Them writer fellers would wait outside the 'ouse for me and pay me for the information."

"My goodness!" I muttered, being lost for words.

"I just wanted you to know, madam."

"And can I expect the same treatment?"

Adelaide assured me that she was a reformed character. "It was the boredom what made me do it," she explained. I realised why she had to fake her references.

"Did Lady Fortescue discover what you were doing?" I asked.

"Yes," she admitted, "someone betrayed me and I was dismissed at once."

I could not reproach her. In the circumstances I might have done something similar. My maid and I were well suited.

As we left the inn to continue the journey Adelaide uttered a scream when Selena and Miles popped out of an adjoining room and accosted us merrily.

"We could not pass this opportunity to take the sea air in good company," my friend gushed to an astonished Mr Getheridge.

"Yes, indeed," said Miles, who declared that he was feeling quite jaded and needed perking up.

My patron did not exactly gnash his teeth, but he appeared to restrain himself with an immense effort. Miles placed an arm affectionately round his shoulders and steered him towards the carriage. Selena quickly drew me aside.

"We could not allow you to continue this ridiculous adventure alone," she lectured. "After the incident with the highwayman I realised that your judgement was seriously awry and that you needed to be protected from yourself." I shook her hand away.

"Do not be ridiculous. You were encouraging me to encourage Mr Getheridge only a short time ago."

"I have had time to review the situation," she said, breathing deeply. "There is a delicate balance to be maintained if we are to advance our position. We cannot afford to outrage society. I am here to restrain you, if necessary." I felt vexed by her remarks and even more so when I admitted to myself, reluctantly, that she was right. Selena was usually right. It was most annoying. I tried to sound confident.

"He has taken rooms for me in George Street," I told her. "He will be staying in his own house. It will look perfectly respectable."

"Then we will take rooms nearby," she said firmly. "Miles says there is an inn on George Street, the King's Head. We will lodge there." I deduced that their finances had taken a sudden turn for the better or that Lord Finchbrook was assisting them.

When I told Mr Getheridge of their intentions he turned puce and began to sweat profusely. "The King's Head you say? No. I would not advise that at all." From then on he huddled in a corner of the coach muttering under his breath. I began to fear that I had taken up with a mad man. Adelaide was obviously of the same opinion. Sitting in the opposite corner she rolled her eyes at me in a suggestive manner while indicating the gentleman in a discreet manner with a jerk of her thumb.

Despite my fears, I was happy to be in Brighton as the coach rolled along the Steyne with the elegant new houses gleaming in the silvery light from the sea.

My rooms were adequate if not luxurious. Mr Getheridge departed promising to arrange delivery of new furniture and furnishings. I left Adelaide to unpack and made my way across the street to visit my friends.

The black and white façade of the King's Head was exactly opposite my lodgings. Miles was already fitting snugly into a window seat with a jug of claret when I entered. Selena and I went up to their room. The innkeeper was adamant that only the rooms on the second floor facing the front were available, although there were very few other guests to be seen.

"There is something altogether odd about this place," Selena remarked when we reached the room at the end of a long corridor. There are scarcely any guests but the upper floor is closed off." I agreed that it was most peculiar. I had already decided to demand that Getheridge rent an entire house for me on the Marine Parade. My friends could then take over the lodgings across the street.

As we had driven into town my patron had pointed out Mrs Fitzherbert's gracious residence. Why could not this widow do as well for herself as that widow? Of course, Getheridge was not the Prince Regent, but he probably had more money than Prinny who was always in debt due to his lavish lifestyle.

The three of us dined at the King's Head in a private room. Other diners were conspicuously absent. Miles was the worse for drink and announced that he would take a stroll up to the Castle Hotel where he would find other drinking companions.

My friend agreed to accompany me back to my rooms to inspect my new yellow muslin gown. A decision had to be made about the choice of a blue or green bonnet with a striped velvet ribbon. How we women must suffer in the cause of fashion. The prospect of promenading on the sea front in the continuing grey, cold and windy weather wearing only muslin and silk was frightful. I hoped that I would not be wearing blue skin to complete the ensemble.

Preoccupied with these details we crossed the street and entered the rooms to find them in complete darkness. There was no sign of Adelaide and my shout was greeted with deafening silence. We groped our way into the drawing room where one candle sputtered on the mantelpiece. I seized the light and looked around the room. Selena grabbed my arm and pointed wordlessly at the sofa which was placed diagonally between two corners.

On it lay a man of about thirty dressed in the height of fashion. His buff trousers were spotless and without a crease, and his Hessian boots gleamed in the faint moonlight filtering through the uncurtained window as they rested on the carved, scrolled ends of the sofa. He was covered in a pale grey riding coat with many capes and silver buttons. A lock of dark hair fell over a white face where a dried trickle of blood emerged from a neat bullet hole in the middle of his forehead.

We clutched each other and shrieked in unison. "He's dead!" With one accord we bolted from the room into the adjoining bedchamber where we sat on the bed shivering uncontrollably.

When we had recovered a little I wished devoutly for some brandy. We found our way to the kitchen where I lit more candles and we discovered a bottle of red wine among the provisions laid out on the table. A glass or two revived our spirits a little and we tried to decide on a sensible course of action.

"We should call the watch," Selena said.

"Think of the scandal, of my *position*." We shook our heads. "We must wait for Miles to return," I said. Selena pointed out that he would be of little use when he returned, if he was not already face down in a gutter somewhere.

"I could send a message to Mr Getheridge." I thought of the fearsome women and decided against that course of action. We agreed to return immediately to the King's Head and wait in Selena's room.

I suddenly remembered the maid. "What shall we do about Adelaide?"

"She was probably murdered or kidnapped by the intruders. There is nothing we can do until morning." We rushed out of the apartment, locking it behind us.

CHAPTER
SEVEN

We were scarcely outside the door when I unlocked it
again and returned inside, to my companion's dismay.
I put my finger to my lips urging silence. I thought I
heard something as we made our hasty exit. Sure
enough, there was a faint knocking sound . . . knocking
on wood.

Selena seized my arm and tried to drag me away.
"Who knows what horrors we shall unearth if we
remain here? One dead man is enough — too much for
one evening."

"At least we know *he* cannot be knocking," I
remarked. She shuddered and pressed herself against
the wall. "It must be Adelaide," I cried, "she is locked
away somewhere. Come, help me to search for her."

We worked our way around the apartment by the
light of two candles, carefully avoiding the salon where
the corpse lay. We found the maid in the closet in my
bedchamber. She had locked herself away when she
heard male voices in the adjoining room and had been
too overcome to open the door when she heard our
voices. We persuaded her to turn the key and she
eventually fell at our feet in a dishevelled heap, her face
green with terror.

When she heard the shot, Adelaide had been convinced that she would be discovered and murdered. Now, when we showed her the corpse on the couch, her face turned from green to chalk white and she collapsed once more.

After pouring a considerable quantity of red wine down her throat she could tell us only that she had heard the voices of two or three men. She had seen nothing.

"I was arranging madam's dresses at the time," she told us. "I heard the men enter the apartment. Their voices were rough and I knew that they could not be friends of madam's, especially at such an hour." She gave me a sly look at this point and I resisted the urge to slap her.

"Go on, child, go on!" urged Selena, recklessly pouring more wine.

"When I heard the sound of something heavy being dragged along the floor, and the threatening voices of the men, I hid in the closet and locked myself in. I thought I was going to be murdered." She started to sob at this point and Selena comforted her while I looked inside the closet. Obviously, Adelaide had burrowed among my gowns. The yellow muslin was sadly disarranged.

When the girl had composed herself a little we all returned to the kitchen and sat at the table. Selena was terrified the men responsible might return but I considered it unlikely. It seemed to me that the body had been brought to this place and left on the sofa quite deliberately. The killers would not return to the scene of their crime. There was now the problem of what should be done with the body. The two women looked at me in horror.

"You surely cannot imagine that we will dispose of it?" said Selena, her voice trembling. "There is no question, we must call the watch, and bring my husband," she added for good measure. I decided that my friend must be deeply shaken if she needed recourse to her uniquely useless spouse.

"You are forgetting the scandal that will ensue," I reminded her. "My name will be besmirched. Yours also. We were both in the apartment, after all." The maid looked from one to the other in fascinated alarm. Then she spoke in a small voice.

"We could carry him down to the cellar, madam. I am strong and between the three of us I think we could manage well enough." I pointed out that we could not leave him there for long. Servants would visit the cellar for coal and other necessities as soon as it was daylight.

"Well," said the helpful Adelaide, "perhaps madam's husband could remove the body before morning."

"We are being ridiculous," said Selena. "Even if my inebriated spouse could carry the man unaided, where would he take him? He could hardly stagger along the Steyne with a dead man on his back and throw him into the sea."

"He wouldn't need to do that, madam," said Adelaide. "He could just take him across the street to the inn. In an hour or two there won't be a soul around. He can take him to the back of the inn and dump him in one of the store houses. I saw them when

I was in the inn's kitchen with the servants. There won't be no scandal to you if they find a body at the Kings 'Ead."

After this little speech Adelaide took another swig of wine while we regarded her with admiration. I had struck gold when I employed this young woman. Her resourcefulness was remarkable. I wondered if she was related to Jerry Sartain.

In the end it was necessary for all of us to assist in the disposal of the body. As we expected, Miles arrived back at the inn in a sorry state. We three women were waiting for him in the room at the King's Head. We were forced to immerse his head in cold water for some time before he was able to understand the bare facts of the matter. Even then, as we dragged him back to the apartment he seemed to be at a loss.

The sight of the body did not alarm him. He was at Waterloo, after all. He muttered something about a "deuced fine greatcoat and boots", then turned unsteadily to me and winked in a gross manner.

"My god, what have you done to the poor fellow, Mrs Wickham? He seems quite overcome." Selena pulled him down towards the couch and held the candle so that the gunshot wound was visible. "Well, I'm damned," he remarked. At this point his exasperated wife placed the candle carefully on the chest of the dead man and smacked her husband's face.

After many reproaches all round Miles accepted the gravity of the situation and agreed unwillingly to the plan. He proved incapable of hoisting the man on his back. The night's activities had taken their toll and the corpse was a good six feet tall.

The quick thinking Adelaide removed the greatcoat and boots to lessen the weight and placed them in my closet. In the coming days we both forgot they were there, which later proved to be a grave mistake.

We began to move the body with some difficulty. A grotesque procession staggered across the black, deserted street, carefully avoiding the lamp lit above the main door of the inn. Selena and I supported Miles on either side while Adelaide went ahead to show us the way. I prayed that no dogs would be alerted on the premises but all was quiet as we deposited the unfortunate man in an outbuilding used for storing furniture.

Like criminals we scuttled back to our respective rooms. My gown was bedraggled and filthy and my own arms ached from holding up the dead man's at an unnatural angle. His shirt had been of the finest linen and his skin as smooth as a girl's. It seemed a dreadful waste.

Within the hour I was lying in my bed turning over certain worrisome thoughts. I presumed that the intruders in my apartment could not have known that I had taken up residence only a few hours before. The intention must have been to terrorise the owner of the property. When a dead man is deposited on one's sofa it tends to send a clear message.

Mr Getheridge told me that he had "taken rooms" for me. Who then, was the real owner of the premises? I had seen no-one in the rest of the house, although there were two other apartments. My patron had said that it was too early in the season for full occupancy. I needed to make urgent enquiries as soon as it was light. I had an uneasy feeling that Mr Getheridge had not been strictly honest with me. I knew he owned a number of properties in Brighton and I suspected that my current residence was one of them.

This led me to conclude that the gruesome warning had been intended for my patron. As to the unfortunate victim, what had he done to warrant such an end? I recalled his handsome, pale face, his elegant body and equally elegant clothes. He must have been a person of some consequence.

I thought about gambling debts, affaires of honour, espionage. Lurid scenes filled my head but they would not serve. I remembered on my first visit to Brighton more than three years ago hearing someone remark that everything that happened in the town centred around the Prince Regent's court. The prince was always short of money and Mr Getheridge was a banker. There were conclusions to be drawn somewhere but I needed to prise the facts from him.

At least my experiences would give me an excellent reason to be moved to larger and more luxurious quarters. I would demand a body guard, my own carriage and definitely more jewellery. Only then could I begin to recover from the shock.

Adelaide said she was too frightened to sleep alone in her room. She insisted on dragging her truckle bed into my chamber. I was kept awake for the rest of the night by her moans, groans, whistles and snores. I was not excessively diverted.

Getheridge arrived at ten o'clock in the morning enquiring about the reason for the commotion at the inn across the street. The body of the unknown man had been discovered an hour or more ago and the place had been in uproar ever since. I had sent Adelaide to investigate and she confirmed the facts.

I gave him a meaningful look before informing him of the events of the previous night. The news had an astonishing effect upon him. He sank into a chair, burying his head in his hands. His face turned a distinctly unhealthy colour. For several minutes he lamented and exclaimed about murder and his own anticipated death, carrying on to such a degree that my insistent request for an immediate change of lodging fell on deaf ears.

This behaviour on the part of my declared protector and patron was tiresome to say the least. It also confirmed my suspicions that the body had been left as a warning to Getheridge. I needed to know what was afoot but I had little joy in prising information out of him. I offered wine and spirits to revive him, brought back from the inn by Adelaide. When he stopped shaking and crying I repeated that I could not possibly stay in this place and he must either install me elsewhere or I would return to London immediately.

"Yes, yes," he murmured feebly, "of course you must leave. I have another property on the Steyne. You can remove there." I assured him that I would not stay in any property of his for fear that misfortune would follow me.

"If you cannot tell me the truth about this matter, sir," I remarked sternly, "I fear our association must be at an end." I made no mention of returning the jewellery and Mr Getheridge had weightier matters on his mind. An inspired thought struck me.

"Has this matter any connection with the Prince Regent?"

He cringed and looked away but I seized his chin and turned his face toward me.

"You must be truthful, sir. My life could have been at stake. If Adelaide and I had surprised the murderers, if we had arrived a little earlier, I have no doubt that we would have been like lambs to the slaughter." Getheridge's lip quivered a little but he remained silent.

"Have you no conscience?" I cried. "Do I mean so little to you that my death is of no consequence?" My companion was by now on the verge of tears. Various parts of his anatomy began to tremble.

"Oh, my dear, I would not have involved you in this matter for the world. It was the most fearful accident. There are matters concerning the prince that I have undertaken. I cannot speak of them, but there are people who wish harm to our rulers and to this country who seek to frustrate my efforts."

I considered this for a moment. If Prinny could not find anyone more resolute to undertake his missions than this heap of jelly before me, then the outlook for the country was a poor one. He would have done better to employ Jerry Sartain, or even Adelaide. I almost giggled at the thought. Then I remembered the dead man and the laugh died in my throat. I also recalled that Getheridge was a banker. I had no doubt that the prince's debts were at the bottom of this matter.

"This is what you must do," I said firmly. "Go at once and arrange lodgings for me that are not connected to you in any way. Adelaide will pack my things and I will repair to the inn where my friends are staying. I cannot remain alone in this house. You must then seek protection from the royal household. Surely the prince will provide you with a bodyguard?" He nodded miserably.

"Yes, I must see His Royal Highness urgently. We had been invited to the *soirée* at the Pavilion this evening but I cannot wait until then. I will arrange lodgings for you and send a messenger to the inn." I brightened considerably at the mention of an assembly. As he scurried out of the door, hastily kissing my hand en route, I remembered something else.

"Who was the man who was murdered?" I asked in a casual manner. Getheridge hesitated; "His name was Adam Von Mecks." The name meant nothing to me but it sounded decidedly foreign which made the whole affair more sinister.

After giving instructions to Adelaide regarding the packing of my belongings I crossed the street to the inn where I found my friends endeavouring to obtain coffee and rolls from the distracted innkeeper. Several maidservants were still suffering from the vapours after finding the body and a large number of determined looking men were swarming over the place. Several of them wore the livery of the Royal Pavilion.

"Thank goodness you are here," exclaimed Selena, "now we can walk into town and find a more convivial place to have breakfast." We walked along the Steyne in a chilly wind to the Castle Hotel where, as we warmed ourselves with hot coffee, she told me what had occurred at the inn. Miles contented himself with an occasional painful nod of corroboration. The effects of the previous night's drinking had rendered him incapacitated.

"The strangest things happened last night," Selena remarked. "We were longing for a quiet night's sleep after our, um, *exertions*," she lowered her voice, "but we were kept awake for hours by mysterious noises, thumps and bangs and smothered laughter. It all came from the basement area. I cannot think what was happening down there. This morning when I asked one of the staff to explain, he gave me a strange look and said it often happened and I should ignore it."

I did not think I could cope with any more mysteries for the moment. I gave them an account of my conversation with Mr Getheridge.

"I shall be removing to more salubrious accommodation," I assured them. "It might be possible for you to join me."

Selena looked relieved but declared that she would like to get to the bottom of the mystery before they left. At this point Miles stirred into life. With some effort he indicated the far corner of the room near the door to the street.

"That fellow has been staring at you, dear Lydia. Confounded impudence! I would deal with him but I am feeling a little, ah, fragile at the moment." He subsided with a groan and I turned to see a man leaving the room, caped and with a hat pulled down over his eyes. For a moment he raised the hat a fraction and looked into my eyes. It was Jerry Sartain.

I looked down at my dish of steaming coffee, at a loss for words. I cleared my throat. "I need your advice about my dress for this evening, Selena dear." Even to myself I sounded false. My friend regarded me with narrowed eyes.

"Are you acquainted with that person, Lydia? He looked a trifle sinister to me."

"Oh, no," I replied in a strange, falsetto voice. "I cannot think why he looked at me; most impudent, really."

"Brighton is full of scoundrels," announced Miles raising his head from its resting place on the table.

"We have certainly found that to be true," sighed his wife. "I hope they will have removed the body from the inn before we are forced to spend another night there." Mention of the elegant deceased reminded me of something. "I know the identity of the poor fellow," I told them. "His name is — was — Adam Von Mecks. A foreigner I think."

"Von Mecks?" Selena exclaimed. "The Von Mecks family is an aristocratic Russo-Prussian one, courtiers to the Tsar and friends of the Prince Regent. There will surely be an almighty fuss about his death." We all paused to recall uneasily how we had dumped this scion of a noble house in a coal hole. I do not know how Selena acquired this information. Her knowledge was quite fatiguing at times. Miles muttered that the man must have fought at Waterloo.

"Probably gave a good account of himself, poor devil." He added that he knew the man was someone of consequence because of his boots. I recalled that those boots were still in my closet.

When we left the hotel one of Mr Getheridge's grooms appeared with a note from my patron stating that he had taken a house for me on Old Steyne, No. 26, known as Halfcrown House. We repaired at once to this address.

The façade of the building was elegantly decorated with two classical pillars set into the wall. A servant answered our knock and showed us around a set of very well appointed rooms. I deduced that Mr Getheridge's conscience was pricking him in a satisfactory manner. There would be plenty of room for all of us. Miles and Selena could occupy the suite of rooms on the third floor. My patron would not like this but he was in no position to argue. The servant assured us that the house was only rented to people of the highest quality. Her lips twitched very slightly as she said this. The neighbours, she added, were charming.

Anxious to escape from the prospect of the grey sea and the equally dull sky we walked back to our lodgings past the Royal Pavilion, observing it in all its peculiar glory. Selena and I believed that the prince drew inspiration for the building from William Beckford's Arabian fantasy *Vathek* which we have both devoured eagerly. I whiled away many a dull afternoon in

Newcastle reading this work while Mr Wickham was away who knew where.

At the inn I found Adelaide installed with all our belongings. She had already pressed my yellow gown and arranged everything for this evening's toilette, as well as preparing a glass of Madeira and some seed cake, "to keep out the morning chill". Truly the girl was a remarkable find. We would stay for this night at the inn and move into Halfcrown House tomorrow.

CHAPTER
EIGHT

I spent a half hour sending notes to my various relatives assuring them of my safe arrival in Brighton where I was staying with the Caruthers. This was absolutely true and would, I was sure, set their minds at rest. While I was resting in preparation for the *soirée* which would commence at six in the evening, a note was sent up to my room from the innkeeper stating that there was a gentlemen waiting downstairs who was anxious to see me.

I knew that the gentleman could only be Jerry Sartain and I did not trust myself to meet him at that time. I sent Adelaide to tell him that I was indisposed and he could give her a note if he wished. My maid returned with a knowing look on her face and a folded missive. It reminded me that I had promised to provide him with a sum of money from my winnings at the card tables. He trusted that I would make good that promise at the Royal Pavilion this very night, otherwise our association was at an end.

You will think me very foolish, dear reader, for allowing myself to be blackmailed in this manner. I knew that I should hand Sartain over to the authorities at once, but my tormentor knew how much I wished to see him again. Indeed, if the truth were known I wished for far more of his company than was decent or respectable and a few guineas at cards were a small price to pay for this pleasure.

I knew card playing was an important part of the festivities at the Royal Pavilion. I was convinced that I could make a profit out of the evening but I wondered uneasily how large an amount Sartain was expecting. At that moment I noticed that Adelaide was trying to attract my attention. Her face had turned quite pink and she was twisting her features alarmingly.

"Is something wrong," I enquired. "Are you unwell, Adelaide?"

"No, ma'am, but I 'ave some bad news . . . that is, sort of bad news if you see what I'm a-drivin' at." She swallowed hard and stared at her boots.

"Oh, for heaven's sake, out with it girl. What have you done?" An injured expression replaced the gurning on my maid's face.

"I 'aven't done nothing wrong, ma'am. It's just that there is something you ought to know. I thought as I was doing you a favour, like."

"For God's sake, Adelaide, will you tell me what it is that is so important before I crack you over the head with the smoothing iron? My patience is wearing thin."

For answer, she ran to the bed and held up the yellow gown.

"*This*, ma'am. I have found out that yellow is completely out of fashion in Brighton. Pink is all the rage this season." To add insult to injury she added that Mr Sartain had informed her of this fact. "He told me earlier today but I was too bedoozled by the murder and everything to mention it to you."

"Do not be ridiculous. What can that man possibly know about fashion?"

Adelaide looked mutinous as she clutched the yellow gown to her breast. "He told me that he had it on good authority that pink was *the* colour among the ladies at court and he hoped as how you would be wearing a pink gown tonight. He said it would suit you admirably." I felt my cheeks turning pink in sympathy as my maid endeavoured to suppress a smirk.

I sank into a chair and closed my eyes. To be cursed with such ill luck! First I choose a worthless husband, then I become a beggar at my brother-in-law's table, then I fall in with a criminal, acquire a hairy patron whose meddling causes a corpse to be deposited on my sofa — and now this. I am fated to be a laughing stock in front of the highest in the land.

Adelaide patted my shoulder. "Don't take on, ma'am, I've sorted it out. You will get the right gown within the next hour."

I looked up at her in amazement.

"What do you mean? What have you done?" My maid's smug expression grew ever more smug. "I knew as there wasn't much time, ma'am, so I run down to Madame Renée's emporium in Ship Street and found the perfect outfit for you. It was the only suitable gown in the shop and I persuaded her to deliver it here with all the accessories." She stumbled a little over that last word.

"And what did you use for money?" Adelaide smiled triumphantly.

"I took Mr Getheridge's card and told Madame Rénee to charge it to 'is account. Everyone knows him 'ere so it was no problem. I found the card on the mantel where 'e left it." She sniffed loudly. "That Madame Renée is no more a Frenchy than what I am."

Once again I was awestruck. I would never let Adelaide go from my service even if I had to chain her to the wall. "You are most resourceful, Adelaide," I said, fanning myself feebly with a lace handkerchief. "What would I do without you?"

She grinned. "I try my best to satisfy, ma'am."

Half an hour later a young man arrived bearing various parcels and packages. Adelaide opened them and laid them out on the bed. The gown was delightful, of pink gauze over a white satin underskirt, with blonde lace trim and fichu. Pearl beads trimmed the underskirt and a pair of pink satin slippers with silver rosettes completed the ensemble. I would carry an ivory fan with my gloves and Madame Renée had provided an elaborate headdress of pink feathers and pearls.

The next problem was what to wear as jewellery. I knew that only diamonds were worn for evening in the highest society. I had the remaining diamond and amethyst bracelet but it could not be worn with pink. Adelaide assured me that pink topaz was all the rage for day wear, and then she produced her trump card. In a small box lay a delicate necklace of diamond links with matching earrings.

90

"They're fakes, just paste, ma'am. Madame Renée loaned them to you for the evening to be of service. I said as 'ow you would be a good customer in the future."

Indeed I would; I intended to haunt that establishment during my every waking hour. My sartorial reputation, at least, had been saved. I was so grateful I immediately gave the yellow gown to Adelaide although I do not know in what circumstances she will wear it.

I was dressed in my new-found splendour in good time while Adelaide arranged my hair and assured me that striped, gauze ribbons were no longer in favour and only plain or brocaded ones would serve. She spends so much time with her ear to the ground that I am surprised she can walk upright.

I was alarmed to find a small blemish on my right cheek despite the fact that I use only Pears soap on my skin. We contrived to cover it with a beauty patch just as Mr Getheridge arrived. He was wearing knee breeches as the occasion demanded but they did his figure no favours. Of course, he noticed my necklace immediately and demanded to know in the frostiest tone who had given it to me.

I told him the whole story of the near disaster with my ensemble and how Adelaide's quick thinking had saved the day. My maid further endeared herself to me by emphasising that Madame Renée had loaned the fake diamonds to me because I had none of my own.

My patron was so overcome by this account that he gave her a half crown on the spot which she received politely while contriving to give the impression that it was no more than her due.

It is true that up to that moment the ball on the eve of Waterloo had been the social zenith of my life, but the Prince of Wales's banquet in the Royal Pavilion would certainly approach it for splendour and cachet. If only my family could see me at this moment. How far I had come from those parochial assemblies in Meryton!

Arrayed in my pink satin splendour with my false jewels gleaming in the half light of the carriage, I muttered under my breath, "Wickham, if you could see me now."

Sadly, my companion was unable to share my joy on this occasion. Apart from patting my knee and telling me that I was "As beautiful as an angel" he appeared to be distracted and upset, offering little conversation and staring morosely at the floor. He had not recovered from the affair of the murdered nobleman which obviously affected him greatly. This subdued creature was most unlike the Getheridge I had come to know. He was usually loquacious to a fault. His tongue was a perpetual clapper.

As the carriage drew up at the Royal Pavilion and footmen hurried forward to assist me, I knew a feeling of sheer triumph. At that moment my companion shocked me by announcing that the banquet was being given in honour of Grand Duke Nicholas of Russia, who was presently visiting England. All the great and the good from our country would be present, as well as many from continental Europe. Thank goodness Adelaide had procured the correct gown for me.

★　★　★

The building was ablaze with lights and the heat in the room was phenomenal, in contrast to the January chill outside. The air was full of heavy oriental perfumes as we joined the long line of people processing through the yellow, green and golden halls with their pink marble columns.

I hoped for a glimpse of Princess Charlotte and her new husband, Prince Leopold. Mr Getheridge did not respond to my nudges and requests as to the identity of the distinguished guests. He remained gloomy and nervous, looking about him guiltily and starting visibly when we were accosted by a lone gentleman.

This man was an astonishing sight. Tall and thin as a beanpole and dressed entirely in white, he looked like a ghost from another age in his tight breeches and court dress. I detected a touch of rouge on his wrinkled cheeks and surely that was a nutty brown wig perched askew on his head, reeking of oil?

I smiled behind my fan at this extraordinary apparition as he made an exaggerated bow and gave my companion a malicious smile.

"Ah, Getheridge, how good to see you. And who is your delicious companion?" I was introduced, a trifle unwillingly I thought, to Lord St Just while the strange creature twirled a lace handkerchief and asked solicitously after Gethridge's household at Hampton Lodge.

I knew this was a reference to my patron's Brighton mistress Maria Bertram, the fearsome woman Selena had warned me against. At the very mention of Hampton Mr Getheridge blanched even a shade paler and whisked me away with a curt farewell to the beanpole.

We made our way through the throng to the magnificent red and gold dining hall where the tables were already adorned with some of Careme's magnificent creations. I gazed in awe at a four feet high concoction of almond paste, puff pastry and icing sugar snow.

The prince, the Grand Duke, and the other important guests were seated at a high table, while we lesser mortals were seated at two long tables before them. Mr Getheridge and I were placed far down on the left side. I had a feeling that either bankers were regarded as little more than servants, or the prince did not want to be reminded of the man who controlled his purse strings.

I caught glimpses of the Grand Duke who was a very tall, fair, handsome man with a serious expression and a military bearing. Our Regent, in contrast, was in high spirits. His conversation and witticisms were passed around to all so that we might laugh immoderately at his *bon mots*. He was speaking of his love for Italian opera which affected him deeply — like drowning in a bath of pure melody. I had heard that brandy had the same effect on the royal personage. His jokes involved a play on words at which my patron pretended to roar with laughter.

"Why are Lord Palmerston's dashing pantaloons like two French towns? Because they are Toulon and Toulouse!"

I raised a polite smile.

All of the forty courses on the menu were placed on a central table, with some towering creations the like of which I had never seen before. Alas, the heat and the heady perfumes in the room combined to destroy my appetite. I normally eat little, but I forced myself to sip a little spicy soup. Mr Getheridge's spirits having revived, he urged me to try one of Carême's most celebrated inventions — *vol-au-vents à la Nesle*: large pastry cases containing meat, surrounded by a rich sauce. He transferred some meat balls on to his spoon, holding them aloft in a salute.

"Chicken balls, my dear!" he declaimed, to my great embarrassment. "You must try some, they are effective for both men and women!" Not content with behaving in this gauche and vulgar manner, he urged our neighbours at the table to join in. Cries of "chicken balls, balls, balls!" could be heard around us as more offal was consumed with suggestive comments and leers.

During a quieter moment I was obliged to listen to the elaborately painted harridan on my right who complained bitterly about the state of society in general. With a glance of contempt at my patron's nodding head she asked me why I was consorting with such "a poor, drawling, cold-hearted, crazy-headed creature". I assured her that Mr Getheridge was quite unlike her description and she turned away with a sneer. I concluded that her family must owe the bank a considerable sum or had been refused a loan.

To reduce my embarrassment I fixed my eyes on a wonderful concoction in the middle of the table — a huge apple meringue hedgehog with almond spikes. I deflected my companion's attempts to feed me the chicken balls with some difficulty, saying that only the apple meringue would pass my lips. He hid his disappointment and procured a dish for me. I was astonished at the speed at which the vast array of food was consumed by the guests, especially those at the top table. I was glad when we eventually rose and followed the royal party from the table, my escort having eaten enough for the pair of us.

A crowd entered the breakfast room where the gaming took place and I followed them, having dispatched Mr Getheridge to search for a conveniently missing glove. I insinuated myself into a likely looking group and embarked on a bout of *vingt-et-un*. I concluded the game with two hundred pounds in hand but my favourite card trick was almost discovered by a sharp-eyed fellow who was only distracted when I accidentally poured red wine over his immaculate lap.

At this point the heavy, perfumed air, the heat and the fumes of the wine caused me to mistrust my own eyes. I became convinced that one of the uniformed retainers bore a startling resemblance to Jerry Sartain. I blinked slowly, and when I opened my eyes I found a gentleman seated across the table was signalling to me in a coy but meaningful manner. I indicated with my fan that I was willing to speak with him and he escorted me from the room. There was no sign of Mr Getheridge.

The gentleman's intentions were obvious as he led me along a corridor into the bare, half finished part of the pavilion. I protested that I did not wish to dally on a building site when my unknown admirer turned abruptly towards a panelled wall and pressed a switch. The panel opened revealing a narrow, dark and uninviting staircase. I recoiled but my companion seized me by the waist and urged me forward.

"This staircase leads to the King's Head Inn. We will not be disturbed there, my dear. The prince had it constructed for that purpose." I broke free and gave the man a hard shove causing him to topple down the stairs with a loud yell. I closed the panel and sped off realising that I had solved the mystery of the noises at the inn. Selena would be gratified.

Immediately I lost my way, taking many turnings in search of the revels before reaching a small anteroom. A door bearing the Royal Arms led into a larger chamber. The door was ajar and I could hear voices. I applied myself to the opening and saw Mr Getheridge talking in an agitated manner with the prince's private secretary. I could only catch a few words but the name of Adam Von Mecks was mentioned several times.

At that moment the sound of approaching footsteps forced me to flee again. Once more I rushed blindly along into the uninhabited section of the pavilion. As I turned back and ran around corners I could hear music in the distance. I must be heading in the right direction. My heart was pounding and I was becoming quite damp from my exertions. My hairdo would be ruined. It would collapse like one of Monsieur Careme's sugar confections after the prince had prodded it with his fat finger.

I slowed down and almost collided with a footman who appeared from nowhere. Dizzy with emotion and relief I seized the man's lapels and begged him to conduct me back to the state rooms.

"Are you in trouble again, my dear?" the footman remarked as I looked up at the sardonic smile of Jerry Sartain.

I gasped out, "So it *was* you! Whatever are you doing here?"

"More to the point, what are *you* doing here? The arrangement was that you would remain in the gaming room earning money for both of us. I have been forced to follow you as you leapt around like a March hare." I knew I should not allow him to speak to me in this fashion but, against my will, I heard myself meekly apologising and explaining my adventures up to that moment.

"Are you going to tell me why you are posing as a footman?"

"To keep an eye on you, of course; you cannot be trusted not to get yourself into ridiculous predicaments." I did not believe this explanation for one minute. I wondered if he knew about the corpse on the sofa but he made no mention of it.

"It is not a pleasant situation for me," he went on. "The footmen sleep nine to a room in folding beds and the atmosphere is far from fresh, I assure you." He took my reticule from my unresisting hand and removed the money. With some reluctance, I thought, he returned a portion of it to me.

I smiled at him as he led me back to the state rooms. "The livery suits you well." He gave me a peck on the cheek and pushed me gently towards the gaming room.

What a fool I was, simpering and complimenting him like a love-sick swain. Our positions have reversed. *I* was paying court to *him* and he knew it very well. I must take care that I do not propose marriage to him. This penchant for penniless villains must be overcome at all costs.

As if summoned, Mr Getheridge appeared from the gaming room, mopping his brow and looking gloomy once again. He did not comment on my prolonged absence. I wondered if he had even noticed.

"Ah, there you are my dear. Shall we take some cold drink and a little fresh air in the gardens? The heat is becoming oppressive." Indeed, the hot, jasmine laden air was playing havoc with my toilette and my constitution. Unfortunately, the contrast of the cold air outside was so great that we were soon shivering and retreating inside once more.

By this time my patron was so overcome with anxiety and depression that he spoke of retiring to Bath for a while. I realised that the Von Mecks affair must have affected him profoundly if he was contemplating such a drastic step. I had it on good authority that Bath had become dreary beyond measure in recent times. He appeared to want me to accompany him. Jerry would not like that at all.

"How long do you intend to remain in Bath, sir? Is it possible for the bank to manage without your presence?" At the mention of the bank Getheridge's face fell even more. He passed a hand across his eyes and murmured to himself, "The affairs of the world are pressing upon me. I need to get away for while; I must rest, perhaps take the waters." I recoiled in horror. To be in Bath would be ghastly enough after London and Brighton, but to take the vile tasting waters in the company of the elderly, scrofulous, broken down dregs of society was too awful to contemplate.

I gave an unenthusiastic nod in answer to his remarks. It occurred to me that the inestimable Adelaide might have heard something concerning *l'affaire* Von Mecks and my patron's part in it. I had a sudden yearning to be back in my bed, alone, if possible. The surroundings of the Royal Pavilion and my delightful gown notwithstanding, I was fatigued in the extreme. At least I had fifty guineas to show for the evening.

"I find that I have an excruciating headache," I told him. In truth, I was wilting like one of Careme's carved celery sticks at the end of the evening. Mr Getheridge agreed to summon the coach and seemed happy enough to deposit me at the door of the inn. He again complained of feeling unwell and I left him contemplating the mournful pleasures of the Bath spa waters.

CHAPTER
NINE

I found Selena and Miles ensconced in my chamber, being served refreshments by Adelaide despite the late hour. As I sank down on the bed I noticed that my friend was in a state of great excitement which she was endeavouring to suppress with little success. I was mortified that she did not enquire about my evening. It is not every day that one is invited to a royal *levée*.

"You will never guess what has happened in your absence, Lydia," she burst out.

"Never guess," echoed Miles.

"It's true, madam, you'll never guess," chorused Adelaide. I felt peeved and tired.

"Have you all gone mad?" I raised my voice in an unladylike manner. "Of course I cannot guess. I was elsewhere at the time — in the Royal Pavilion as a guest of the Prince Regent," I added for good measure. They brushed this aside.

"We have solved the mystery of the cellar," Selena rushed on. "It is droll beyond words. There is a secret passage from the inn to somewhere, I don't know where as yet. During the evening, just as we were having supper, a great noise came from under our feet."

101

"The innkeeper turned the colour of old liver sausage," Miles contributed. "He rushed off to investigate and came back with this queer old party in fancy dress, knee breeches and such, all covered in dust and in a fine temper. The innkeeper sent him off in a carriage and pretended it was nothing out of the ordinary."

"I know all about that," I said, watching their faces fall. "Now if you will excuse me I am exhausted and must go to my rest."

On the following morning we were so preoccupied with moving our belongings into Halfcrown House that I did not have an opportunity to speak to anyone until lunchtime. We assembled in the dining room and ate a picnic lunch obtained from a nearby hostelry and pie shop.

As we ate I told my friends about my evening at the Royal Pavilion. Selena was agog for information about the gowns, the jewellery and the general ambience. Miles wanted to hear about the swells who milled around the Prince Regent. I did my best to entertain them while Adelaide's ears twitched in the background.

When I reached the part about my escapade in the corridors and the secret passageway to the inn, Selena almost fell off her chair with excitement. Of course, I did not mention my meeting with Jerry. I called to Adelaide and asked her if she had heard the name of Von Mecks mentioned anywhere. She shook her head saying that she had been too occupied with her duties concerning the move to go about the town. Selena frowned in an effort to remember something.

"I caught a glimpse of a strange looking woman at the inn after you left, Lydia." She turned to her husband. "Surely you saw her, Miles? The creature had a hoisted up look about her. Her eyes were bloodshot and her lips parched. She looked as if her shoes were too tight."

Miles seemed doubtful, saying that the description might have applied to him after a night on the town. Selena turned to me impatiently. "Miles can never remember anything. The strange thing is that the woman was at the inn one moment and then she disappeared. I am sure she did not leave by the front entrance. She must have gone into the secret room."

"One of the prince's floozies," Miles added. I agreed that this was intriguing, if not altogether surprising, given the prince's known preferences, but it told us nothing about the murder of Von Mecks and my patron's connection with it.

"Getheridge is up to something, mark my words." Miles tried to look solemn for a moment. "Up to his ears in it, that fellow . . . not a gentleman, if you get my meaning."

"But he's a banker!" Selena and I chorused. Miles agreed that money counted for a great deal. The prince spent lavishly and his only daughter had just been married with great splendour.

"They say that Prince Leopold hadn't a penny when he married Princess Charlotte," Miles added. "When the Archbishop came to that bit in the marriage service about 'For richer, for poorer', Charlotte laughed out loud." Seeing our baffled expressions he added, "My point is that money — or the lack of it — is at the root of everything."

Selena agreed that it certainly was in his case.

Adelaide begged leave to speak at this point saying that she knew someone who might ferret out the truth of this matter, "Being a lowlife hiself, in a manner of speaking, and acquainted with others of the same ilk." She gave me a meaningful look and I blushed furiously. I collected myself sufficiently to mutter an agreement.

Miles conveniently changed the subject remarking that the house across the Steyne from our own belonged to Mrs Fitzherbert, the prince's former mistress, the mother of his children — and his real wife, according to gossip.

"What has she to do with this?" Selena asked.

"She receives Getheridge and half the *beau monde* of Brighton. I saw some of them arriving this morning." It was agreed that we would contrive to visit the lady as soon as possible. Adelaide would talk to the staff at the Royal Pavilion.

At this point Miles, having finished his meat pie, sprang to the window exclaiming that someone should keep watch on the Fitzherbert house.

"As you are so interested, I can survey the place from here. This window is an excellent vantage point."

Selena said she hoped that he would not take to loitering in alleyways. Miles looked aggrieved, saying that he was not some Johnny Raw up from the country. "Surveillance was part of my role as a military man, you know."

My friend and I immediately decided to leave a card at Mrs Fitzherbert's home. We put on our bonnets and crossed the Steyne, accompanied by Adelaide. As we mounted the steps to the house I saw Miles watching us from the window and waving encouragement. It occurred to me that my highwayman friend might well decide to keep watch on Halfcrown House itself. The alleyway afforded an excellent view.

As we retraced our steps a carriage rolled up. An unprepossessing woman wearing too many furs and furbelows descended and was admitted to the Fitzherbert residence. Selena clutched my arm excitedly. "That's her, the woman from the inn last night. Who is she?"

The inestimable Adelaide was quick with the answer. "That is Maria Bertram, ma'am. She's well known in Brighton." I was horrified. She was none other than Mr Getheridge's long standing mistress — the fearsome woman! It appeared that everyone was invited to the Fitzherbert house. All except Lydia Wickham.

"We have only just arrived, my dear," said Selena in answer to my sudden howl of outrage.

We rushed back to the house and Miles confirmed that he had witnessed the arrival of a strange-looking woman. "The plot thickens!" he gurgled with predictable relish.

Selena said she had one of her headaches and must lie down at once — always her reaction to a problem. I retired to the window seat in preparation for a long, tiresome afternoon and evening. Mr Getheridge had not called or sent a message. There were no invitations on the mantelpiece. Brighton was not taking us to her bosom.

Adelaide announced that she too needed to retire promptly. The meat pie at lunch had been questionable and she was experiencing an attack of the wherry-go-nimbles. I sighed and picked up a copy of *Pamela: or Virtue Rewarded*.

After two hours of this occupation, varied by staring out of the window, I was startled by a loud knocking at the front door. Several moments passed, followed by renewed knocking. Eventually, Adelaide appeared, looking wan, but collected.

"There is a messenger here, ma'am, from Mrs Fitzherbert across the way. She urgently requests that you and Mrs Caruthers take tea with her this afternoon." I sprang from my seat with such alacrity that I almost knocked Adelaide against the wall. She turned green and rushed from the room so that I was obliged to answer the messenger myself, saying that we would be delighted to accept the invitation.

I rushed to rouse Selena from her bed where she was not sleeping at all but reading a story by Mrs Thrale. We hurriedly prepared ourselves and left the house. As my maid was in no condition to accompany us, Miles escorted us to the door of Mrs Fitzherbert's residence.

The house was spacious and well-appointed and the lady herself was most affable in her manner. One or two gentlemen of the highest fashion, a type known as Corinthians, bowed to us as they were leaving. A young woman of my own age, dressed in blue muslin, also left the room quietly. I wondered if she could be Maryanne

Smythe, the unacknowledged daughter of Mrs Fitzherbert and the prince.

I had a few moments in which to observe the lady. Although advanced in years, she bore the remains of the beauty that had captivated the Prince Regent. Her large hazel eyes and excellent skin were still in evidence and her once blonde hair, now grey, was still silky and fine. She had gained a great deal of weight in her middle age. The watered silk of her gown strained across her ample bosom and her ill-fitting false teeth clacked somewhat alarmingly as she patted the seat of a striped silk chaise longue and urged us to sit comfortably with her.

"Now, my dears, tell me everything!" she commanded. We were somewhat startled to hear these words issuing from the mouth of the woman who would be, if justice prevailed, the next queen of England. Selena and I stared at each other and then at our hostess.

"We . . . we cannot imagine," I stammered, "to what you are referring, madam."

Mrs F laughed, leaned forward and patted my knee.

"Very little happens in this town that does not reach my ears." I was impressed. Her network of spies must be formidable. I imagined a whole army of Adelaides stationed below stairs. As we drank tea and nibbled ginger leaves she set about enlightening us.

"Mr Getheridge took tea here a few days ago. I thought he was not looking at all well. I hear his affairs at the bank are proceeding badly." My ears pricked up at this. "And, of course, there is his connection to the Prince Regent who is indebted to him." She leaned forward and patted my hand. "Take care, my dear. I fear it will not end well for him."

I almost choked on my ginger leaf. How could she know of my connection with Getheridge? I remembered the look on Mary Bertram's face and shuddered.

"Of course," Mrs Fitzherbert continued, "the prince is indebted to half the merchants of London, but the news about Mr Getheridge's affairs is very worrying." Selena came to life at this point. She reminded us about the matter of Von Mecks.

"Yes," our hostess nodded, "a strange ending for one who seemed more concerned about the knot of his necktie than matters of high politics." I assumed the deceased had also taken tea in this house. "I do not know why he was killed but I hope to discover something quite soon." Selena and I were rigid with astonishment. I had no idea that the Prince Regent's morganatic wife headed her own espionage service. My friend recovered her wits quickly.

"What was he doing here? Did he have business with the prince?"

"He undertook a commission for HRH on the continent, before returning to England. I do not know what the commission was but it must have been of great importance if murder was involved. The prince will be greatly perturbed. I did not care for Von Mecks myself. His conversation was facetious, full of sparkle of the first water, but I was saddened to hear of his death and the manner of it."

I recalled that my patron had also been badly affected by the incident, to the extent of forgetting my existence. I pointed this out to our hostess who patted my hand again and said it was just as well. I would in that moment have told her all about Jerry Sartain as well, were if not for the suspicion that she already knew. For a moment I longed to be back in London with nothing to worry about but the date of the next card party. I had progressed from a living death of boredom at Pemberley to an uncomfortable proximity to the criminal underworld.

"Mr Getheridge is so cast down by the Von Mecks affair that he speaks of retiring to Bath to take the waters," I commented. Mrs Fitzherbert looked startled and then an expression of distaste crossed her face.

"If one cannot be in Brighton, then London is the only place to be. In no other place can fortune be so successfully wooed." She gave me a meaningful look as she spoke. How comforting it was to be advised by one who was well-disposed and in possession of great wisdom. I felt that this gracious lady had taken me under her wing in some way and I knew I could count on her advice.

As if she read my thoughts the lady remarked that it was fortunate we were living just across the Steyne. "You must come to visit me frequently, my dears." Our kind hostess then enquired after the health of Selena's spouse. How was he faring in peacetime and were his prospects good? My friend sighed that life on an officer's half pay was not easy.

"My husband is ill-fitted for life outside the military, madam. Miles is, of course, a gentleman. That is to say, he keeps his hands out of his pockets and has no visible means of support."

Mrs Fitzherbert clucked sympathetically. "And have you no fortune of your own my dear?" Selena shook her head sadly.

"I will inherit a small estate in Ireland should my uncle and his son expire suddenly."

"Anything is possible," remarked the lady enigmatically. She rose to her feet. "Always think of England my dears," she said with great feeling. I reflected that I preferred to think of Lord Byron at moments of great emotion. We made our farewells.

Selena appeared to be quite bemused by the experience. She made her way unsteadily across the street to Halfcrown House and remained blindly unaware when Jerry Sartain materialised from the alley alongside the Fitzherbert house and whisked me away.

"We have urgent matters to discuss," he muttered as he seized my arm. He was still wearing the livery of the royal household under his great cape. I protested that my companion would be dismayed by my disappearance but he was not impressed. He hurried me towards the Royal Pavilion, lowering his voice in a conspiratorial manner.

"You know about the Von Mecks affair?"

"I have heard it mentioned far too many times. I do not want to be involved in whatever you're planning."

He leered at me in an attractive way. "Jewels, my dear. I know you cannot resist them."

110

"What do you mean?"

"I refer to the jewels Von Mecks brought back from the continent. I know where they are hidden in the Royal Pavilion."

"Where?"

"In the prince's bedchamber."

"You will never manage to steal them from there," I said scornfully.

"No," he agreed, "but you will!"

CHAPTER
TEN

I cannot adequately describe my feelings of terror at hearing this remark, dear reader. I knew immediately that I would have to agree to whatever Jerry was planning. He was an irresistible force. That is the only excuse I can give.

By the time we reached the servants' entrance to the Pavilion my companion had outlined his plan and had explained my part in the scheme. We slipped through the door unobserved and found an empty room where we could talk without interruption. Jerry continued in his most persuasive manner.

"Von Mecks went to the continent in pursuit of Princess Caroline. The prince wanted to recover a priceless set of jewels known as the Cambridge emeralds — a set consisting of a necklace, earrings and bracelets which were in the possession of his estranged wife."

"Surely she had a right to them?" I said. Jerry gave me an amused look.

"Perhaps. But he had cast her off and the jewels were the property of the crown. He had a right to demand their return."

"I suppose he wanted to give them to his latest doxie."

"No, I believe they were intended to be a gift to the Princess Charlotte on her marriage. The prince thought that Von Mecks might be able to charm the old hag — I mean the Princess Caroline. I heard he was prepared to make the ultimate sacrifice."

"You mean . . . death?"

"No, you cuckoo, I mean his body. The princess is not only as ugly as sin and as randy as a goat, but it is said she bathes infrequently. The prince always needed a large brandy before doing his marital duty, which was not often."

I pointed out that this was all quite fascinating but it had little to do with us. Jerry disagreed, saying that the jewels were now in the prince's possession, although not before Von Mecks had been murdered by person or persons unknown.

"There are many people who would like to acquire those jewels, including yours truly." He drew closer and breathed in my ear. I felt a tingle start in my toes and move rapidly up through my body.

"This . . . this is monstrous," I stammered. "How could you dispose of something so valuable, should you manage to steal the jewels? The Cambridge emeralds cannot be traded in a house of ill repute in Seven Dials, surely?"

"We would take them to the continent, to Amsterdam. They could be split up, it would be easier than you suppose."

I swallowed hard. "And what do I have to do?" He toyed affectionately with a lock of my hair. "My royal master cannot resist a pretty face. He craves novelty. Your part will be to keep him occupied in the usual way and then to slip a sleeping draught into his wine. You will need to let me into the bedchamber whereupon I will take care of everything. There is a secret passageway from the royal apartments to a nearby inn . . ."

"Yes, yes," I interrupted, "I know all about that."

"There is a secret panel in the prince's chamber leading to the staircase out of the building. He is afraid of assassination attempts. That is why I need you to be in the chamber so that you can open the panel after the prince has taken the sleeping draught." I tried to protest again but he ignored me.

"I will have to introduce you to the prince as the latest novelty."

"And so I must keep the prince occupied in the usual way, must I?" I stuttered with rage.

Jerry raised a surprised eyebrow. "Surely that will not be a problem for you, my dear — an experienced woman like yourself."

"How dare you!"

"I mean only that you are a married woman. You are no trembling virgin. Think of the jewels and what they will mean to us."

Many things raced through my mind at that moment. Visions of the stately façade of Pemberley and the shocked faces of my sister and brother-in-law, followed by an image of my childhood home with my

114

parents weeping into their soup. This was swiftly followed by a vision of the Prince Regent divested of his brocades and corsets. I closed my eyes and tried to think of Lord Byron. Jerry was holding me close and placing his lips near my ear.

"It will only be for a short time. I hear the prince has little stamina for such matters these days — or rather, nights." I shoved him away indignantly.

"It seems that I will be the one making all the sacrifices in this little escapade. It is all very well for you, my friend. You will merely be acting normally, arranging fast horses and knocking people on the head."

He frowned. "On the contrary, I shall be taking all the risks. Just by donning this uniform I put myself at risk of discovery. I am a wanted man, remember."

"And I shall be a wanted woman," I cried miserably, "as well as a wanton one!"

He shook his head at me. "I had thought you were more ambitious and determined, my dear. I cannot enter the royal chamber through the secret panel unless you open it for me, so you see; your role is a vital one." He went on to assure me that fast horses would be waiting at the inn and we would be away at sea before anyone missed us.

I am sure you can imagine, dear reader, how this little scene played out. Jerry escorted me back to Halfcrown House after I had promised to return to the Pavilion at midnight whereupon I would be "introduced" into the Prince's bedchamber. He assured me that I would be painted in glowing terms to HRH.

115

When I outlined the plan to my friends, in defiance of Jerry who had sworn me to secrecy, they were struck dumb for a full two minutes. Miles slowly found his tongue. "Well, blast my breeches, this is a scheme and a half."

Selena fanned herself; she looked quite pale. "I only agreed to a little finagling with the cards," she said plaintively. "It was never my intention to be involved in treason and grand larceny."

"Quite so, my love," her husband agreed. "I have no love for the Germans," he waved a hand in the general direction of the Royal Pavilion, "but treason is treason. I fought at Waterloo, after all." I hastened to assure them that I would not involve them in this ridiculous scheme under any circumstances.

"You have been good friends to me and I am telling you this so that you will know what happened to me and you will be able to notify my unfortunate relatives when I am hanged at Newgate." Selena began to weep and Miles dabbed at his eyes with a large cambric *mouchoir*. (I am still continuing with the French language.)

"We cannot let you take part in this madness," he said firmly. "You must be saved from yourself, don't you agree my love?"

His wife nodded and blew her nose loudly. "You are in the grip of a grotesque *folie d'amour*, Lydia. What became of your simple ambition to dance at Almack's?"

I pointed out that I could not refuse at this stage. Jeremy Sartain was not a man to be crossed. I shuddered to think what he might do if I did not arrive for this rendezvous. Miles began to think furiously, his face turning purple at the unfamiliar exercise.

"I think I have an idea," he said slowly. I began to feel anxious.

"I trust it does not depend on Adelaide?" I said. "I do not think in the circumstances . . ." Miles waved his hand airily.

"Leave it all to me, my dear." At that point there was a loud knock on the front door. "Ah, here comes Lord Finchbrook, just the man I need. He is down from London and we persuaded him to dine with us." He patted my knee. "Don't fret, Lydia. We will save you from yourself." I went upstairs to change, trying to establish in my mind whether I wanted to be saved or not. I prayed that reason would triumph in the end.

After dinner, during which I was somewhat quiet and distracted, the men retired to smoke and drink port while Selena and I paced miserably around the small salon. Later, the men emerged looking conspiratorial. Lord Finchbrook announced that he would drive me to the Pavilion in his phaeton. I could not, of course, walk through the streets of Brighton alone at that hour. Miles assured me once more that all would be well. "We have everything in hand," he insisted, while his lordship nodded agreement. Selena and Adelaide started to cry as I left the house, adding to the funereal atmosphere.

As we drove the short distance to the Pavilion the night suddenly became so still that I could hear the muted roar of the sea acting as background music to the latest drama in my life. Where were all the revellers who usually thronged these streets? I wondered, and shivered. Lord Finchbrook told me not to be afraid.

"I suppose you think me little better than a harlot?" I remarked.

"Indeed I do not," he replied. "Members of my family, male as well as female, have been offering themselves to the royal family for centuries. In fact, it's something of a family trade. I am descended from Nell Gwyn, you know." I laughed, reflecting that Charles Stuart was by all accounts a handsome fellow. I would have changed places with Nell if I could.

His lordship watched as I entered the servants' wing once more where Jerry was waiting to whisk me along to the royal apartment. The clock struck midnight as the valet, looking bored and fatigued, let me into the bedchamber. An equally bored looking guardsman was the only other person on duty slumped on a seat in the antechamber.

I walked forward and curtsied before what looked like a small white mountain in the middle of the room. The soft candlelight was playing tricks on my eyes. Then the mountain moved and I saw it was the prince dressed in a white nightshirt flowing to his feet, a nightcap and gold Turkish slippers. This ridiculous vision was made even more incongruous by the blue sash of the garter worn across his chest. He greeted me eagerly and kissed my fingers before I removed my velvet cape and hood.

"How *delightful* to see you, my dear," he murmured, drawing me towards a small table where two cups of wine had been placed. I smiled sweetly, at a loss for

118

words. "How kind of you to let me come," was all I could muster in return, and it seemed inappropriate in the circumstances.

We sat on a love seat sipping our wine while I glanced anxiously at the prince's imposing bed with its Chinese silk and gold brocade hangings. I tried to establish where the secret door might be but the panelled walls gave nothing away. HRH mumbled and murmured beside me but I could not concentrate on the conversation. Brandy fumes wafted in my direction as he fumbled for my hand and peered down my bosom.

I wondered what the etiquette might be in these circumstances. I remembered reading that the concubines of the Great Turk approached their master via his feet. This thought made me giggle which seemed to please the prince.

"Delightful, delightful!" he burbled. "Have we met before, my dear?" He removed my glass and pulled me towards the bed none too gently. "No time to waste," he announced as he proceeded to throw himself onto the bed where he became stuck, half on and half off, undulating like a giant, gilded caterpillar. He signalled that I should assist him and so I found myself lifting the royal legs and attempting to hoist the future king onto the sheets.

When this manoeuvre was completed I reluctantly began to remove my own clothes. I approached the bed clad in my shift but not before I had poured more wine while the prince was arranging himself in the bed. I contrived to slip the sleeping draught into his glass. Jerry had given me the powder in a twist of paper.

I climbed into the bed and passed the glass to the Regent urging him to drink a toast to our meeting. He obediently swallowed it down and proceeded to business with gratifying enthusiasm, but his bulk somewhat limited his abilities. There was a great deal of huffing and puffing. He eventually had his way with me but I was thinking of Lord Byron at the time and I contrived not to notice.

I lay politely under the royal bulk for some time listening for the sounds indicating that my ordeal was over. When he began to snore and whiffle gently, I carefully began to slide away from the regal mountain. Once upright I dressed hastily and began to examine the wall panels wondering how I might find the right one.

As I was running my fingers over the walls there was a knock that seemed terrifyingly loud and Jerry's muffled voice could be heard calling my name. I froze, thinking that the prince must surely hear the sound — but he continued to emit soft whistling noises.

I located the panel and after some frantic examination of the woodwork there was a loud click and a panel slid back. Jerry emerged, gave me a swift kiss on the cheek and began to open a drawer in a gilded writing desk using a tiny gilt key.

"How did you get that key?" I hissed. He gave me a warning look and whispered, "I stole the original from the valet and made a copy." He removed a long blue box with gilt clasps. With a sigh of pleasure he relocked the drawer, seized my arm and propelled me towards the secret door and the darkness beyond.

He lit a small candle and I stumbled after him for what seemed an interminable hour but must have been around fifteen minutes. We mounted a flight of stone steps and entered the King's Head where Jerry hailed the landlord in a familiar manner.

We were led to the stables where I was heaved onto a large black horse which rolled its eyes in a disagreeable fashion. Jerry jumped up behind me and we were soon trotting through the narrow lanes of the town and out into the woods. A half moon and a sky full of spring stars gave us a good light and Jerry set the horse at a gallop.

"We are off to a new life, my love!" he gave an exuberant wave at the night sky. "How will you feel as the companion of a successful outlaw? Perhaps we should be married when we reach Amsterdam."

My thoughts on this subject were very mixed.

I wondered when and where my rescuers would appear and whether I truly wanted to be rescued. I was soon to find out, as a shot rang out. The horse reared, and then fell to its knees throwing me painfully into a heap on the hard ground. I heard my highwayman utter a curse as he knelt down trying to reach the brace of pistols he carried in the saddle bag. Another shot rang out and I saw him fall. A familiar voice cried out, "I think you winged him, Miles."

I was raised up by Lord Finchbrook who allowed me to lean against his manly chest and sob with relief and who knows what else. Miles called out again. We saw him bending over Jerry and shaking his head.

"Surely you have not killed him?" I wailed. Lord Finchbrook patted my head.

"He was a villain and a highwayman. Eventually he would have been hanged and taken you with him as his accomplice. It is better this way." I snivelled again and made to run over to the body to make a last farewell. His lordship restrained me gently and lifted me onto his horse. Miles removed the blue box and the pistols from Jerry's body and we rode away leaving the corpse under a tree.

I shall never forget my last sight of that still form lying under the black, midnight branches of an oak tree, with pale moonlight shining on the cape spread out around the body like wings. Jerry's face was turned away from me but one pale, lifeless hand rested on the grassy verge.

That night was the longest of my life. We returned to Halfcrown House where Selena and Adelaide were awaiting us, white with fear and anxiety. I felt more dead than alive but we huddled round the table fortifying ourselves with brandy while the men outlined their plan of action.

The blue box lay open in the centre of the table. A magnificent pendant necklace of diamonds and emeralds with matching pendant earrings and a wide bracelet — all set with delicate oval shaped stones of a deep lustrous green lay on a bed of black velvet. Lord Finchbrook closed the box and we sat staring at each other.

"At first light Miles and I will present ourselves at the Royal Pavilion and tell the whole story." I looked alarmed and he quickly reassured me. "We will explain that you were abducted from the prince's bed by the villainous Jeremy Sartain who intended to steal the jewels. He took you because you were a witness. Miles and I came upon you both in the woods and in the attempt to liberate you the villain was shot dead. We were thus able to rescue a lady in distress and to recover the royal jewels." He gave a broad smile. "Naturally, we were delighted to be of service to the crown!"

"How will you explain the opening of the secret door?" I asked. Miles gave an even broader grin and slapped the table. "We will simply tell the truth, that we have no idea how it was done. Naturally, you had nothing to do with it. Perhaps Sartain discovered the secret of the mechanism."

"Can you imagine the prince's gratitude, my dears? There will be a handsome reward for this and Lydia's unfortunate connection to the highwayman will remain undetected." I felt tears pricking my eyes once more as an even more unpleasant scenario passed before my eyes.

"If the prince is really grateful he might demand my presence in his bed on a regular basis. I do not think I could contemplate that." Lord Finchbrook assured me that he would tell the prince that I was prostrate with shock and unable to leave the house.

Selena chimed in at this point. "I think it might be a good idea if we removed ourselves to Bath. We could say that Lydia needed to take the waters after the shock to her nervous system. After a while Prinny will have forgotten all about her. I hear that his attention span is very short."

"Among other things," I remarked silently.

Miles and Lord Finchbrook did not appear overjoyed by this suggestion.

"I shall remove myself to London," Finchbrook declared. "The Bath waters always give me a deuce of a headache and I can't abide the company of the ancient and the broken down."

With that we retired to snatch a few hours of sleep before the dawn broke although Miles was heard to say that he felt fit for anything and fancied a bowl of mutton and beans and a heavy wet.

"Fighting and bloodshed always cheer him up," Selena remarked as she led him away. I felt more tears pricking my eyes and I sought oblivion in slumber.

When I rose again to face the world it was almost time for nuncheon and the menfolk were in high spirits. Everything had gone according to plan. There had been some consternation in the royal quarters when the prince woke alone. Amazingly, no-one had thought to check the jewels which were still unmissed when Miles and Lord Finchbrook presented them while the Regent was having his breakfast.

Jerry Sartain's treachery would be a nine days' wonder at court. The prince avowed that it was a pity he had escaped a good hanging. He was full of praise for the two heroes, especially for Miles who had done the actual deed. He promised a generous reward but we all knew how parlous the royal finances were. I wondered if he planned to sell the Cambridge emeralds after all, or merely to raise a loan through Mr Getheridge.

That gentleman suddenly reappeared after his strange absence — or rather he communicated by letter in the most forthright and unpleasant manner. No doubt he had heard of my elevation to the royal bedchamber and was jealous.

His letter, delivered soon after nuncheon, stated that he could no longer support me in "lavish" style in view of our apparent estrangement.

"He means because you have not spent time in his bed," remarked Selena. He requested that we vacate Halfcrown House within the week. I knew I had only to plead with him in person and trip lightly into his bed and all would be well, but I had no intention of doing so. A royal mountain was one thing but a gorilla was quite another. Once again I remembered my brief moments of pleasure with Jerry and felt emotion overwhelming me. I fled the room as Selena said firmly,

"We will definitely go to Bath."

I remained in my room for the next twenty-four hours, reading quietly and writing in my journal while Adelaide packed our belongings. Selena loaned me a Gothic mystery to distract my mind. It was Mrs Radcliffe's *The Confessional of the Black Penitents*.

"Is it horrid?" I asked her. "Are you sure it is horrid?" While I immersed myself in the terrors lurking behind the black veil a messenger arrived from the

Royal Pavilion. He delivered an elegant note from the prince assuring me of his devotion. He hoped that the enclosed gift would mitigate to some degree the terrible ordeal I had suffered. The gift was a row of perfectly matched pearls with a diamond pendant.

By an astonishing coincidence another messenger arrived hot on the heels of the royal emissary. I opened an ornate, gilded card bearing the arms of a foreign court. A note said briefly that Count Ferenc Esterhazy of the Austrian Embassy in London had caught a glimpse of me at Mrs Fitzherbert's house and wished to make my acquaintance.

"You have found a new career, my dear," Selena remarked quietly.

CHAPTER
ELEVEN

Bath, Spring 1816

We left the town on the following day. I realised that we needed to get away from Brighton after our recent experiences — but we had been there for such a short time! There would be no more *soirées* at the Royal Pavilion, no more invitations to take tea with Mrs Fitzherbert — and no chance to patronise Madame Renée's establishment. I sighed and again sought comfort in a novel as we bowled along, but I could not help wondering about my mysterious Austrian admirer. What should be my response? Would this be my opportunity to rise in the world? Visions of a countess's tiara swam before my eyes. Such carriages I would have. And the gowns, the *entrée* to royal courts, my own château . . . The coach jolted me back to reality. There was a possibility that I would merely receive another invitation to an assignation. I clutched the box containing the prince's necklace in frustration. Adelaide sat opposite giving me speculative looks. I fear she can read my mind.

Lord Finchbrook continued to befriend us in the most gallant manner, acting as go-between with the royal household, assuring the prince of my deepest gratitude for his gift and my prostration with shock necessitating a stay in Bath, as agreed. He also offered us the use of his house in Laura Place in that city.

"It is really my aunt's house but she is seldom in residence and I have the run of it whenever I want." In addition, he arranged to meet us in London and convey us to Bath in his own carriage. We were extremely obliged to him. It was obvious that he still yearned after Selena. I must have a serious conversation with her on that subject.

When we reached London we broke the journey by putting up at the White Horse in Piccadilly for two nights. My friends had given up their London house for financial reasons. My spirits remained low and I thought often of Jerry. I knew he was a rogue and no gentleman, but the heart cannot be swayed by logic. I tried on the prince's necklace, admiring my image in the mirror, but finding that I was only partly comforted by this.

News has come to London that Lord Byron has taken a villa on the shores of Lake Geneva where he holds court with the mad poet Shelley and his wife, his paramour, and a household of fallen women and strange doctors. How I wished I could join them. If I am to be an outcast and a scarlet woman what better company could I have? Instead, I am en route to Bath and the company of elderly invalids and twittering debutantes. I can only hope that my admirer, the Count, will seek me out. If only we had been introduced when we visited Mrs Fitzherbert. I recalled the two elegant gentlemen who left as we arrived. Which one of them had been smitten by my charms?

Selena had not recognised either of them and even Adelaide had nothing to report.

My friend confined herself to commenting that she hoped the Count was in possession of a good fortune. Did I detect a note of jealousy in her voice? Once again, I confided my exploits, hopes and fears to my journal before leaving London. There was much to tell.

Adelaide knew that Bath was no longer the height of fashion. As we resumed our journey she remarked that some trollopy servant at the inn had told her it was stupidish to visit the city. Nobody of any account was travelling there. I looked meaningfully at Selena but she was busy writing lists of things to do.

"We must have cards printed immediately," she told her almost insensible husband who was nodding off in the corner of the carriage.

"We have left a good deal of unfinished business in Brighton," I remarked. "There is still the matter of how Von Mecks was killed — and why, and how Mr Getheridge was involved."

"It is not for us to trouble ourselves with such things," she rebuked me. "What have we to do with matters of state and the prince's finances?" I reflected gloomily that we were already involved and we had surely not heard the last of them.

Although we contrived to sleep through part of the journey we were weary and out of humour when the carriage rolled into Bath in the late afternoon. We were soon conveyed to Laura Place where we found the household in immaculate condition. Lord Finchbrook bade us farewell and left us to the care of the requisite steady cook, giddy housemaid and sedate, middle-aged manservant. Fires were lit and a meal prepared in the greatest comfort. I retired early to seek solace with my novel while Selena contemplated the joys of shopping in Milsom Street.

Adelaide remarked darkly that the serving maid looked the type that was always on the gad. I have noticed that my maid affects to despise other servants. I was disturbed to discover that she had brought along Von Mecks' boots and cape which I had forgotten about. I felt uneasy as I contemplated the tasselled Hessians and splendid cape. Surely it was bad luck to be carrying around the possessions of a murdered man and I had attracted enough of that already. My maid obediently tucked them away at the back of a closet. They were too fine to be given to a beggar.

Miles declared that wild horses would not compel him to drink the spa waters but he had no doubt that blue ruin was as readily available in Bath as elsewhere. Selena placed a restraining arm on his.

"We must first be seen at the Assembly Rooms. If we consult the visitors' book we can discover who is in residence and leave cards." I could tell that my friend's mind had turned to financial matters once again. She was planning a card game, I had no doubt. Something altogether more sedate than the London gathering, however. Perhaps a lethal game of whist.

The dawdling, genteel atmosphere of Bath served, unaccountably, to put my friend in the highest of spirits, while Miles and I remained downcast. At least I was able to buy some good lace and borrow books from

Duffield's library in Milsom Street. Selena, who knew Bath well, could not wait to drag me along to Sydney Gardens. I made a decision and wrote to the Count that I was in Bath and I would be delighted to receive him either in that city or when I returned to London. I am sure, dear reader, that you would have done the same in my position.

I agreed with Selena that the wide, tree-lined thoroughfare that was Sydney Place and also Great Pulteney Street were most impressive to stroll along. The warm, honey-coloured stone of the houses with their classical lines, white doors, black railings, set against the green hills in the distance, cannot fail to lift one's spirits. Selena ecstatically described the routs and gala evenings held in the gardens with fireworks and dancing. As we wandered among the grottos and arbours I had to agree that Bath could be delightful and was certainly less frantic than London.

"Wait until you see this place filled with three thousand people," Selena enthused. "What fun, and what opportunities for clandestine meetings!"

"Were you thinking of Lord Finchbrook?" I asked. "You know he hates Bath."

"No, you silly creature. I was thinking of you." I sighed, thinking again how tiring the life of a scarlet woman might become. Within a few days of our arrival we duly went to the gardens for the public breakfast, escorted by a reluctant Miles.

"The weather is far too chilly for alfresco meals," he complained. "I could be at home, warm and snug and pushing a glass about."

"Is it not a little early in the day, my love, even for you?" Selena's tone was more acid than usual. Adelaide was dragging her feet too. I knew she was disappointed to leave Brighton but as my maid she cannot expect to have any say in the matter. I was paying her seven pounds a year and all the tea and sugar she required. This was more than generous bearing in mind my paltry allowance from Darcy. Only this morning she surveyed my wardrobe with some disdain and asked when I planned another card game. She has realised her usefulness to me and takes advantage. My mother always advised me to be firm with the servants. It was the only sensible piece of advice she ever gave me.

Our low spirits were soon revived when we arrived at the gardens where pretty booths could be hired. We ate our rolls and drank our chocolate to the soothing accompaniment of a trio of musicians playing stringed instruments. The gardens were delightful to wander about in with grottos, waterfalls, plants and shrubs arranged to give the maximum pleasure to the eye.

After breakfast we returned to the house but Selena insisted on going back to the gardens at dusk. Crowds of people were pouring through the gates and the night sky was lit up with fireworks. A military band was playing near the hotel and the sounds of dancing and singing could be heard.

Sir Winthrop Meyers and Lady Dorothea, our neighbours in Laura Place, graciously agreed to escort us on this occasion, leaving Miles to find his own distractions in the less salubrious parts of the city. Sir Winthrop was most attentive, introducing us to some of the gentlefolk of his acquaintance. Sadly, none of them were less than fifty years old.

One of them escorted me to supper and told me an improbable story.

"Did you know, my dear Mrs Wickham, that at least one former resident of this fair city believed that the breath of virgins could prolong life and ensure good health?" He winked at me in an inappropriate manner and I gave a sour response.

"The number of decrepit citizens on the streets of Bath would indicate that virgins are not as easily come by as they once were." My companion sniggered and attempted to pinch my rear. I stepped aside quickly and returned to the main party where a dowager was extolling the merits of the adjustable mattresses for invalids available at a Milsom Street store. A Catherine wheel exploded overhead in a shower of pink and green and violet.

The delights of the gardens and the shopping possibilities of Bath began to pall after a few weeks, but as we left the premises of Smith & Jones in New Bond Street, one morning Selena announced triumphantly that she had arranged a card party.

"It will be held at Laura Place, I am sure Lord Finchbrook would not object."

"How can you possibly do that?" I cried. "There are not enough people in sufficient health in this city to undertake gambling for high stakes. Any losses would probably result in heart failure." Selena gave me a playful rap with her reticule.

"You exaggerate, Lydia. I have chosen the victims carefully. There are some members of the *ton* here at the moment. Most of them are in possession of their own hair and teeth and, more importantly, large sums of money that they are anxious to lose." I realised that Selena had researched her prey carefully at the Assembly Rooms. Even Miles could be useful at such times, striking up conversations in unlikely places.

I remained doubtful of the wisdom of this enterprise, even though I knew we needed to replenish our funds. I wondered how our neighbours would react when they realised what was happening, but Selena had thought of that too.

"Of course we shall invite the Meyers. They will take part in a sedate game of whist and a hand of loo while we gather a small number of enthusiasts to play for higher stakes in another room. There will be an elegant supper. It will be the talk of the Assembly Rooms."

"It might be as well to ask Lord Finchbrook to come down from London with some friends. It is his house, after all — or his aunt's." I had a sudden vision of the ancient aunt making a surprise visit in the midst of all this. "Finchbrook will do anything for you," I added slyly, "you know he is sweet on you." Selena blushed and turned away. I resolved to wear the prince's necklace in public for the first time. Of course my friend was able to win me over by persuading me of our urgent need for ready cash.

"Miles is already talking of buying more etchings," she complained. "He is frequenting those little shops near Abbey Churchyard. You know his spendthrift ways, Lydia." Indeed, and I also knew that acquiring some expensive jewellery was no substitute for ready money. My friend gave signs of being on the fret like a thoroughbred horse. Her nostrils quivered and she gave a low whinnying noise of distress. I stepped back hastily and agreed to everything.

There remained the problem of the staff at Laura Place. Disgruntled by the sudden appearance of three strangers who were taking up residence and disturbing their comfortable existence, they were aghast at the notion of entertainment and cards at the house. The manservant assured us that Miss Worthington disapproved of gambling and rarely entertained. We were forced to assure him that Lord Finchbrook had given permission. A generous gratuity settled the matter. Our meagre finances were spent on the preparations for the evening's entertainment. Recovering our outlay was essential, if only to keep Miles in blue ruin.

He had been greatly cast down at not receiving a financial reward for his part in rescuing the royal emeralds. A messenger had brought a small oil painting of the prince and a signed letter of commendation before we left Brighton. Selena and I had expected nothing else, given the state of the royal finances.

We placed the portrait in a prominent position in the room at Laura Place where our neighbours would play a staid hand of whist. In the main salon the table was arranged for gaming and the servants were instructed to bring plenty of food and drink. Miles was given the task of preventing the two sets of guests from mingling or even meeting, if possible.

"He should be good for that if he keeps a clear head," Selena said without much conviction. I was looking forward to the evening with impatience, not only for the chance to repair my finances, but to relieve the genteel monotony of this place. There was only the elegant stupidity of dinner parties and trips to the pleasure gardens. Lady Dorothea told us that it would be unseemly to visit the theatre, and the balls seldom attracted anyone of note.

Sydney Gardens remained the height of gaiety — all very well if one had a beau to dally with in the grottos and flirt with among the arbours. I remembered Jerry with a pang at such moments.

"If we raise sufficient funds tonight we must return to London," I told Selena, thinking of my Austrian admirer. "I cannot achieve my ambition to reach Paris, or indeed dance at Almack's, while we remain in this deathly watering hole. You are in a similar position," I reminded her. Selena looked thoughtful.

"Might it not be wiser to avoid London altogether and take a house in Paris? The Duke of Wellington is leaving soon to become the French Ambassador. Many influential people will accompany him, and the rents are lower in Paris."

"What about Almack's?" I cried. "When will I dance there?" Selena withered me with a look. "Sometimes, Lydia, I fear you have a remarkably shallow nature." She swept out of the room and I called for Adelaide to place the royal necklace around my neck. I wore a gown of the palest grey lace over pink silk. All pretence of mourning had vanished since the *soirée* at the Royal

Pavilion. In Bath I told everyone that I had been widowed for some years.

My friends managed to assemble a reasonable crowd of people for the gaming. A few members of the *ton* needed a little persuasion to part with their money with the degree of abandon common in the capital, but Lord Finchbrook and his party encouraged them and the brandy and wine began to flow.

I urged everyone to wash away the taste of spa water, and casually lowered my bodice. Things began to liven up immediately and large amounts of money changed hands. Selena and I agreed to take turns to visit our other guests. Thank heaven for sturdy doors that kept in the noise from the gambling room. The fact that most of our neighbours were elderly and in various stages of decrepitude worked to our advantage; their hearing was none too sharp.

My eye fixed on a Mr Charles Lennox who was reputed to have an income of ten thousand pounds per year, as much as my dear brother-in-law. Selena and I tried our womanly wiles upon him without success. I wondered if he might prefer Miles's attentions. Society is full of depravity and Mr Lennox's arrogance needed puncturing.

I circled the room, leaning over shoulders, cooing encouragingly and trying to glimpse the cards. Mr Lennox was not fooled. He carefully blocked my view. I had to admit that he was a handsome fellow — dark haired, straight of nose and broad of shoulder. It was unseemly to be so wealthy, so attractive, yet impervious to womanly charms.

"Offer him some game pie," Selena whispered, "it might distract him."

I procured a plate of pie and surreptitiously laced it well with black pepper. Mr Lennox took a large mouthful and fell into a paroxysm of coughing and spluttering. Coins, notes, food and drink scattered across the table as Selena and Miles ran to offer assistance. In the confusion I was able to rearrange some cards to our advantage. I slipped from the room as Miles poured champagne down the throat of the unfortunate man.

I fortified myself with a little more champagne and remembered to hitch up my bodice before opening the door of the other salon. A discreet hum of voices abruptly stopped and several pairs of eyes regarded me with alarm. I looked down and realised that I had pulled up my bodice on one side only, revealing even more on the other.

"Oh, Mrs Wickham," cried Sir Winthrop Meyers, "you must join us for a hand of whist!" His wife shot him a poisonous look.

"Forgive me, sir," I cried, "but I am a fiend at cards and I would not want to incommode you." This speech was greeted with a puzzled silence broken only by a loud hiccough — mine.

"We heard some commotion earlier," said Lady Dorothea suspiciously. We did not realise you had other guests."

"Oh, that? Just Captain Caruthers meeting with a few old regimental friends. They can be a little unruly at times." An expression of alarm crossed her ladyship's face.

"Perhaps in the circumstances, dear husband, we should leave."

"Not until I have persuaded our fair hostess to play a hand with us."

"How can I refuse?" I found I was leaning against the door at this point. I must have taken more champagne than I thought.

The door opened a crack behind me and Selena whispered urgently. "Come at once, Lydia. There is chaos in the gaming room." I backed out of the room waving my fan distractedly at the guests and promising to send in some refreshments. I rushed back to the gaming room, lowering my bodice once again and hoicking up a stray lock of hair. Adelaide rolled her eyes at me as she passed by. I found Lennox prone on the floor gasping like a fish.

"I think he's dying," declared Miles who was purple in the face from his attempts at resuscitation.

"Nonsense! Give him *sal volatile* and take him out into the fresh air."

Several people raised Lennox and began to drag him away. Overcome with heat and annoyance I took a few more sips of champagne realising that I had scarcely found an opportunity to play at the tables. I had turned my attention, a trifle unsteadily, to the remaining players when scuffling noises and raised voices reached my ears.

Selena and I rushed into the entrance hall just as our whist-playing neighbours emerged from the small salon ready to take their leave.

"Will you not stay for supper?" Selena begged.

"That was our intention," replied Lady Dorothea icily. "But supper was not forthcoming." We had been sabotaged by the servants. That same manservant threw open the front door triumphantly revealing the figure of Mr Lennox vomiting over the railings outside, assisted by Miles and Lord Finchbrook. Curled up on the bottom step was a figure I recognised with horror as Mr Getheridge.

The guests picked their way neatly through this scenario and I retreated back to the gaming room where I collapsed into a chair and finished off the champagne. I leaned my arms on the table and bowed my head in momentary despair. When I looked up a large cheese reproached me from its china dish in a way that cheese often does, especially the kind with holes.

Eventually Getheridge staggered into the room and sank to his knees in front of me.

"For the love of God, madam, allow me to stay," he begged. I stared at him in amazement. His clothes were dusty and covered with white smears. Even his face and hair had a curiously moth-eaten appearance.

"You appear to have been savaged by demented pigeons, sir!" I remarked, giggling at my champagne wit. When questioned he would admit only that he had been set upon by footpads — an unlikely event in this quiet area. I asked him where he was staying but he evaded the question.

We gave him food and drink and he revived a little and begged to join the gaming. I was surprised because he had told me he disliked gambling. Selena and I exchanged worried looks as Getheridge played with

140

feverish intensity. He had no money but as a banker he was considered good for any amount. After a few early wins, he lost heavily and was forced to withdraw. He collapsed in an inconsolable heap in a corner and we found him there after everyone had left and we were counting our winnings.

Miles wanted to throw him out but I was curious to hear the real story from our uninvited guest. Selena discreetly left the room and I sat beside him.

"My dear, my dear, things are not going well for me," he moaned.

"Is this a matter connected to the prince's affairs?" I enquired. He nodded miserably. "That is but one thread in this complex tapestry of misfortunes. There is the matter of the bank. Its affairs are not in order. There will be . . . repercussions."

"And you will be held to account for them?" He nodded again and put his head in his hands.

"What is the connection with Von Mecks?" I asked innocently. He started at the name and looked up. "I was the prince's banker and I tried to be of service in other ways."

"The emeralds?" He nodded again. "Unfortunately, criminal elements became involved and I was vulnerable to blackmail."

"Was Von Mecks murdered as a warning to you or to the prince?" This was an inspired guess on my part. Getheridge's eyes filled with tears.

"Yes, I will have that man's death on my conscience always. I must pay the price. We will not meet again, my dear. It is best if you are not associated with me in any way."

"Surely the prince will not see you cast down?"

He shook his head. "His Royal Highness cannot afford to be involved in any more financial scandals. He will disown me rather than incur the wrath of Parliament."

I could not help reflecting on my bad luck once more. The only banker I had managed to snare had turned out to be a fraudster.

We took pity on Getheridge, allowing him to stay the night. His clothes were righted and he was offered breakfast. Miles called for a chair to convey him to the London Mail and I surreptitiously placed a few coins in his pocket. He did not ask for the return of the diamond and amethyst bangle, which I thought very sporting of him in the circumstances. We all retired to bed muzzle-headed and exhausted.

As if the lamentable scenes at Laura Place had not been enough to try us, the next morning, as I nursed a champagne headache of Napoleonic proportions, Miles brought more bad news. Having supervised Getheridge's departure he told us that we could not take breakfast in Sydney Gardens because a ruffian was at large in the grounds. Selena waved this excuse aside; she was furious with the servants and tried to prod her husband into action.

"You must remonstrate with them, Miles. Their behaviour was disgraceful and we will be shunned by our neighbours from now on. If you cannot do that then we will immediately leave to breakfast in the gardens regardless. I will not eat another meal in this house!" Miles looked wretched; he disliked confrontation except on the battlefield.

"Now, now, my love. As they are not our servants and this is not our house I can scarcely dismiss them."

"We paid them well," Selena insisted, "and we deserve good service at the very least." I tried to pacify my friend by pointing out that if the house was not ours then the neighbours were not our neighbours. Impasse resulted and we all departed for the gardens.

CHAPTER
TWELVE

We arrived at the gardens in tolerable weather although the general hubbub did little to restore my low spirits or assuage my pounding headache. Nevertheless, the spirit of the place catches at everyone as they enter, gazing at the mural of the god Apollo in the loggia.

Miles had purchased a season ticket for one guinea against Selena's wishes. My friend has become very unpredictable of late. First she wished to remain in Bath, her favourite city, and then she urged me to return to London — or even Paris as soon as possible. I wondered if Lord Finchbrook's attentions were unsettling her or whether she was anxious to curtail Miles's visits to a certain Miss Coleman, a lady chiropodist at No. 5 Abbey Churchyard. He swears that his corns need expert attention but Selena is not convinced.

We sat in a thatched booth sipping chocolate and trying not to think about last night's disasters. A thin, watery sun struggled through the treetops before expiring into the general greyness. Summer has decided to avoid the British Isles this year. Miles read his newspaper and we listened contentedly to the music playing even at this hour. A small boy appeared with a handbill advertising the appearance of Madame Naqui, an acrobat and tightrope walker, direct from Vauxhall. She was depicted perched confidently on the rope like St Simeon on his pillar.

Selena could not be persuaded to take a walk and so I set off in the direction of the labyrinth. I encountered few visitors as I wandered along. Most people were in the booths or gathered to hear the musicians at the hotel.

My melancholic thoughts about my situation in life, my feelings for Jerry and other missed opportunities oppressed me so much as I walked that I was forced to brush away a few tears. If only I could be indifferent to the slings and arrows of outrageous fortune. I have observed that those who care least for the outcome, whether in love, in cards or in life itself, are the most successful. It is a curse to be needy, but I am too passionate by nature to be indifferent to anyone or anything. I needed to meet the Count as soon as possible. Perhaps then my life would change for the better.

As I was immersed in these thoughts I heard a low whistle from the bushes on my right. Taking it for a simple bird call I continued on my way, but the whistle was repeated and was followed by my name called out in a low, throaty voice. I jumped several inches and felt my heart leaping about my chest. I walked slowly towards the bush, looking right and left to check that I was alone before peering into the boughs.

"You took your time, madam." A low voice was followed by the head and shoulders of Jerry Sartain. I gave a shriek and my legs turned to jelly. I clung to a willow branch for support as he urged me to keep quiet.

"But you are dead!" I choked.

"And I intend to remain that way as far as the world is concerned, my dear. With your able assistance, of course."

"I think I am about to faint."

"Don't be a goose, Lydia. I am alive, you are not being visited by a spook. Let us go into the labyrinth where we can wander undisturbed." He emerged from the undergrowth enveloped in a dramatic cape and hood. I noticed that he looked pale and thinner than before and he had grown a small beard — or affixed a false one.

He took my arm and we entered the labyrinth as the sound of pan pipes floated over the garden. The band had been replaced by the Pandean Minstrels.

I was overwhelmed at being reunited with my highway-man lover although I knew my value to him was purely a monetary one. Taking a deep breath I blurted, "I want to help you but I have no money at present. I have not been lucky at cards of late."

"Never mind that, for the moment. There is the little matter of how your friends knew where we were, how they managed to apprehend us in the forest. Did you betray me, my dear?" His voice was still low but full of menace. He tightened his grip on my arm until I almost squealed with pain.

"They forced me to tell them," I cried. "I had no idea they would try to kill you. They were concerned for my reputation."

146

"How touching. And you left me for dead. I was forced to crawl through the forest, wounded, until I reached a hovel where a poor creature took me in until I was healed." My eyes filled with tears. "I am so sorry, Jerry, they told me you were dead."

"Did you not hear that no body was found?"

"No, we left almost at once for Bath."

He moved closer to me, his eyes still shadowed by his hood so that I could not read their expression. His voice assumed a pathetic timbre that I wanted to believe was genuine. "You do not know how much your desertion pained me, Lydia. I thought of you constantly during my long hours of convalescence. When I remembered the ecstasy of our moments together in that bedchamber, I —"

"Stop!" I moaned. "I cannot bear it. Forgive me." His mood changed abruptly. He seized my arm again and asked sharply, "What of the jewels . . . did your friends keep them?"

"Of course they did not. How can you think that? They were returned to the prince. Miles hoped for a reward, a financial one, but it was not forthcoming." I decided not to mention the royal gift to me. Jerry would surely force me to hand it over.

"It was a wild and witless scheme that could never succeed," I continued. "Only a mad man would have attempted such a thing." He suddenly released me and gave a growling laugh. "You are right, of course, sweet Lydia. It *was* a crazed scheme but it just might have succeeded — and had it, it would have been the crime of the century. Would you not have wanted to be part of that, my dear?"

I licked my dry lips and whispered, "I do not know. I have not . . . I am not as daring as you." A small voice in my head was telling me that Jerry had little to lose. He was already an outcast from society while I was still clinging on by the skin of my teeth. He began to walk quickly, dragging me along with him. We had not paid any attention to the pathways since we entered the labyrinth and now we were lost. We darted to and fro unsuccessfully while Jerry said he would send me a message later. "But first we must get out of this confounded maze before we are seen together."

"Where are you staying?" I asked.

"In a low rookery on Avon Street, where else?" He named a place in a district of the city notorious for every kind of vice.

At that moment we turned a corner and found an exit just as a crowd of people walked towards us. Jerry said that I should meet him tomorrow in the gardens. "And bring some money." These were his last words before he slipped away into the shadows.

Tomorrow was Sunday. I would have to plead an indisposition while Miles and Selena went to the service in the abbey, for appearances' sake more than religious feeling.

I returned to the breakfast booth and found it empty. My friends had walked to the hotel to listen to the musicians. Selena had been too preoccupied to notice my long absence. I wondered what Jerry would expect me to steal next. The crown jewels?

Dinner that evening was a melancholy affair. Selena was obsessed with our presumed loss of reputation among the boring Bathonians in the neighbourhood. I was wrapped in thought about my position in Jerry's affections and my status in Society. I realised that the two things were precariously linked.

Miles found the atmosphere oppressive and escaped as quickly as possible to one of his drinking haunts. Selena barely noticed his departure as she chewed on a fingernail.

"I am afraid that the Meyers and their friends will cut us if we appear at the Assembly Rooms. Word may have spread already," she moaned.

"Then we will not go there," I replied. "What is the point? They are all half dead and of no consequence in society." Selena ignored this and moaned on. "I dare not even contemplate attending divine service at the abbey." I remembered my assignation in the gardens and hastily urged her to do her duty.

"They cannot cut us dead in a house of worship. We must do the right thing and put on a brave face." Of course I had to promise to accompany my friends. I would need to develop a sudden indisposition at some point so that I could remain behind and sneak off to the gardens.

In the event it proved difficult to evade Selena's commands. She assembled us all with military precision and led the way, chin held high, towards the abbey. I feigned a twisted ankle and insisted on returning to the house leaning on Adelaide's shoulder. That young woman was not fooled for a moment and said she would follow me at a distance as I made my way into the gardens, "for your own good, madam," as she put it. That would not do at all so I insisted that she return to the house.

Once again Jerry popped up from the bushes like one of Mrs Radcliffe's lurking ghosts. He gave me an affectionate peck on the cheek and came straight to the point.

"Do you have the money, my sweet?" I handed over my meagre winnings from the ill-fated card game while he complained at the paltry amount. I had kept back only a small part, dear reader. I urgently needed a new bonnet and Adelaide had not received her wages.

"I must return to London forthwith if I am to capitalise on my ghostly status," he declared as he stowed away the money beneath his cape. "Bath is too small, the pickings are slim these days." He gave me his wicked smile. "How say you Mrs Wickham, shall I become Willy Raikes henceforth? The name has a certain ring to it. Or shall I be William Theophilus Raikes, gentleman's gentleman? That could be a useful profession." I shook my head.

"Are you not afraid of Captain Townshend, the Bow Street officer? He terrified me when we met. If he decided to investigate . . ." My voice failed. Jerry patted my cheek reassuringly. "He will not pursue Jeremy Sartain. That man is recently deceased, do you not recall?"

"Your body was not found," I reminded him. "Townshend is no fool, he will remember that."

Jerry refused to be cast down, declaring that he did not fear the little man in his kerseymere breeches, "Although he is a sharp one." Suddenly he broke off, mid-conversation, and peered out from under his hat at one of the servants from the hotel who was staring in his direction. "I believe that confounded rascal suspects something or has recognised me." He took my arm and we walked rapidly in the opposite direction, passing the waterfall.

Visibly relaxed now that the danger appeared to have passed, Jerry picked me up, deposited me playfully in one of the swings, and soon had me soaring aloft, despite my protests. Soon there was a disturbance, as at least a dozen passers-by congregated around us laughing, pointing and shouting ribald comments. Two officials from the hotel pushed their way through the crowd, one seized Jerry and the other caught hold of the swing bringing me down to earth rapidly. I was all aflutter, clutching my bonnet to my head as the officials angrily demanded to know our names, telling us that we had flouted one of the local by-laws. The crowd agreed, chanting as one, "No swinging on Sundays!" as we were dragged away. Several more respectable looking couples turned away in disgust as we passed.

I was crimson with mortification and I knew instinctively that I could not rely on any assistance from my companion. This proved correct when Jerry wrenched himself away from his captor. "I swear I'll spoil your daylights," he said, before knocking the man to the ground. We were near the canal bank at that point and Jerry took a flying leap onto the passing

London-bound boat, to the accompaniment of cheers from its occupants.

My captor unwisely released me and rushed to the canal bank shouting at the disappearing boat. I hitched up my skirts and fled towards the nearest exit. Adelaide was waiting for me in the street having observed my humiliation from afar. Fortunately she had not recognised Jerry, but I cannot imagine what she had made of the situation.

"I was about to return to the 'ouse, madam," she assured me as we hurried homewards, "when I had a feeling you was in trouble." We had walked for barely five minutes when a carriage rattled past and stopped suddenly a few yards ahead of us. I was convinced that I was about to be arrested and exhibited in the stocks or some such fate when an elegant arm waved from the window of the coach followed by the head of a man with a mane of blond hair.

I climbed in without a moment's hesitation and collapsed on the seat followed by Adelaide. I gasped my thanks to the handsome man sitting opposite. He seemed familiar, but I could not place him.

"You appear to be in some difficulty, my dear," he remarked in a charming foreign accent. "I observed some of the scene in the garden." I blushed again.

"I am afraid I inadvertently desecrated the Sabbath and I am sure the penalty for that is most unpleasant." He laughed and patted my hand.

"At least it enabled me to meet you again, Mrs Wickham." At that moment I realised why this elegant gentleman seemed familiar to me. I had glimpsed him at Mrs Fitzherbert's house. This was the Count, my mysterious admirer!

The knowledge caused me deep embarrassment. Aware of my disordered appearance and the circumstances of my departure from the gardens — all witnessed by the Count — caused me to blush to the roots of my hair. I hastily patted my curls into place and adjusted my bonnet.

"I assure you, sir," I began to stutter. "My behaviour is not usually so wild. I was caught up in an unfortunate escapade. I am quite mortified." My voice faded away and my blush deepened as the Count smiled reassuringly.

"I am quite sure that you were the innocent party, my dear Mrs Wickham." There was a hint of sarcasm in his voice.

I took a deep breath and leaned back against the luxurious upholstery. Adelaide in her corner watched us wide eyed. The Count was staying at No. 33 The Paragon as a guest of Mrs Sarah Siddons, the celebrated actress, and her husband. "I am a great admirer of her artistry." As the coach rattled along I collected my wits sufficiently to give the Count directions to Laura Place. I entreated him to join us for a dish of tea but he preferred to continue in his mysterious fashion, saying that he would call upon me in London when I returned. He deposited us outside the house and drove away immediately.

CHAPTER
THIRTEEN

We entered the house and I had only a few minutes in which to compose myself and rest my foot on a stool before Selena and Miles arrived, the former gazing suspiciously at my injured limb before announcing that they had been ignored by everyone at the abbey and we might as well return to London forthwith.

Later, I recounted to Selena my meeting with the Count and his refusal to enter the house. "He must have something to hide. Like a wife," she said. My friend can be very cynical at times.

"He simply wished to avoid incommoding us," I insisted. Selena smiled in a superior manner. I fear she is jealous of my good fortune in attracting such an admirer. Sometimes I catch her looking at Miles in a speculative manner. I decided not to confess my other misdemeanours at this stage. There was no point in adding to the household woes. I did venture to point out that if we returned to London we would not have a roof over our heads and I would not be able to receive the Count.

"I have a little money," Selena said. "We can rent some rooms in a more modest part of town."

"That would not be the thing at all, my dear," Miles argued. "If we are to continue with the card parties we need suitable surroundings."

"And what do you suggest, husband dear?" Selena snapped at him before putting her head in her hands. I felt downcast for all of us. Our dreams and fantasies were destined to remain nothing more. Miles did not seem at all upset. He patted his chest in a self-congratulatory manner, patted his wife's head and announced that he had some capital news.

"And I have not even had to resort to selling more etchings." He explained that he had met an old military acquaintance in one of Bath's drinking dives who had offered him the use of his house in Portman Square for six months at a peppercorn rent.

"My friend will be abroad for that time and we will act as custodians. We must make our fortune quickly, my dears." He sat down with a silly smile on his cherubic features while Selena rushed across to him and covered his face with kisses. She vowed to overlook his visits to the lady chiropodist — for the moment — and pronounced him the finest of husbands. To this touching scene I added my congratulations and promised to contribute what I could. I still had Mr Darcy's allowance if I could keep it from Jerry.

Lord Finchbrook was expected down from London later that afternoon and he brought gloomy news.

"Getheridge has been arrested for fraudulent dealings. They say the bank will fall." Everyone looked meaningfully at me, no doubt expecting lamentations, but I had not been exactly intimate with the man.

Selena remarked that she was glad not to have had money in that particular establishment. The men agreed and I remembered my modest allowance again.

"My money!" I squealed. "Mr Darcy deposits it quarterly at that bank." Lord Finchbrook said he was sure that Darcy could bear the loss. "I must write to him at once," I muttered. The news quite destroyed my appetite for the boiled mutton in white sauce with boiled onions — a favourite of the Prince Regent, according to the cook. We were attended assiduously by the servants in the presence of Lord Finchbrook but it availed them little. Selena remained determined not to give them a penny when we took our leave.

I retired to my room later and composed a gloomy note to my brother-in-law informing him of the bank's affairs and begging him not to leave me destitute. My small allowance from my father was also paid into that same bank.

Afterwards, I sat by the window trying to collect my thoughts and formulate a plan. I wondered whether my friend was right about the Count. Did he have a wife and were his intentions, therefore, strictly dishonourable? I wondered also whether in fact I cared, especially if he offered to take me to the continent.

My family would be excruciatingly mortified. That thought cheered me somewhat.

There was little else to be cheerful about. The news was all of riots in the streets, failed crops and bad weather. The Duke of Wellington was to leave London soon to become our ambassador in Paris, but I was no nearer to achieving my goal unless I had the help of my new admirer. And what would become of Getheridge — or Jerry? I shuddered when I thought of my involvement with two men who were both felons. I needed to meet the Count soon. At least an aristocratic diplomat would be unimpeachable, unless there was another outbreak of revolution on the continent.

After his somewhat precipitate departure Jerry lost no time in returning to Bath, despite his avowed contempt for the city. I fondly hoped that his swift return meant that he could not bear a parting from me. Alas, I was to discover that he had more pressing financial reasons and my assistance was needed.

He contrived to meet me at St Aldhelm's church, an unlikely spot where we could converse undisturbed on pretence of inspecting the memorials. I was to notify him in advance whether any runners were in the vicinity.

After I had satisfied myself that there was no danger I found a child from the perishing and dangerous class who could be entrusted to deliver a note to the Crown and Thistle public house in Avon Street where Jerry was lodged, in what circumstances I shuddered to think. Later, he announced quite casually that he was sharing a room with several hobbledehoys and a prostitute calling herself Freelove Flower.

He told me that he had *marked* a certain gentleman in Bath, Mr Nathaniel Davenport, and planned to burgle his house knowing that he kept large sums of money at home. If that stratagem proved to be too dangerous he planned a spot of blackmail. Jerry knew of the man's activities in Walcot Street where there was a home for fallen women who were persuaded to follow

157

a new occupation as laundresses. Davenport recruited women from this place to attend lewd gatherings at his house with groups of men. Messages and instructions were conveyed to the women in Davenport's laundry.

Jerry had already befriended one of the women who called herself Belle Fleur. She acted as a spy for him — and who knew what else? Jerry had an effortless way with females, as I knew to my cost. He was irresistible, a force of nature.

"I will need your assistance, my love." I had been dreading an announcement of this kind. I knew I would be called upon to give aid in one form or another. Jerry had subtle and not so subtle ways of reminding me of our original agreement and, as always, I felt powerless to refuse.

"You must distract Davenport while I gain access to the house," he informed me.

"What about the servants?" I offered this feeble resistance and he dismissed it. "There are only two male servants living in the house and I have arranged for Freelove Flower to keep them occupied." This was the woman from the inn of doubtful virtue. Some shreds of self respect came to my defence.

"I will *not* distract anyone in the manner you required of me in Brighton," I said vehemently. "The Prince Regent was all very well but —" Jerry interrupted me using the caressing, wheedling tone I knew well.

"There will be no need of that, my love. You will simply need to engage Davenport in conversation long enough to enable me to enter the house unseen."

158

"We have not been introduced!" He sighed and instructed me to be outside the house with Adelaide at the hour when Davenport always left the premises, at eleven o'clock. "Appear to twist your ankle, or anything that will oblige him to assist you for a few minutes. You will think of something. Leave the rest to me."

I attempted to strike a bargain, but instead, I found myself begging for some moments alone with him. He gave me a smile and a peck on the cheek before departing swiftly. He would promise anything to gain my assistance. Jerry was truly cast in the same mould as my late husband. I am always attracted to cads of the worst kind.

Unfortunately, Selena insisted on accompanying us on the walk. I fussed over an imaginary stone in my shoe outside No. 26 Bennett Street while both Selena and Adelaide eyed me with suspicion.

"What ruse are you employing, Lydia? You have had a number of trifling accidents recently and you make an astonishing recovery from them." Truly one's friends cannot always be relied on for support at crucial moments.

Adelaide contented herself with a sarcastic, "Modom?" I replied with a terse.

"Trust me."

Mr Davenport duly appeared but he seemed reluctant to be of assistance. He had a narrow face and a ferret-like visage. It was not difficult to imagine him indulging in all kinds of perversions behind closed doors.

I was invited to rest on the doorstep but he made no move to invite me inside. Selena became impatient; she tugged at my arm and grew fractious.

"We must return at once to Laura Place," she announced firmly, then hissed in my ear. "Whatever game you are playing, Lydia, stop it at once!" Adelaide grasped my other arm and I almost became the centre of a tug of war. Mr Davenport looked on impatiently with a few by-your-leaves, but made no attempt to depart. The front door remained obstinately closed and I wondered how Jerry would gain entry.

At that moment a woman I assumed to be Belle Fleur arrived clutching a pile of laundry which obscured her face. She disappeared rapidly down the area steps, ignored by Mr Davenport. I gave up and allowed myself to be led away. Later, I discovered that the laundress had been Jerry in one of his disguises. His assistant entertained the servants in the kitchen while Jerry had the run of the house.

I heard nothing from him for a few days while Selena and Miles made preparations for our removal to Portman Square. No doubt my highwayman had also departed for London with his spoils. There was a report of the robbery in the *Bath Chronicle* and extra vigilance on the part of the watch, but the mysterious laundress had vanished. I wondered what financial advantage I had gained from the enterprise. Jerry was not keeping the terms of our agreement.

Miles made a last visit to the lady chiropodist in Abbey Churchyard where he met "a bluestocking kind of woman called Mary Shelley" who lived in the rooms above. Selena and I looked meaningfully at each other.

"Does she by chance have any etchings to sell?" My friend asked in a dangerous tone. Miles looked astonished, saying that they had merely exchanged good mornings as they passed each other.

It was the lady chiropodist who had offered the gossip.

"The woman is said to be the wife of the notorious poet Shelley. He is elsewhere, it seems, and she occupies herself with sketching and writing books. Most unwholesome for a woman," he added.

At the last moment Selena was reluctant to leave Bath, despite the allure of a free house in London. She loved the place and insisted that we should all attend the Assembly Rooms one more time before our departure, having overcome her fear of public disapproval. Miles and I agreed with a noticeable lack of enthusiasm, but whenever my friend set her mind on something she could not be dissuaded. You may imagine my lack of interest in this event, dear reader, when I say that I wore a simple, pleated, blue silk gauze gown much altered and reworked. It did not seem worthwhile to go to any great trouble. My spirits were low and brought even lower by my latest encounter with Jerry. I resolved to start afresh in London with the Count, if the fates allowed.

We entered the blue ballroom, Selena having confirmed that the Meyers and their friends were not present. Miles was itching to hide away in the gaming room but he was restrained by his wife.

"You must be our attendant for the evening," she instructed. "We cannot be left alone like two unlit tapers in a glittering candelabra."

"Do you so despair of our finding dance partners?" I asked. "Then why have we dragged ourselves to this tiresome event?" My friend narrowed her eyes in that strange way I have often noted. "Who knows what may happen on such an occasion? I merely wish us to have a permanent escort to hand." Miles objected to being relegated to the status of a piece of furniture, but Selena was adamant.

"You know your dancing skills are lamentable, my love. Guard us. That is your forte."

We stood like two of the three wise monkeys blankly surveying the undistinguished assembly. Even the faithful Lord Finchbrook had abandoned us temporarily. Miles and Selena went to greet an old regimental friend, leaving me alone for a moment.

Suddenly, as they returned to me, the crowd parted a little and a handsome figure of middle height appeared before us as if transported by a magic Persian carpet. He was clad in the finest broadcloth coat and snowy linen. A diamond pin sparkled in his cravat and the shine on his dark hair, caught in the light of a hundred candles, matched the glitter in his brown eyes and glanced off his sharp cheek bones.

With the merest nod to my companions he raised my hand to his lips saying,

"I must appropriate this fair damsel for the evening." As Miles and Selena stood agog he led me into the throng to dance a cotillion. It was Jerry Sartain.

162

Immediately, the Assembly Room became an antechamber of the gods and I was treading on air. As we danced he murmured sweet nothings in my ear, telling me that I looked divinely fair, like an Italian Madonna in my blue gown.

I tried to whisper questions about Bow Street Runners and the danger of discovery, but he silenced me with a wink or a whisper. In truth, no-one would expect to see a felon in such finery in these surroundings, especially one who was presumed deceased.

"I hear there are some daring, dastardly laundresses in this city," he remarked as he led me into supper, and I almost collapsed in hysterics. I heard Miles in the distance complaining of the dangers of dancing.

"I heard that a fellow dropped dead after dancing thirty-three rounds in this very room." Selena told him to be quiet.

"The devil!" muttered Jerry. "It's the villain who shot me in the forest. I did not recognise him for the moment." A terrible look passed over his face and I was afraid that he would drop his impersonation of a gentleman and leap upon Miles with murderous intent.

"No! No," I whispered, hoarse with emotion. I squeezed his arm so tightly that he tried to shake me off, but I hung on.

"I will save you from yourself," I hissed. "Lay a finger on him and all will be lost." Jerry, with huge effort, managed to control himself. I would not have been surprised to see steam issuing from his ears.

"It is imperative that Miles does not see you at close range," I added as I pulled him away from the tables into an anteroom. "Whatever made you come here tonight?" It was pure chance that Miles had not recognised Jerry when he came to claim me, but Miles had not the quickest of wits and one does not expect to see a dead man walking. Of course I was delighted to see him but Jerry was behaving in his usual reckless manner, relying only on his changed appearance for protection. He could put us all in danger. As if he had read my thoughts he turned to me and smiled.

"People see what they expect to see, my love. I learned that a long time ago. I am happy to dice with death in order to spend a little time with you!"

I was overcome by this remark — the most romantic, indeed, the only truly romantic pronouncement Jerry had ever made.

He seized my hand and drew me along. "Let us find a more secluded spot." We squeezed ourselves into an alcove shielded from view by columns. He held me close and whispered in my ear. Indeed the alcove was so tight that there was no other option.

"You are firing my blood tonight, sweet Lydia. His mouth was suddenly hard on mine as he kissed me long and passionately. I could feel the pressure of his fingers through the thin silk of my gown as the familiar thrill started to run around my body, the feeling I remembered so well from our first wonderful encounter. He was kissing my throat, my shoulders, my breasts. I felt my knees tremble.

"Jerry," I protested weakly, "we cannot . . . we are in a public place." At that moment a liveried servant stopped by the alcove waving his hands in an agitated manner.

"You must leave the building, madam, and your honour. There has been a disastrous incident in the gaming room. A gentleman has been stabbed. We must close the doors until the matter has been resolved." Jerry cursed quietly as we dislodged ourselves from the alcove.

"I must leave, my love. The watch will be called, not to mention a magistrate. I cannot risk being recognised." As I opened my mouth to speak he closed his own over it with a last kiss. Then he vanished into the night.

Selena and Miles found me standing like a statue.

"A stabbing in the Assembly Rooms!" Selena mourned. "Society is crumbling around our ears. Let us return to Laura Place."

On the following day we caught the Bath Regulator at six a.m. which was due to arrive in London at eight p.m. We fortified ourselves with brandied coffee en route and arrived in an exhausted state in the capital. I have little recall of the journey, being in a daze for most of the time.

CHAPTER
FOURTEEN

London, Spring 1816

Our spirits lifted somewhat when we were installed in a delightfully appointed house in Portman Square. How wonderful it was to be back in London and away from damp and deceitful Bath. For a while we were taken up in a mad social whirl which had an almost hysterical edge. A Mrs Willoughby and her daughters lived at No. 19 in the Square. The widow of a wealthy merchant who had acquired his money by providing boots for the British army, she gave many balls and suppers and she lost no time in making our acquaintance. We were invited out so often that we scarcely had time to draw breath, although we were able to organise a card *soirée* at our house which we hoped would improve our financial health greatly.

Finally, I had an excuse to invite the Count to join us and he accepted with alacrity. Few men in London would refuse such an offer. The proximity of a guards' barracks in Portman Street was a great advantage. The victorious soldiers were as willing to throw away their money as ever.

However, Miles was having an unaccustomed fit of caution. Gaming on unlicensed premises was unlawful and he feared the attentions of the upholders of the law.

A procession of military men entering the house would surely attract attention and Mrs Willoughby could not be relied on for discretion.

"But military men are always so willing to lose money," I protested.

Finally, the matter was settled by the size of the salon where the gaming would take place. It was a modest but charming room decorated in the Chinoiserie style with the finest yellow silk curtains bordered with red dragons. The dragons distracted me as Selena was preparing discreet invitations by hand for the selected gamesters.

"There must be a handsome supper, Lydia," she reminded me. "Could you not take responsibility for that? Do not allow the cook to be too extravagant. Chicken and salmon of medium quality will suffice and Miles will order champagne, hock and claret from Priddy's." I protested that I had little inclination for domestic matters. Left to me the household would survive on bread and cheese. I offered to ensure a good supply of candles.

Selena had been happy to invite the Count. Although she did not approve of my involvement with him she was more than willing to have him as an ornament at the tables, especially if he proved to be a keen player.

"He must be wealthy," she mused. "Let us hope he is also reckless and unlucky."

All that remained was for Miles to recruit a former sergeant from his old regiment to act as doorkeeper. This man had such a violent appearance and tongue that he was positively operatic. He declared that he

167

could "spot a wrong-un at ten paces". Meaning a representative of the law.

On the night of the *soirée* I donned a gown of lilac brocade while Selena wore dull gold and white taffeta.

When the Count arrived he drank a glass of wine with me and insisted I should stay by his table to watch him play a game of picquet.

"You will bring me good fortune, my dear."

"Are you a good player, Count?"

"I believe I am considered to play a very fair hand. I have always believed that a steady nerve was more important than skill in games of chance." I nodded rather doubtfully. Wickham always said that a certain low cunning was the principal advantage in card playing.

As I stood behind his chair I noted that nature had favoured the Count with a fine figure, broad shouldered with a slim waist, but I observed a certain puffiness in the chest that indicated some tight lacing under his bright blue coat and pristine linen. As I leaned closer to observe the cards I inhaled the smell of his skin — lemon and vanilla with a hint of mint. My hand brushed against his thick blond hair. He shook out the ruffles at his wrist and cut the cards with a snap. His opponent watched carefully.

"What stakes will you play for, Excellency?"

"Shall we start with ten shillings a point?" My eyes widened. The Count was either reckless or a confident player or extremely wealthy — or possibly all three.

Abruptly he seized my hand which was resting on his shoulder. "Sit where I can see you, my dear. You must be my lucky charm!" I quickly took a seat near the other player facing the Count. I smiled sweetly at him and raised my eyebrows to signify victory, but my presence appeared to distract him rather than anything else.

My admirer negligently lost several hundred pounds before pausing to call for more champagne. His game rallied a little before diving again just before a halt was called for supper. When he fetched chicken and salad for me I commiserated with his losses which stood at two thousand before I remembered that I was a joint custodian of the gaming salon. The Count brushed the amount aside saying that it did not signify. "It was worthwhile if it allowed me to spend a few hours in your company, my dear."

Later, we played picquet together and I allowed him to win five hundred pounds. Selena then took my place and won the money back. The Count did not stay long, to my regret. He drew me close as we stood in the entrance hall and gave me a lingering kiss. "Until the next time, *Cherie*."

The guard on the door obligingly looked the other way. Then my admirer was gone saying only that I would hear from him very soon. Once again I wondered why he behaved so mysteriously.

"He is a diplomat," said Selena. "They have to be circumspect. Either that or he has a vigilant wife." She gave me a spiteful look. We rejoined Miles and a few hours later we were able to count our winnings which were satisfactory enough despite Selena bemoaning the ruinous amount of wine and spirits consumed during the evening.

A few days later, when we were still basking in our comparative wealth, Selena horrified me by declaring that I should visit Getheridge in his prison.

"I will do no such thing. How can you suggest it, Selena? Do you want me to become embroiled in this affair?" My friend gave a mysterious smile and tapped her nose.

"That man has many financial secrets. Why should he take them to the grave? You may learn something to your advantage."

"I say, dear heart, don't wish the poor fellow dead just yet. He hasn't even been tried," protested Miles. Selena shook her head knowingly.

"Lord Finchbrook assures me that he will hang." I shuddered again and devoutly wished myself in Paris. Even Pemberley was beginning to appear attractive in the circumstances. Apart from the mad whirl of evening activity the atmosphere in the capital was grimmer than ever. In addition to the dolorous weather and the bread riots, cholera had appeared in London striking terror into every heart. It was reported that wells had been poisoned which led Miles to declare he would drink only brandy for the sake of his health. This regime differed so little from his usual habits that we scarcely noticed a change.

Furthermore, London society was agog with the scandal of Mr Getheridge and the bank. He pleaded with his creditors but they showed no mercy. He was duly tried at the Old Bailey for fraud and embezzlement and sentenced to be hanged. While he was incarcerated in the Fleet prison before his execution at Newgate, I began to think of Selena's words. Was it possible that I could persuade the man to reveal any secrets he might have? We had not exactly had a happy relationship but we were reconciled in Bath and he had been grateful for my assistance.

On the other hand, if he had money hidden away would he not have used it to help himself? I suggested this to Selena at breakfast one day but she disagreed.

"Any money he admitted to possessing would have been seized by his creditors. No doubt he wishes to make some provision for his family."

"I am not his family."

"I am including his mistresses in this group."

"I was never his mistress, strictly speaking," I pointed out. Selena told me I was being tiresome. She tapped her nose in that irritating way she had.

"Stratagems, Lydia, stratagems. Would not a person *in extremis* be overwhelmed with gratitude towards anyone who offered to stand by him, to help him in some way?" I continued to look puzzled and my friend shook her head in despair.

"You must visit him, tell him you will do anything to help him."

"Anything?"

"Of course, you have no money, but you might be able to help in other ways. Remind him that *we* recovered the Cambridge emeralds for the prince. Tell him something that will raise his hopes. In return urge him to tell you everything so that you can make plans."

"What exactly do I want to know?"

"Oh, really, Lydia, must I spell it out? You need to know if he has any money hidden anywhere. Offer to marry him if necessary." I almost choked on my chocolate.

"Marry him?" I squealed.

"Have you never heard of a Fleet marriage?"

"Surely they are not legal. And he already has a wife." She brushed this aside.

"We do not know if his first marriage was legal either. It does not matter, he will be hanged. I am speaking of gaining his trust."

I was momentarily horrified by my friend's words. She was revealing a side of her character I had not previously seen. Suddenly, it seemed she had metamorphosed into Jerry Sartain's twin sister, perhaps separated at birth.

As always, these schemes involved no inconvenience to anyone except myself. The thought of entering the noxious confines of the Fleet prison was terrifying.

"There is plague in the city," I whispered, adding, "All I want is to dance at Almack's and go to Paris with the Count." Selena rolled her eyes impatiently.

"Believe me, my dear, your plans will come to nothing for want of a fortune."

"I am sure that poor Getheridge does not have a fortune and why should he bestow it on me?" My friend frowned and stood up in a decisive manner.

"If I cannot convince you, then this is an end to it. I must await the apothecary, Miles is to be bled this morning." As she left the room she paused and remarked over her shoulder, "I would not suggest this action to you if I had not heard that Getheridge's mistress has abandoned him." With this parting shot she withdrew leaving me to ponder on my next step.

Lord Finchbrook called at the house later that morning and found me in the red drawing room with a book open. He took one look at my book and reproached me for reading "the merest trash from the common circulating libraries".

"Why should I not read a Gothic novel in this delightful room?" I replied. No. 27 Portman Square was furnished in exquisite taste. The room in which we were sitting was a smaller version of one in Carlton House with five gilded Gothic arches and crimson silk curtains. What better surroundings for reading *The Monk* by Matthew Lewis? A truly horrifying and disgusting novel, I would never have been permitted to read it in other circumstances.

"This book is the talk of London," I assured him. His lordship shrugged in the manner of one who never read anything but the *Sporting Times*. He did not mention Almack's to me. I needed to remind him of his promise. Whoever escorts me, it must surely be before I visit Mr Getheridge. I looked down at the book resting on my lap. It was open at a page describing particularly gruesome scenes in a subterranean prison. I thought again of the Fleet and shuddered.

It was surely a malign fate at work that caused a servant to appear at that very moment with a note from Jerry. He had wasted no time in discovering my whereabouts. Then I recalled that I had given him the direction. Of course, he knew about Getheridge's imprisonment and he agreed with Selena that I should visit the man.

"In fact," he declared when we met later that day, "I can smooth your path in a manner of speaking. I have an acquaintance with one of the jailers."

I could well believe this: the jailers were notoriously easy to bribe and Jerry had probably spent time in the prison at some stage. No doubt he would use my money for the purpose. He generously offered to escort me "at a distance", in view of his own dubious status. My own life was beginning to resemble the plot of an unsavoury novel. How could I, poor little Lydia Marianne Bennet, have come to such a pass?

My wants in life have always been modest. A few pretty gowns, a sprinkling of diamonds, a matching pair of footmen (so, so fashionable) and of course a respectable roof over my head, some land and a handsome, attentive, wealthy husband. These are the dreams of any well brought up female. I cannot imagine how they became entangled with outlaws, royal plots and fraudulent bankers.

Inevitably, I agreed to visit Mr Getheridge although I was in a state of terror the whole time. I could not pursue the matter of Almack's as Mr Getheridge was due to be hanged in two weeks' time. Even Lord Finchbrook declined to accompany me, so great was the fear of cholera. Chivalry had died a death.

Selena pointed out that I must remain anonymous. I therefore travelled in a common hackney carriage wearing a dark cloak and hood that covered every part of my body and face. I carried a plentiful supply of lemons as an antidote to disease as well as a basket of food and drink to comfort the prisoner. I saw no sign of Jerry but no doubt he was lurking somewhere in the background. He was probably spying on me from a corner. That would be his idea of escorting me.

I was greatly relieved to discover that my poor friend was not in the insalubrious prison itself but in nearby lodgings that were available to the better class of prisoner for two guineas a week. I offered some silver coins to the evil-smelling guard who hovered outside and he let me into the premises with a sneer.

Mr Getheridge's room was far from well appointed: the pockmarked plaster was peeling from the walls and the furniture consisted of a wooden chair, a small wooden table bearing a candlestick, and a narrow trestle bed. He was gratifyingly pleased to see me, weeping a few tears over my hand and thanking me for the food in sepulchral tones.

Selena had instructed the cook to prepare some broth and a few meat patties, bread and honey and a small bottle of brandy. There were also some pills to purge the head which Miles swears by, although I cannot think that the prisoner will have much use for them in the circumstances.

My former patron offered me the chair and sat on the bed to eat a little bread and honey. For a while we exchanged pleasantries and discussed food. He confessed that he had made a request for a final meal of hind of pork and rout cakes with a glass of champagne.

"I am glad you have not lost your taste for the finer things in life," I remarked, then regretted the sharpness of my tone. The poor man was facing a dreadful end with some fortitude after all.

He gave me a reproachful look. "I know that I am regarded as a great villain, dear Lydia, but my intentions were never evil. I believed that I could have resolved everything if I had been given time. I was also greatly distracted by the prince's affairs." He heaved a deep sigh.

"Has the prince abandoned you to your fate?"

He nodded sadly. "His Highness cannot afford any more scandal." I thought it a poor thing for any man, prince or pauper, to abandon a man to the gallows who has rendered him a considerable service. I remembered my papa declaiming, "Put not your trust in princes" although I cannot remember the source of the quote.

I tried to bring the conversation delicately around to the subject of Getheridge's own fortune and its whereabouts, if any, but he had other matters on his mind. Reminding me that he had been deserted by his womenfolk he patted the bed and smiled winningly.

"I entreat you to visit me again, my dear, before my end. We will be undisturbed here for a while!" I was so startled I bit down on a lemon and almost choked at its bitterness. Selena's instructions ran through my head. How could I broach the subject of money not to mention convincing him that I could help him to escape?

The scent of lemon hung in the air and I felt juice dribbling down my chin. He was looking at me expectantly.

176

"Of course I will, you dear thing," I cried. "But you must not despair." I launched into a breathless description of our rescue of the prince's emeralds. "If we can accomplish such a thing why should we not, my friends and I, rescue you from the gallows? Of course, it would necessitate considerable expense," I added. He shook his head.

"It is too late for me, dearest Lydia. All I can hope for is a little comfort at the end." He looked meaningfully at me and then at the bed again.

"I would do anything for you, my dear," I declared, trying to keep a note of desperation out of my voice. "We could even become man and wife if you wish." He seized my hand and drew me towards the bed.

"I already have a wife and little use she is to me." How was I supposed to resolve this situation? Selena was far too glib with her suggestions.

I allowed myself to be deposited on the hard and none-too-clean bed and I patted Mr Getheridge on the cheek. "My regard for you is too great, sir. I could not forgive myself if we did not put together a plan for your deliverance."

"Oh, whatever you say, my dear." He pulled me towards him and two fat lemons suddenly shot out from my bodice where I had secreted them against the fetid airs of the prison. My companion was so startled that he fell backwards across the bed and on to the floor. He rose to his knees, shaking off the dust and looking petulant. I seized my cloak, waved my hand and fled, promising to do everything in my power to remove him from harm's way. Jerry was waiting for me outside.

CHAPTER
FIFTEEN

"Did he tell you where the money is hidden?" The question was predictable and I heard myself replying in the whining, wheedling tone I usually adopted with him. I despised myself for this but I was helpless, having never truly been in love before, dear reader, except for my passion for Lord Byron which remains unrequited — for the moment.

"He did not tell me anything. I do not believe he has any money. Surely that was the point of the embezzlement?" Jerry shook his head sadly.

"You are naive, my sweet. The man had fingers in many pies. He has swindled everyone from the highest in the land to the humble tradespeople. Did you not read the reports in the *Times* newspaper?" I acknowledged that I had heard rumours to that effect.

"If he has not made a secret profit then he is a spectacularly bad example of a banker." Another thought occurred to me. "Surely that is the reason why he is being hanged at Newgate, because he was not successful?" My highwayman laughed. "He was not quite clever enough but he fooled many people for a long time. You must try harder with him, my dear."

We were standing in the street called Faringdon as we spoke. Suddenly, the great doors of the Fleet prison opposite slowly opened and foul, stomach-clenching fumes wafted over us. I knew that Getheridge would be transferred to Newgate forty-eight hours before his execution and I had no doubt that the environs of that place were every bit as ghastly as this one. I swallowed hard and whined again.

"There is so little time left, only a few days before he goes to Newgate. We have enough money for now. Cannot we spend a little time together, my love?" I rested my head against his lapels and looked up imploringly at him. Jerry remained unmoved. He looked down at me incredulously. "And lose the chance of a fortune? Stop this girlish nonsense. We must make plans." He loosed himself from my grasp and sped off promising to contact me "soon". He had not even offered to escort me home. As I ran off to find a hansom cab I began to wonder whether he cared for me at all.

On the journey back to Portman Square I kept the lemons pressed against my nostrils until we reached a more healthful area of the city. I had once passed the place where the Fleet Ditch outfall empties into the Thames and that hellish stench was the worst thing I had ever known. The odours floating around the prison had been almost as unbearable, and there was cholera in the city. Panicstricken, I rushed into the house leaving Miles to pay the cabbie.

I commanded the servants to bring hot water as soon as possible and to burn the clothes I had been wearing all day. As the gown had a charming and most becoming cherry print border one can imagine the desperation I felt. Even after bathing in hot water and lemon juice I felt unclean. At dinner I ate little and while the others enjoyed fig tarts I sucked on more lemons until my face was wrinkled up like a bleached walnut kernel.

Miles, none the worse for his recent bloodletting, gave us a vivid description of a hanging and its attendant rituals which he described as the finest entertainment imaginable.

"Your banker friend will soon be doing the morris, my dear." When I looked perplexed he explained that the squirming and writhing of the prisoners at the end of the rope was known as doing a morris dance. My blood ran cold at the thought.

"Do they not die instantly?" I asked in a low voice.

"Oh dear, no!" carolled Miles. "But if the prisoner pays something to the hangman the matter is concluded faster. The executioner will grab the prisoner's knees and pull on them to assist the process."

"That is quite enough of that, Miles," said Selena with a glance at my face, but her husband was not to be suppressed.

"Of course, we must secure a place at the Magpie and Stump Inn where we will have a good view of the proceedings. A window will cost at least ten shillings but their breakfasts on these occasions are famous, the devilled kidneys are a triumph." At this point I lost my appetite completely and retired to my bed where I lay awaiting the first symptoms of whatever deadly disease might afflict my body. I recorded these facts in my journal fully expecting it to be my last testament in this life.

Whatever poor Getheridge had done he surely did not deserve his fate. He had rendered services to the Prince Regent and that alone should have secured a reprieve, but perhaps death was preferable to imprisonment for life in a sewer. Of course, there was transportation, why had I not thought of that? He could begin a new life in Van Diemen's Land if it could be arranged.

I turned my head and saw in the faint light of the candle the diamond and amethyst bangle lying on my dressing table. Getheridge had expected something in return for that and I had not provided it. Wickham's words came into my head to torment me.

I bought you my dear . . .

What is a young woman to do? Urged on by Jerry's commands and my own feelings of guilt I waited for forty-eight hours to pass before returning to Mr Getheridge. He was already in Newgate prison and this time the guard had to be more heavily bribed in order to turn a blind eye.

"'E's a marked man," the fellow commented, jerking a thumb in the direction of the prisoner's door. "Off to the dance 'e is, tomorrer. You, madam," he sneered, "are by way of bein' 'is last visitor."

I hurried in to Mr G's room to find him with his head resting on the bed and his knees on the floor in an attitude of complete dejection. He had been writing letters — the pages were strewn over the thin coverlet.

"I have been putting my affairs in order, Lydia, writing my last letters. You are kindness itself for making this visit." He waved away the basket of victuals I offered, saying that he was not hungry. His depression was in marked contrast to his manner on my first visit. I was relieved that he no longer had designs on my person. After I sat gingerly on the bed the unfortunate man placed his head in my lap and wept bitterly. He poured out a good deal of stuff about the bank and its affairs, letters of credit, guarantors, gold reserves and other matters that I did not comprehend. I had never before received anyone's last confession and I felt ill-equipped for such a role. It appeared that he had little time for religion and had not asked for any spiritual comfort.

I ventured to ask him as tactfully as possible about the mechanics of the execution. In fact, there was no tactful way to broach such a subject.

"Have you thought about your, er, knees?" I whispered.

He nodded, "I will pay for such comforts as may be obtained in the circumstances."

"And your families . . ." I continued, "are they well provided for?" Perhaps I should not have used the plural but it slipped out without warning. He did not appear to notice.

"I have provided for all my dependants. I made sure of that before things began to go wrong." He gave me a pitiful look. "It all started with the prince, you know." He did not enlighten me further.

I patted his unadorned, thinning grey hair. It was strange that a man so hairy in the body should have so little upon his head. He gave me another woebegone smile.

"If things had gone according to plan, my dear, I would have settled a charming little house on you. It is in Richmond, I have the deeds still."

My heart skipped a beat. Had I heard correctly? A man had planned to give me a house — a roof over my head. Only my papa had ever provided such a thing, and that one entailed. What did he mean if things had gone according to plan? Was it because I had not become his mistress, or was it because of the circumstances?

"In Richmond, you say?" I struggled to breathe slowly. "I am gratified that you wished to provide for me, sir. I have nothing in this world, as you know." I allowed a tear to trickle down my cheek. I am always touched by my own predicament.

He shook his head sadly. "It is all too late now . . . too late." Suddenly galvanised into action I cried out, "But if we were to be married I could inherit the house! Allow me to be your wife even if it is in name only." Mr Getheridge regarded me seriously for a moment. His spirits were returning somewhat.

"Yes," he declared, "and there might be time to consummate the marriage if we are quick about it." He leapt to his feet with surprising agility and called for the guard. There was a hurried consultation, a few coins exchanged hands and the man disappeared. He returned

183

within ten minutes accompanied by a dishevelled, grease-flecked fellow of middle height who wore a clergyman's collar askew over a shirt heavily marked with his last meal. The fellow swayed a little on his feet and almost tripped over the basket of food.

"Always happy to be of service to a fellow prisoner," he leered at us while holding out a hand to Getheridge who dropped some coins into it. This time I saw the glint of gold.

"Are you really a man of the cloth?" I asked. I eyed him doubtfully as he smiled revealing several missing teeth.

"I am the closest you will get in these parts, madam. Reverend Abel Imray (unfrocked) at your service."

"Hurry, man, hurry," urged Getheridge. "There is no time to lose. The sands of my life are running out." I stood up and we joined hands. He tore a signet ring from his finger and gave it to the reverend who produced a tattered prayer book from a pocket and muttered a few lines from the marriage service. The ring was placed on my finger and then removed because it was too large.

"I pronounce you man and wife," he remarked before collapsing on to the bed and requesting some strong liquor "to toast the happy couple". At that moment the guard reappeared and ordered me to leave. I was shooed away as Getheridge argued loudly with the man.

"The deeds, the deeds!" I called frantically. "Where are they?"

184

"At Jasmine Cottage," shouted my new husband. I was never to see him again.

"A Fleet marriage is not valid in the eyes of the law, Lydia. You are aware of that, I trust?" Selena gave me one of her superior looks when I returned to Portman Square in a distracted condition. "You must flee to Gretna Green these days." I clenched my hands in fury. Had she not urged me to ingratiate myself with a condemned man, advising me to do everything in my power to take his money? I found myself raising my voice in an unbecoming shriek.

"How can you adopt that tone with me, madam? Have I not succeeded in doing what everyone wished me to do?" I was including Jerry in this statement although Selena could not know that. She ignored my rage and looked excited.

"Do you mean you have his money — or some of it, at least?" How easily the need for solvency overcomes our finer feelings. I lowered my voice just as Miles entered the room.

"I do not have his money, but I have a house. It is called Jasmine Cottage and it stands in Richmond Park. We have only to go there and make a claim. The deeds are at the house and I am his wife — for a short while."

Selena rang for tea at this point and we sipped it slowly, thinking over the events of the day. Miles suddenly frowned and again gave evidence of some thought processes at work. He seized my left hand and peered at it exclaiming,

"You have no wedding ring." I explained that we had used Mr Getheridge's own ring for the ceremony and it was too large for normal wear. "If you have no ring, no doubt you are without a marriage license also. Your lack of forethought is astonishing," Selena chimed in. I was temporarily crushed by this evident truth, but I pointed out that the likes of the reverend Abel Imray were unlikely to be in possession of such a thing in the circumstances.

"Surely it does not signify, if the marriage is illegal?" Miles remarked brightly. "Did you not tell me, my dear, that Getheridge already had a wife or two?" His wife tapped her teacup impatiently.

"All the more reason to stake a claim quickly before the authorities discover the truth. Miles, you must hire a carriage and take us to Richmond Park immediately." He protested that it was already four-thirty in the afternoon and time for a "libation" as he put it, but his wife was unmoved. I was touched by their enthusiasm on my behalf. I knew that Selena was concerned about where they would live after Portman Square.

In my mind I could see myself departing for Paris with the Count and leaving my friends in charge of Jasmine Cottage. I would be a woman of property at last, even if it was only a small one. I wondered uneasily about Jerry and his plans for me but if my future lay with the Count Jerry would have to be jettisoned at some point, however hard that would be for me to accept.

We were soon rattling through London on our way to the park while Miles reminded us that Getheridge would be hanged on the following day. He had arranged places at the Magpie and Stump but I knew I could never watch such an event.

"Surely a wife's place is among the onlookers on such a day?" Miles was grinning and being provocative again. I protested that I had no stomach for such a thing and least of all for the devilled kidneys afterwards.

"It hardly matters," said the practical Selena. "I am sure at least one of his wives or mistresses will be present."

"I daresay the poor fellow will have other matters to worry about," added Miles. "A hanging must concentrate a man's mind in a wonderful fashion." We spent the rest of the journey in silence except for a brief account from Miles about an acquaintance of his who had over indulged in morphine and had subsequently developed what he referred to as "man boobs".

"A devilish business." He shook his head.

"That will be quite enough of that," was Selena's response.

When we eventually found Jasmine Cottage it was indeed a small cot, more suitable for a shepherd than a lady but Miles declared it to be a bijou residence and when we managed to gain entrance we found it to be pleasantly, if sparsely, furnished. Miles had climbed through an open window in order to admit us through the front door. Selena declared that the cottage in its isolated corner of the park was obviously intended as a love nest.

"Never mind that, we must look for the deeds. The deeds. He said they were hidden somewhere." I set them both to searching and although we made a thorough inspection of the rooms and peered in all the drawers and closets, we found nothing. Then Miles put his hand into the chimney space and pulled out an oilskin package containing documents. A quick look inside confirmed that these were the deeds. We left immediately and returned speedily to Portman Square. I resolved to visit a notary on the following day to make my claim. Before I retired to bed that night I remembered to put a curtain ring on my left hand in lieu of the real thing. My Wickham wedding ring had been quietly stored away.

Miles and Selena left early the following morning in order to make their way through the huge crowds assembling for the execution of my friend/husband/ protector. I admit that I cowered in my bed for some time, unwilling to face the day. Adelaide told me that large numbers of people were making their way to Newgate. She implied that nothing would give her greater pleasure than to join them, but I already had two witnesses to the event and I did not need another.

I made a late breakfast and sat listlessly reading a novel when a loud knock at the front door caused me to run to the window where I beheld two rough looking fellows who closely resembled bailiffs trying to gain admittance. I assumed they must be in search of Miles but Adelaide burst into the room saying that the men wished to speak to me. She was closely followed by the men themselves, who, when I protested at the outrage, ignored my words and simply demanded the deeds to Jasmine Cottage.

My astonishment at that moment was genuine. How could they have known about this matter? They soon explained themselves.

"We are here to execute a warrant for the possessions of the late felon, Thomas Getheridge, executed but one hour ago at Newgate. His possessions and property are forfeit to the state."

"But I am his wife," I squeaked.

"They all make that claim," retorted the first bailiff.

"May we see your marriage licence, madam?" The second bailiff sneered at me.

"I have the deeds!" I squeaked again. "The deeds to Jasmine Cottage. It belongs to me."

"Then you will hand them over, madam, seeing as the house is forfeit and seeing as how you are only his latest wife." The bailiffs seemed to think this was a great joke. Just as I handed over the deeds with the utmost reluctance a commotion in the street outside indicated that a number of carriages were jostling for position. I saw Lord Finchbrook's phaeton tangling with an elegant maroon, blue and gold vehicle. To my horror I saw my brother-in-law descend from the carriage and mount the steps to the house, casting a disapproving glance at Lord Finchbrook who followed him twirling a cane with gusto.

I tore the ring from my finger and dropped it quietly under a chair before running quickly to my chamber and replacing my legal Wickham wedding ring on my left hand. When I returned downstairs I saw that Adelaide had bustled the bailiffs out as quickly as she could but Darcy's sharp eyes missed nothing.

"Are you in some kind of trouble, Lydia?"

"Oh no, dear Fitzie," I replied gaily. "Just a little matter connected with Miles." Mister Fitzwilliam Darcy's cheeks began to turn purple.

CHAPTER
SIXTEEN

My brother-in-law was never noted for his sense of humour. I doubt that he would have recognised a jest if it ran up the main staircase at Pemberley and bit him on the nose. It seemed that he could not bear a little light joshing from his sister-in-law, either, although I have seen a faint smile appear when Lizzie teased him.

My ability to look on the bright side of life at the most distressing moments was either an enviable gift or a dubious one, depending on your point of view. On a morning of death, dashed hopes and unwelcome visitors I could not resist annoying Mr Darcy. He was so easily annoyed. I watched the purple hue rise in his cheeks as I smiled pleasantly and offered my guests a seat. At that moment I heard the front door close with a loud bang as the bailiffs finally left. I hastened to make the introductions.

"May I present my dear brother-in-law?" I said to the beaming Lord Finchbrook, who shook the hand unwillingly proffered, giving the impression that he had waited all his life for this meeting. "I am sure you must have met His Lordship in London at some time, dear Fitzie!" I remarked wickedly.

"I have not had the pleasure," Darcy retorted, adding between gritted teeth, "Do not address me by that ridiculous name, Lydia."

While I rang for Adelaide to bring sherry and ratafia wafers for the visitors, Darcy unbent sufficiently to remark that he had endured a "dashed difficult journey" from his London lodgings on account of the crowds gathered to watch the execution of some felon.

Lord Finchbrook nodded enthusiastically. "Yes, that would be the unfortunate Getheridge. We knew him quite well, did we not, Mrs Wickham?" I almost congealed with fright wondering what this ridiculous lordling would blurt out next. The man had the brains and sensitivity of a feather duster. Darcy turned to me with an expression of horror.

"You, my sister-in-law, were acquainted with this felon?" Lord Finchbrook interrupted hurriedly having realised his mistake. "Oh, do not be alarmed, sir. Everyone of consequence in London knew Getheridge. He was, until recently, a respected banker and confidant of the Prince Regent. His end was a most melancholy matter." I swallowed my sherry too quickly and choked a little. Thank heavens Lord Finchbrook had not poured out the details of my Fleet marriage. I was sure Miles would have told him of it. My brother-in-law wreaked vengeance on a ratafia wafer with his excellent teeth and regarded me suspiciously.

"Your sister and I have been concerned about you, madam. Your letters have been sparse, to say the least. We were naturally concerned with your welfare, as a young widow in London." There was a wealth of

192

unspoken accusation hanging in the air. I knew that his concern for me meant a fear that I might disgrace his august family in some way. I was the disreputable relative, the woolly-headed creature who had eloped at sixteen with the dastardly Wickham.

That episode had cost him ten thousand pounds. I had no doubt that he wanted something in return. Men always want something from women. In my case it would probably be an undertaking to remain of nun-like virtue for the rest of my days. Lord Finchbrook must have read my thoughts.

"I can assure you, dear sir, that the Caruthers and their friends, of whom I am one, have taken the utmost care of dear Mrs Wickham. You need have no fear on that account." Darcy raised an eyebrow and gave him a look that would have chilled a sorbet in an ice house.

"I am much obliged to you." He was probably wondering whether I planned to elope with this dandy. If only I could. His lordship was wealthy, affable, titled and stupid — the perfect spouse. Unfortunately, I knew that he was mooning after a married woman and that his family would disinherit him if he took up with any females in this household.

At that moment I heard the front door opening and I realised that my friends had returned. I could only pray that Adelaide had managed to warn them before they entered. My hopes were dashed when Miles burst into the room braying loudly;

"My dear girl, you missed a splendid event. Hordes of people gathered to see poor old Getheridge. You would have been proud. Oh, there you are Finchbrook.

Why did you not join us?" He was pushed aside momentarily by the entrance of his wife who rushed across the room crying, "Lydia what happened with the deeds?" They both noticed Mr Darcy at the same time as I closed my eyes and waited for the world to end.

I shall be eternally grateful to Lord Finchbrook. I repent of my harsh judgement of him. Gesturing frantically to the newcomers behind my brother-in-law's back, he startled them into silence and drew Darcy towards the door.

"Please be good enough, sir, to give me your opinion on a new Arab I have harnessed to my phaeton. I have heard you are an acknowledged connoisseur of horse flesh." He steered the surprised and unresisting Fitzie out of the house while I reproached my friends unfairly for their precipitous entrance.

"If he has the slightest notion of what is going on I shall be cast into the gutter," I moaned.

"We could not be expected to know he was here, Lydia, do not be unreasonable," said Selena.

"If only you were not so agog with hangings and such," I continued. "You are obsessed with the affair." Miles wagged his finger at me.

"And so is half of London. You could not move for the press of the crowd. And the carriages, my dear. Half of the aristocracy turned up."

"That would be because they had all borrowed money from him," his wife added. I twisted my hands and begged them to forget Getheridge for the moment. They finally realised the importance of removing Darcy as soon as possible and gathered their wits as Lord

Finchbrook and my brother-in-law returned and introductions were made.

Selena took a deep breath and assumed the gracious hostess mode.

"You will dine with us, of course, Mr Darcy? I hope we will have the pleasure of meeting your wife later in the season. Any sister of my dear friend Mrs Wickham would be an honoured guest." Miles beamed at the visitor in support of these remarks but indecision was writ large on my brother-in-law's face. Courtesy finally prevailed and he accepted in his usual stiff manner. Lord Finchbrook was also encouraged to join us. I would have invited half of London if I could have, so as not to have to make conversation with Darcy.

I knew he was itching to quiz me about my activities and my plans for the future, but I did not intend to let him have the opportunity. His untimely arrival had quite distracted me from the disaster of the deeds and Getheridge's tragic demise. My luck was deserting me once more. It needed only a surprise visit from Jerry Sartain during the meal to seal my fate.

As I was dressing for dinner that evening Selena came to talk to me saying that we must soon visit Hatchard's bookshop in Piccadilly and the Burlington Arcade where all the Bucks and Bloods paraded. "There is not a man among them worth less than twenty thousand pounds a year," she declared, adding that I must surely catch the eye of one of them.

"But I have already caught the eye of the Count," I said. Selena discounted this saying that I knew nothing of his circumstances and that a bird in the hand is worth any number of mystery admirers.

Without waiting for my comments she went on to say that cook had prepared an apricot tart for dessert. "It is the favourite of every man of quality." Tamarinds were available at the greengrocer but cook had no idea what to do with them. Selena always managed to cover every angle in life simultaneously.

Dinner was a somewhat strained affair. Mr Darcy made little attempt at conversation and others made too many. Lord Finchbrook wore a pair of excessively elegant lavender gloves.

"You are the very tulip of fashion," Selena told him and he gave her a look of adoration, blushing a shade of pink that clashed only slightly with the gloves. He always failed to detect the irony underlying my friend's remarks. We were all on our best behaviour as we contemplated the quails in blankets which constituted the main course, but as the evening wore on and the wine was poured, tongues loosened and talk grew careless. I sat on tenterhooks waiting for the remark that would bring the wrath of Fitzwilliam down around my ears.

Miles made the inevitable reference to the execution but got no further than remarking that, "the fellow was neatly dressed" — before receiving a well-aimed kick on the shins from his wife. I enquired politely about life at Pemberley and my relative launched into a lecture on the burden of running a large estate. We all nodded sympathetically while I thought wistfully of the little cottage that had almost been mine. An estate indeed!

When would I ever have a roof over my head that was truly mine?

In an attempt to change the subject Lord Finchbrook twittered about an exhibition of portraits he had seen by the artist Thomas Lawrence who was the talk of London. He had painted vastly flattering portraits of the Prince Regent — his corpulent fifty-two-year-old body rendered as a well-built thirty-three — and of the Duke of Wellington. We all recalled seeing the great duke's large nose, bleak eyes and bristly jaws greatly improved by Lawrence's skills.

Selena exclaimed that she would die happy if she could leave behind her likeness executed by Mr Lawrence. Miles looked startled and shamefaced when she made a few barbed remarks about an oil painting being worth any number of crude etchings. Darcy nodded agreement but could not resist a criticism of Lawrence whom he called a "popinjay".

"They say he is entirely self-taught and has never had a lesson in his life." This was said with the self-satisfaction of one who had an old master or two adorning his ancestral walls. Nobody dared to disagree with him as he warmed to his subject.

"I have seen prints by Gillray that were vicious and crude in the extreme. I believe the fellow must be a republican and a sympathiser with those Jacobins across the Channel." There was general agreement that the continent was now a much safer place since Napoleon's overthrow and the restoration of the monarchy.

I remembered that the duke was about to become our ambassador in Paris.

"I hear he will take a large entourage with him," I said wistfully.

"Indeed," said Lord Finchbrook, "Paris is becoming the centre of European culture once more. There is a vast English colony assembled there, I believe." I wished silently to be among them as my brother-in-law remarked that England and its rural pleasures were good enough for him.

To my surprise Darcy invited us to ride with him in Hyde Park on the following day. I wondered uneasily about Jerry Sartain. I had not heard from him recently and any equine setting would be a likely place to stumble across him. I had hoped that Selena would politely refuse Darcy's invitation, as she had promised Miles a visit to John Trotter's Soho Bazaar where more than one hundred young women were employed. It would have enabled him to ogle the fair sex while pretending to buy artists' materials, cakes and any other non-essential items. However, everyone accepted enthusiastically and it became obvious that my friends believed they were doing me a favour. Then yet another disaster loomed from the saturnine gentleman sitting opposite, frowning at me.

"You must return with me to Pemberley, madam. I leave in two days' time. Your sister expressly commanded me to bring you back." Reluctantly, he turned to my friends and remarked that they would be most welcome if they chose to accompany us.

Once again, to my astonishment, Lord Finchbrook saved the day. This was the second time he had played the knight in shining armour, but I was truly amazed by his words.

"Sir, I must beg your indulgence for a few days. Mrs Wickham has an invitation to Almack's Assembly and I shall have the privilege of escorting her. She could not, in all conscience, refuse or postpone such an honour."

"Almack's?" I shrieked, while Selena hastily intercepted, saying loudly, "Surely you have not forgotten, Lydia?"

I gulped and gathered my wits together, assuring Darcy that I was overcome at the very mention of the event. He looked nonplussed for a moment and then reluctantly agreed.

"Then we shall expect you in due course. Your sister is most anxious."

Selena and I then retired leaving the men to their brandy and cigars. I collapsed onto a chaise longue fanning myself assiduously and trying to recover from the shock. At least I had a reprieve for a few days. How clever of our favourite aristocrat to think of the perfect excuse. If only it were true. My friend apologised for not offering anything similar.

"I could only think that Miles had already been bled. I could not persuade him to offer up his vital juices so soon, and such an excuse would not do for you."

Eventually, a very long evening drew to its close and Darcy bade us farewell. Only then did I have an opportunity to thank his lordship for his timely intervention.

"Oh, it was nothing, madam — nothing but the truth!" With an air of triumph he produced an elegant, gold-embossed card and waved it in front of my bedazzled eyes.

"Your wish has been granted, my lady. Never let it be said that Finchbrook ignored a lady's wishes. Though it will be a dashed boring evening, just chit-chat with dragon-like chaperones and simpering virgins with nothing stronger than fruit punch to fortify us."

"But we shall dance!" I cried, pirouetting around the room with delight. "And I will have gained an *entrée* into the finest circles in the land."

"We shall expect you to snare a duke at the very least," chirped Miles, while Selena looked a little sour. I continued dancing around the room thinking about my gown for the occasion, whether the Count would be present, and meaning to ask Lord Finchbrook how he had procured such a favour, but as I drew near to the window I spied a figure leaning nonchalantly against Finchbrook's phaeton. It was Jerry. Truly, fate never allows me unalloyed pleasure for more than a moment.

Behind me the voices in the room suddenly seemed far away. I heard the men discussing neckties appropriate for Almack's. Miles was agreeing that the ballroom tie would be best. Lord Finchbrook remarked that only the best white linen was suitable — *blanc d'innocence virginal* — fastened in the Napoleonic manner without a knot.

Muttering an excuse I fled from the room and retrieved Adelaide from the depths of the kitchen where she was eating the remains of the apricot pie. I was forced to acquaint her somewhat summarily with the details of Jerry's resurrection from the dead. She gave a little scream before reluctantly agreeing to take a note to him begging him not to perpetrate any atrocity upon his lordship who was playing an important role in furthering my fortunes. I then amended this to "our fortunes" for better effect. I was under no illusions about Jerry's motives.

Adelaide reported back that he insisted on speaking to me personally on a matter of great urgency. I sighed, knowing what that meant. He wanted money, probably a great deal of money. I resolved that things would be different this time. Chiding myself for a ninny with a sorry lack of resolve, I threw a cloak over my gown and slipped out through the kitchen.

He was waiting in the shadows and his appearance startled me so much that I instantly forgot myself and became overcome by concern. His face was worn and haggard, with stubble darkening his chin. His eyes were red as if he had not slept for many nights, and his clothes were dusty. Looking down at his boots I observed that the soles were peeling away from the uppers. Was this the same man who had romanced me in Bath?

Horrified, I grasped his arm urgently. "What has happened, Jerry? Are you in danger?" He gave me his wry smile.

"Of course I am in danger, my dear. I am a wanted man. Sadly, an acquaintance betrayed me to the runners. I was in an ale house when Townshend and his men arrived. I was lucky to make my escape but they

201

are close behind me and I have no place to go now. Townshend will not give up until he has my head." Alarmed by this horrid vision I immediately asked how I could help.

"It is not merely a matter of money," I urged. "You must have a place of safety." Jerry gave a mirthless laugh.

"Such a place no longer exists in this country. You must help me to escape. I will be safe if I can get to America."

"America?" I echoed. "Must you go so far?" I knew how stupid this remark sounded. He shrugged; "There is a Yankee ship in the Port of London. She sails for New York tomorrow. Townshend will find it difficult to get on board a foreign vessel even if he suspects that I am there. The Americans have no love for the British. If I can pay my passage they will guarantee to keep me hidden. "May the devil take me away to hell on his black horse before I surrender to Townshend."

His words barely registered in my mind. All I could think of was that he was leaving me, just as my hero Lord Byron had left me. Why was everyone able to escape from England while I remained trapped?

"Do you not have any family? Someone who could shelter you for a while?"

Jerry gave a bitter laugh. "My mother threw me out of her house a long time ago. There is no-one else."

Of course, dear reader, I gave him all the money I possessed. I would probably have been foolish enough to give him Getheridge's diamond bangle if he had

202

asked for it, but fortunately he was content with the money.

"I cannot reconcile myself to your loss," I whispered as he stuffed the money into various pockets.

"It is better this way, my dear. You cannot share my way of life. Snare yourself a fop like that lord you were entertaining."

Impulsively, I flung myself into his arms and enjoyed a last passionate kiss with the only man who had truly aroused my deepest feelings and desires.

"We had so little time together," I sniffled into his lapels.

"But we had a fine adventure, did we not, my dear? We almost stole the Prince Regent's emeralds!"

"Almost is not enough in this world," I replied sadly. He slipped away after warning me to remember the name of Von Mecks.

"That affair is not yet concluded." Those were his last words to me. At the mention of that name I remembered something. Hastily running to my room I seized the boots and the cape from the closet and instructed Adelaide to run after Jerry and give them to him. The sight of his worn out footwear had moved me almost to tears. At least my highwayman would arrive in the New World well dressed and warm.

I returned to my bedchamber unable to face my friends at that moment. Full of tears and regrets I remained there until Adelaide returned waving the Almack's invitation card in the air in a purposeful manner. "Whatever are you doing with that?" I snapped.

"Testing it, madam."

"For what, gout?"

My maid ignored the sarcasm in my voice and tapped the corner of the card. "This here card is a fake, ma'am," she announced.

"Do not be ridiculous, who would want to fake such a thing?" I already knew the answer; anyone who was desperate to gain an *entrée* into society, as I was.

Adelaide was adamant. As the daughter of a printer in Cheapside she had seen enough forgeries to know the true from the false.

"Have you seen any other cards?" I demanded. "You must be able to compare it with others." Always full of surprises, Adelaide claimed that she knew the printer who made the cards and this one did not have his mark. "That's 'ow you can tell, ma'am. Every printer 'as his own secret mark on his work."

My first thought was why had she not obtained one of the real cards if she knew the printer. It was most unlike my enterprising retainer. She read my mind in an unnerving manner.

"You wouldn't get past the door, ma'am. Your name would not be on the invitation list." I was sure that Lord Finchbrook could arrange that. Finchbrook! Was he the person who had obtained a forgery in order to humiliate me? Surely not? It was more likely that someone had sold it to him for a large sum. The fool! I would have to speak to him as soon as possible. For now I had other things on my mind. It was late and I needed to sleep.

"Adelaide, lay out my walking clothes for the morning. Something dark and unremarkable. We will be leaving the house very early." She raised a questioning eyebrow. "Going where, madam?"

"Ships leave on the dawn tide, do they not? We will be watching a ship leave London."

"I don't know anything about that. Printing and ladies' fashions, them I know about, don't know nothing about ships and tides." She sounded peeved. Adelaide always hated early mornings. "It wouldn't be something to do with that Jeremy Sartain, would it, madam?" My guilty expression gave the answer. My maid nodded in a knowing manner. "'E didn't look none too 'ealthy to me. I s'pose you don't when you come back from the dead!" She gave a macabre giggle while I sniffled and prepared to retire to my bed.

As she helped me to undress Adelaide added that she doubted the wisdom of giving the boots and cape to Jerry.

"And why not?" I asked.

"Well, madam, the clothes of a murdered man . . . they might 'ave some sort of curse on 'em." She was definitely in a strange mood. I told her that poor Jerry had worse things to worry about. If there was a curse attached to the Von Mecks incident it had surely transferred itself to me.

CHAPTER
SEVENTEEN

Very early the following morning we crept out of the house in the chill, overcast dawn light. Adelaide managed to hail a cab whose driver was so sleepy that the sight of two well-dressed women creeping around Bloomsbury at that hour did not bother him in the slightest.

It was a long drive to the docks and I feared that we might be too late. After instructing the cabbie to wait for us we climbed up a small hill where we had a good view of the river and its traffic. In among the ships leaving on the early tide I spied the merchantman flying the Yankee flag: *Pride of Boston* was its name, and small figures scurried around its decks like frantic ants. Of course it was impossible to recognise anyone at this distance.

Tears flowed down my cheeks as I watched the ship's progress. The river was like rippling grey silk and the masts and rigging were so high that even from our distant hill the ship looked like a giant's vessel crewed by manikin men. He was gone — the only man who had ever inspired deep affection in my heart, gone thousands of miles away to a land I would never see. I sobbed quietly and Adelaide handed me a lawn handkerchief saying briskly, "You don't know as 'e's on board, madam. He could have taken your money and 'oled up in the stews of London." I thought of Townshend the runner and shook my head.

"No, this time he had to leave." Certainly he had taken all my available cash. I was forced to borrow the cab fare from my maid's wages when we returned home.

I sent a note to Lord Finchbrook telling him of the situation regarding the invitation card and requesting him to attend on me to explain the situation. He came to the house promptly after riding with Darcy. He looked quite concerned.

"Well, sir?" I waved the card at him. "It is definitely a forgery. Am I to go to Almack's or not?" Finchbrook examined the card and visibly relaxed. He sat down carefully in his tight pantaloons, spreading his coat tails.

"Unfortunately, dear madam, I had to obtain a forged invitation because all the cards for our appointed evening had been allocated. Rest assured our names will certainly be on the guest list."

"Surely they will check the cards against the list and realise that they do not tally?" I protested. He waved away this problem.

"It is all in the hands of the stewards and I have given them a small *reward*. The main thing is that we must pass the scrutiny of the dragons — I mean the distinguished ladies who preside over these matters." He did not explain how we would manage this without, in my case, appearing before the guardians and I did not wish to ask. Lord Finchbrook gave me a roguish smile and explained everything.

"It only remains for you to be presented to the guardian tomorrow morning so that we may attend the assembly on Wednesday." I knew that the balls were always held on that day.

"I know how much it means to you, my dear," he added.

At that moment Selena came into the room, golden-haired and fresh in sprigged lawn, and I saw from the expression on his face that he would have loved to take her as his partner. It made his gesture to me all the more sweet and unselfish. I felt a lump forming in my throat. Miles followed her remarking to everyone that my brother-in-law was a fine fellow but easily roused to anger.

"You could tell from his expression, from the nodules of rage on his forehead. I had a commanding officer like that," he added.

"Never mind about Darcy," I assured him. "Just avoid enraging him whenever you meet him." Selena and I had made our excuses, leaving the men to accompany him.

The next morning I prepared my toilette with the utmost care, endeavouring to appear modish yet modest, for my appointment with the guardian. My dilemma was that I was still officially in mourning — or in half mourning at the very least. I had no intention of appearing at Almack's in black, and if the guardian knew of my situation I would never gain entry. Once again, his lordship came to my rescue.

He presented me to Lady Sefton as Mr Darcy's sister-in-law, Miss Mary Bennet. What a stroke of genius! The Bennet family was, naturally, unknown to her ladyship but my brother-in-law's name worked its magic. She graciously approved me and issued me with a stranger's ticket for the evening. Nothing more was required and we left without any further formalities. I hoped that no officers would recognise me at the ball, but it was unlikely.

After that it only remained for me to borrow money from my friend for some silk for my gown. She agreed with an ill grace, reproaching me in private for my stupidity in giving mine to Jerry. I had been obliged to confess to her my encounters with him in Bath and London. There was also an element of jealousy, I suspected. When Miles said that he would prefer to go to All-Max in the east, a notorious drinking den, his wife gave him an evil look.

And so, dear reader, my night of nights arrived. Arrayed in blue silk and white lace, wearing the Prince Regent's necklace, a dead man's bracelet and other finery borrowed or purloined by Adelaide, I awaited Lord Finchbrook's arrival.

"What a lark it will be!" I announced gleefully to my image in the mirror. My partner did his best to be enthused but could not refrain from commenting as he handed me into the carriage that, in his opinion, only the lower orders really knew how to enjoy themselves. I was too busy congratulating myself to heed his words. Almack's was the very meridian of fashion, style, elegance and manners — from the alpha to the omega.

It was seventh heaven of the fashionable world. To breathe this rarefied air would surely elevate me to a different level of society. It must be a stepping stone to something great.

Overcome with deep gratitude I turned to Lord Finchbrook and kissed his hand, which startled him considerably. "Pon my soul dear lady, it was but a little thing."

The clock wanted but five minutes of half past nine when we entered the ballroom and my dazzled eyes took in the diamond encrusted aristocrats, the mistresses of the famous and the infamous, the dandies, the generals, the ambassadors and a number of very ordinary looking people, both male and female. I was not, however, totally overcome by the throng passing before me. Had I not danced with a prince at Wellington's ball? I had also shared a royal bed but I preferred not to dwell on that incident.

It did not escape my notice that the many guests who came up to greet Lord Finchbrook paid scant attention to me, although my escort introduced me with the greatest respect. One woman in particular who was swathed in dark red velvet with ruby and diamond jewellery behaved as if I had suddenly become invisible. Lord Finchbrook said that she was wealthy Lady Sarah Sugden, much courted by fortune seekers. I noticed with satisfaction that the heiress's abilities appeared to be restricted to being able to smoulder and walk in a straight line at the same time.

I wondered why she was wearing velvet when everyone else wore the fashionable muslins and silk. I mentioned this to Lord Finchbrook as we perambulated around the ballroom.

"She wishes to stand out from the crowd," he replied. "It is not enough that she is the richest heiress in England."

I was disappointed to discover that supper would consist of thin slices of bread and butter and pound cake, accompanied by tea and lemonade. I could have been back with my mother and sisters at Longbourn.

We joined another two couples for a cotillion called Mr Fortune's Maggot, the same dance that first brought Lizzie to the attention of Mr Darcy, and then the orchestra struck up a lively quadrille. My heart skipped with joy but despite my entreaties my escort could not be persuaded to venture on the dance floor again claiming that he would end in a heap in front of the dragon guardians.

At that moment who should appear at my side but the Count himself, handsome in burgundy and pristine white linen, his splendid hair vying with the gilt on his Austrian decorations and the ruby pin glowing in his cravat. He gave a deep bow and asked if he could partner me. With a flourish he signed for every dance in my card and whisked me off around the ballroom floor which seemed to my eyes to be sprinkled with gold dust and starlight.

The red silk-covered window seats and the high mezzanine balcony were crowded with observers, including those disconsolate wallflowers and their chaperones who had not been asked to dance.

My partner held me in a pleasingly firm manner and after a few extremely elegant turns around the floor he gave me some personal details at last. I knew he was a diplomat but he informed me that he was, in fact, the military attaché at the Austro-Hungarian embassy.

"I am about to take up a new post at our embassy in Paris." I refused to be downcast at this news, exclaiming, "Oh, but you must be adept at dancing the waltz. What a pity it is not danced here." The Count assured me that it was. "But you must obtain permission from the guardians for your first waltz." Within seconds he had deposited me before the Countess Lieven who gave me permission with a brief nod of disinterest. She bestowed a dazzling smile on the Count, I noticed.

The Count was then able to sweep me out into a small salon where we waltzed around at such speed that my feet hardly touched the ground. Music was unnecessary. I heard it in my head.

When we returned to earth I told him that it was my dearest wish to spend time in the city of light and romance; he smiled, held me tighter and invited me to join him there. He assured me that it would be done without any risk to my reputation. I was so taken by surprise by this sudden invitation that I was struck dumb for a moment or two.

"That is a most improper suggestion, sir!" I felt obliged to say this for propriety's sake. What did the Count really think about me? Had he assumed that I was now Lord Finchbrook's mistress? I was not a debutante or an aristocrat, after all. In our brief

212

meetings I had told him little about my background. I remembered the incident in the Sydney Gardens at Bath and immediately became flustered. I tried to hide my chagrin by fixing him with a haughty look. "You must know, sir, that I am a gentleman's daughter. His lordship is a friend who has generously offered to escort me this evening."

Obviously the Count had recognised something in me. Perhaps I gave off an air of worldliness that marked me out from the simpering virgins being exhibited by their mamas. He saw me as someone helping to operate a clandestine gaming house in Portman Square. In addition I was forced to explain why I had posed as my sister in order to gain admission.

The Count was immediately full of apologies claiming that he was so overcome by my charms that he had forgotten himself. As he said these words he gave me a brilliant smile and spun me around the room again until I saw stars everywhere. When he slowed the pace somewhat he nodded at the glittering throng and remarked, "There are many highborn ladies here who are the mistresses of the most powerful men in the land." And quite a few of the other kind I told myself silently.

The Count looked into my eyes, "Are you sure, *Cherie*, that you would not like to be my guest in Paris? It could be arranged with the utmost discretion."

I fought another brief battle for my virtue and lost. How else could I achieve my ambition? Even Jerry had urged me to snare an aristocrat. I wondered if such a man might be a safer proposition than a banker. It was evident that the Count was not proposing marriage but his reluctance in that department might be overcome, I told myself. Stratagems. Stratagems were required.

The Count must have sensed that I was weighing the possibilities. He watched the expressions of doubt and longing which I knew were passing over my face. As if in a trance I heard myself accepting his proposal. As he led me back to Lord Finchbrook who was to escort me in to supper, the Count whispered, "Let us dine together soon and discuss the matter thoroughly. I leave London in three weeks."

Of course I told the entire story to his lordship and asked for his advice immediately but my escort was not in quick thinking mode.

"Pon my soul, madam, you are a fast worker and no mistake," was his only reaction as he trifled with a trifle.

"Yes, but should I go?" I pressed him as I tried to steer him away from the desserts.

"I am not qualified to advise you, dear lady. Perhaps some enquiries should be made about this gentleman. I might be able to discover something from the Countess Lieven but it will take a little time — and courage. She is a formidable woman." And with that I had to be content.

As we drove home his lordship declared that there had been a monstrous deal of stupid quizzing and commonplace conversation at the ball, as usual, but the trifle had been excellent.

In the cold light of the morning after, I realised that I had also forgotten about my brother-in-law. How could I present this new opportunity in a blameless light? Before breakfast I sat down to write to my sister Kitty telling her about the Count and the probability that I would join him in Paris. I would have to hesitate a little more for decency's sake but I knew I could not resist such an adventure.

Kitty had always been my confidante in the family and I knew she would be enthralled by my adventures. Not so my friends who left me in no doubt as to their opinions.

"Lydia, are you telling me that you agreed to leave for Paris with a man you scarcely know? You have met him only three or four times, if my memory serves." Selena's expression was one of mingled awe and outrage when we sat at breakfast next morning.

"And a foreigner to boot," Miles complained.

"He is a diplomat," I explained, "titled and charming — and he dances like a dream. I have promised to discuss the matter. I have not given a definite answer." This was not strictly true but it was at least half true. There would be more discussion but in my heart I knew I had made a decision. I was not likely to receive a better offer in the near future.

"It is obvious that this man does not intend to make you a respectable offer," Selena sniffed, reading my mind once again. "You will achieve nothing with him except the ruin of your reputation." Of course my friend was probably right but in the sober light of day I was beginning to realise that my expectations among the aristocracy would not include marriage. I would have to accept what was on offer.

For the rest of the day my friends warned and reproached me for my actions, emphasising that they could not escort me to Paris or rescue me if the situation deteriorated. "Unless we are lucky at the tables," Miles added.

I scarcely paid any attention to their remarks. I was already plotting in my mind how I might present the situation to Darcy without exciting his suspicions. I could not afford to outrage him in any way. My parents might disapprove of my behaviour but they were not my main source of support. No matter how my fortunes turned in the future I needed to know that my finances would always be in place.

When the Count took me to dinner on the following evening everything was resolved. We dined in gilded privacy in one of the rooms at the embassy. I wore deep rose-coloured lace and he complimented me on my looks and my vivacity saying that I would be an ornament to Parisian society. He assured me in his delightful accent that French women in general were affected and boring in their conversation.

Ferenc promised me that I would receive a formal invitation to Paris from his mother. This would satisfy my family. He would arrange suitable lodgings for me.

"Will your mother not wonder where I am if I do not arrive at her house?" I asked. The Count smiled. "My mother is elderly and forgets very quickly."

The evening was agreeably romantic. As I prepared to leave, the Count drew me close. I felt his soft kisses on my eyelids and the tips of my ears, his fingers smoothing my hair and caressing my neck. He made no other attempt to seduce me before he handed me into a carriage. I told Selena that his behaviour toward me continued to be honourable.

"To a degree only," my friend gave a move of disapproval. "Why did he invite you to dine alone with him if he has honourable intentions? The news will be all over Portman Square tomorrow." I refused to be cast down in any way. My future had not looked as promising for a long time.

All that remained was for me to visit Pemberley, beg or borrow more gowns from Lizzie, bid farewell to my parents en route and perhaps persuade my brother-in-law to give me some extra money for the trip. I had quite forgotten Lord Finchbrook in all this and when he called on us I was able to thank him once again for his kindness.

"I owe it all to you," I cried. "I knew that if I could appear at Almack's my life would change forever."

He patted my hand and smiled saying, "I have heard nothing untoward about your Count. The Countess Lieven speaks highly of him. He is quite a high ranking diplomat, I believe."

"Do you not think it madness?" Selena demanded of the room. "You should not have encouraged her in this, my lord." Finchbrook looked stricken at the thought of displeasing his goddess, but rallied when she added, "I do not blame you entirely. Lydia is so headstrong and she seems determined to be someone's mistress rather than a wife."

I was infuriated at this cruel jibe, dear reader, considering that my friend had urged me into the bed of the Prince Regent and practically forced me into a Fleet marriage with a felon. Sometimes one's friends are not all one would wish for. As for me I could scarcely believe that my dream was about to come true. It was unfortunate that Lord Byron had moved on to Italy but our paths might yet cross. I had a great deal to confide to my journal that evening.

A few days later a page arrived from the embassy with an ornate invitation card embossed with the Count's coat of arms. Adelaide pronounced it a very fair piece of work. I think she was referring to the card rather than the Count, although he is a very handsome man. I have offered to take Adelaide with me to Paris. I shall certainly need a maid. She is thinking the matter over. I know she has become involved with a footman but she cannot resist a challenge, although she speaks unflatteringly of Frenchies.

I endured the long, tiresome journey to Derbyshire sustained by the thought of my forthcoming stay in the city of elegance. At last I had the opportunity to enter more rarefied social circles and who could say where that might lead? At least my daydreams of marrying into the aristocracy whiled away the tedium and discomfort of the long journey.

CHAPTER
EIGHTEEN

Pemberley, Summer 1816

Lizzie greeted me affectionately and I duly remarked on little Charles Fitzwilliam's progress. The child bears an unfortunate resemblance to his father. Many people find my brother-in-law handsome but I cannot see it myself. Mr Darcy appeared a little more mellow than usual probably because there are rumours of a forthcoming engagement between one of the neighbouring squires and Miss Georgiana Darcy. No doubt he will be pleased to have her off his hands. I feel a strange bond with the woman, part pity, part loathing — after all, we were both Wickham's cast offs, in a manner of speaking.

My invitation was acknowledged with a mixture of bewilderment and pleasure by my relatives. Miss Georgiana actually had the temerity to suggest that I might be invited to fulfil the role of companion to the dowager countess. She made this remark when we were gathered in the music room one evening, where she had carefully arranged herself alongside a marble statue of St Cecilia, the patron saint of music, in order to display herself to the best advantage in an elaborate new gown of silver tissue and lace. The effect was to make her resemble an outsize Christmas package. Only a wreath of holly berries and mistletoe was lacking, but she was vastly pleased with the ensemble.

"You will be greatly favoured, Mrs Wickham." She gave me a patronising smile, while her brother nodded in agreement. If only they knew.

When I was able to speak privately to my brother-in-law I was assured that my allowance would reach me in France. Lizzie gave me many warnings about the dangers of being a woman alone in a foreign city, although I do not know how she can presume any knowledge. She has never left these shores. Her honeymoon was spent touring Scotland.

During the following week mysterious packages arrived at the house addressed to me. They contained small gifts and knick-knacks guaranteed to please a lady. Fine gloves, an ivory fan, a beaded and jewelled reticule and an antique, miniature pack of playing cards were among the trinkets. These last were perhaps a joke at my expense. The Count sent messages with them assuring me of his devotion to my needs and of his admiration and respect for me. I carefully disguised them from the prying eyes of the family saying that they were necessities for the journey.

With the assistance of Lizzie's French maid I was able to refurbish my wardrobe somewhat. I prevailed upon the woman to teach Adelaide a few words of her language — she has decided to accompany me after all. The time passed less ill than I had anticipated. I doubted that I should be at Pemberley again for some time.

Perhaps I should have anticipated the disaster that was about to befall me but I am of a sunny and optimistic disposition. I always believe in a good outcome — a tendency often disappointed by reality. I was sitting alone in the library with a book open on my knees day-dreaming of my Parisian future when Mr Darcy stormed into the room waving a letter. His face turned purple and pale in turn and he appeared to be speechless with fury. He threw the letter into my lap and to my horror I saw that it was the one I had sent to Kitty. How could she have betrayed me? Is nothing — not even the bonds of sisterly devotion — sacred?

My brother-in-law found his voice as I clutched the arms of the chair in panic.

"What is the meaning of this, madam?" he thundered. "What mindless folly and treachery are you planning? Thank goodness your sister has acquired a modicum of sense and decorum even if you have not!"

He went on in this vein for some time, reminding me of the circumstances of my marriage to Wickham and the disgrace narrowly avoided on that occasion. I was threatened with virtual imprisonment at Pemberley until I saw the error of my ways. There would be no communication with my friends in London unless I wished to forgo his protection and financial support. He stormed out of the room ordering me to attend a family conference later that day where my wickedness would be discussed by everyone.

I anticipated a biblical stoning at the very least. The servants would probably be allowed to throw rotten vegetables at me as I stood chained to a post wearing sackcloth. My imagination has always tended to the Gothic.

In the privacy of my room I wept bitter tears over Kitty's betrayal, the loss of my golden Parisian future, of the Count, of Jerry — even of Mr Getheridge. Would nothing ever be right in my life, and what should I do now? I had no doubt that Darcy had something unpleasant planned for me. I hoped that Lizzie would stand by me but I was learning a harsh lesson in family values.

I was summoned to the drawing room an hour before dinner. To my disgust, Georgiana Darcy was also present and sending speaking looks in my direction. Lizzie appeared to have been crying. Everyone stared at me as if I had been turned to stone.

After a few silent moments which seemed to contain aeons of recrimination, Mr Darcy remarked with startling originality, "What do you have to say for yourself, madam?"

"I have nothing to say, sir," I replied, more defiantly than I felt. "I am sure you will have enough to say for both of us."

"Oh, Lydia!" wailed Lizzie, "How could you, after all my husband has done for you?"

"Indeed," chimed in Georgiana in an unnaturally deep voice, "and at such a time, when my engagement is about to be announced." She added a pathetic vocal wobble at the end of this sentence for maximum effect. So it was true — the little sister was finally to be sold off, pardon me, betrothed to a suitable spouse. No doubt Darcy paid a handsome dowry whereas I — I am distracted. My brother-in-law is speaking again.

"If you cannot be trusted to live a normal respectable life as befits a gentlewoman there are only two options open to your relatives."

"Yes?" I enquired with some interest.

"Either we contrive to have you detained as befits an insane person or we find you a suitable husband."

For a moment I was torn between these exotic opportunities, but I merely lowered my head and dabbed my eyes with a kerchief endeavouring to squeeze out a tear for the benefit of my tormentors.

"I am sure that Lydia has seen the error of her ways, dearest," pleaded Lizzie.

"I devoutly hope so," he replied between gritted teeth. I was dismissed to my room where I was forced to remain for three days until summoned to greet Georgiana's intended, the Hon. Theodore Whitworth, whose family estate lay several miles north of Pemberley. On the second day I was obliged to pay to receive a letter written jointly by Kitty and Mary which went on at great length about the loss of virtue in women that led to irretrievable ruin. My parents refused to communicate with me. I was not greatly diverted.

CHAPTER
NINETEEN

While I was imprisoned in my room the faithful Adelaide had been busy on my behalf. By judicious listening at doors (and who knows what means besides) she had discovered that Kitty's unexpected fit of decorum was caused by her recent engagement to a clergyman. The man was a mere curate, hardly a catch, but Kitty had no dowry and little in the way of looks. No doubt she was grateful but it did not excuse her betrayal of me. Needless to say my parents had not intervened on my behalf.

I wore the deep rose lace gown to the dinner at which I was to meet the Hon. Theodore who was the younger brother of Lord MountStephen. Was it not strange that Georgiana, with all her advantages of wealth and breeding, could snare only the younger brother — even with the inducement of a large dowry?

The rose gown was another act of defiance. I have no doubt the guests expected me to appear in deep mourning as befitted the wicked widow. I did not dare to wear the Prince's necklace, however. That would have been a provocation too far. I would not have been able to explain how I had come by it without tying myself and my tongue into knots.

When I entered the room a definite *froideur* descended on the occupants except for the Hon. Theodore who greeted me with surprising warmth. I made him a modest curtsey without raising my eyes.

Darcy introduced me as "my sister-in-law who will be leaving us soon". At least he did not grind his teeth when he spoke. I had decided not to engage in any unnecessary conversation and I addressed myself to the soup. No member of the family spoke a word to me but I found the Hon. Theodore sitting opposite me and slightly to the left. He cast a few warm glances at me whenever Georgiana looked elsewhere. She kept a remarkably tight grasp on her intended spouse scarcely letting him move a foot in any direction.

The man did not interest me in the slightest although I noted that his looks were tolerable and his legs were well-shaped. I have always admired that in a man. I had no doubt that he would find Georgiana as dull as everyone else did, but he would have her fortune to console him. The evening wore its way to a bland conclusion and I retired to bed early.

At breakfast on the following morning my brother-in-law informed me that he would soon secure a place for me as a lady's companion in the Bath area. Letters had already been dispatched. Bath of all places; I could not bear the thought of returning to that city with its uncomfortable memories.

It appeared that a suitable spouse could not be found for me at short notice so I must, therefore, be dispatched as soon as possible. At least he had not chosen the asylum option, although I had no doubt that there was such an institution in Bath.

At least my friends might visit me. I had not heard from Miles and Selena since I arrived at Pemberley, but Darcy had said there would be no communication with them. It was possible that the wretched man had confiscated my correspondence. The thought made me so furious that bile rose in my throat.

I remembered that Selena loved Bath and she would surely come when she heard of my predicament. I needed to contrive a way of contacting her. My maid would, as always, think of something. A few more days dragged by in which I scarcely spoke with anyone except Adelaide.

On the fifth day I donned my warm cape and stout boots and went to walk in the grounds as far away from the house as possible. I enjoyed the feel of the lush, late summer grass under my feet. Already there was an autumnal chill in the air despite the abysmal summer we had endured. Flowering shrubs were past their best and even the wild flowers in the hedgerows were hanging their heads in a dispirited manner as if in sympathy with my own despondent thoughts.

I walked and walked until I came to the far edge of the estate where a narrow lane ran alongside the boundary. A light rain began to fall and I sheltered under a large chestnut tree that spread its huge branches over me in a paternal fashion. As I waited I heard the clip clop of horses' hooves and I spied a gentleman riding towards me on a fine black horse.

226

"Good morning, Mrs Wickham, can I be of assistance to you?" said the Hon. Theo. He was on his way to Pemberley to pay a call on Georgiana. I assured him that I was not bothered by a light shower and I was enjoying a little exercise.

"But you will have another long walk back to the house," he objected. "And you will be exhausted if not drenched. I insist on taking you back with me."

Without waiting for a reply he jumped down, placed an arm around my waist and lifted me on to the horse. An unexpected thrill coursed through my veins for a moment. Did I really find this man attractive, or was it the thrill of doing something calculated to enrage the Darcys? I smiled down at him and fluttered my eyelashes, thanking him for his solicitude. Assuring me that he was honoured to be of service he remounted and we trotted off with his arms securely encircling me.

It seemed to me that my rescuer was in no hurry to reach the house and we passed the time very agreeably, chatting and laughing before reaching the stables. As we entered the house Georgiana was waiting. When she saw us both in a damp condition she turned quite green with emotion, a shade matching the virulent viridian velvet gown she was wearing. Her fiancé explained in great detail how he had found me at the side of the road in the rain and had carried me back to Pemberley.

"Indeed," I murmured gratefully, "you were most attentive." Georgiana directed waves of hate towards me as she half dragged Theodore away. I wondered how long it would be before Darcy was informed. I returned to my room to change, feeling far more cheerful than of late, until Adelaide came to tell me that there was still no mail for me. How can they all have deserted me — the Count, Selena and Miles? Of course, my brother-in-law was at the root of this. I would have my revenge in due course.

Adelaide read my mind yet again. She declared that even she was not able to pilfer letters from my brother-in-law's desk, if that was where they were hidden. If only my lost highwayman were available. After pilfering from the Prince Regent, my brother-in-law would not have presented a challenge.

At lunch I could not detect any change in my sister and Darcy which meant that Georgiana had not yet had an opportunity to blacken my character further. Excusing myself from further socialising I retreated to the library where I was re-reading William Beckford's exotic novel *Vathek*. Quickly, I lost myself in its pages scarcely noticing when the door opened and the Hon. Theodore appeared.

"I trust you have not come to rescue me again, sir?" I twinkled at him. He walked across the room and peered over my shoulder at the book.

"I would be delighted to rescue you whenever necessary, madam." He added, "I see we share similar tastes in reading."

"I love a man who enjoys a good novel!" I exclaimed. He perched on the arm of the chair, adding in a lowered voice, "I am sure we have many things in common, Mrs Wickham."

"And I am sure that your fiancée would be most aggrieved if she heard you express such sentiments." He smiled a roguish smile and put his hand on my arm, apparently unperturbed by the prospect.

At that very moment the door opened and Georgiana stood on the threshold. She took in the scene with one glance, noting her fiancé's hand on my arm. She uttered a loud scream and fled, calling for her brother. "I fear, sir, there will be repercussions." I looked pointedly at his hand and removed it from my arm. The Hon. Theodore laughed and walked over to the bookshelves.

"I was merely admiring my host's collection. You happened to be here already. Can we be blamed if my fiancée is given to hysterics?"

"I think I shall retire to my room for a rest," I declared, offering my hand. He kissed it and ushered me out of the room. I left him to face whatever would result from our meeting. Adelaide and I laughed a great deal as I recounted the story. She declared that the Hon. Theo had a reputation as a womaniser and had sired a child by a village girl whom he still visited. I wished Georgiana joy of him.

I had not been in my room more than an hour when from my bed I observed a note being surreptitiously pushed under the door. I replaced my facemask, lay back and continued thinking about Paris. I had no stomach for more intrigue, but Adelaide was soon waving the note under my nose.

It was in the form of a wager — unsigned. It read:

T bets Mrs W one guinea that her charms will overpower a certain person before the week is out.

The effrontery of the man! My position was difficult enough at the moment without the Hon. Theo's attentions. Indeed, a novel could be written on the subject entitled *Parlous at Pemberley*. Adelaide, as usual, had an opinion.

"Either 'e don't fancy being married to Miss Georgiana or 'e 'as some kind of 'old over Mr Darcy and can do whatever 'e pleases," she declared.

"That is absurd, Adelaide. The idea of my brother-in-law allowing anyone to have a hold over him is fanciful in the extreme."

"That depends, 'e must want to get 'is sister married off real bad." She gave me a sly look. "Will you take the bet, madam?" I gave her a light slap and commanded her to fetch me a dish of tea.

When I descended the stairs that evening for a pre-dinner sherry in the salon, the atmosphere was as icy as ever, but no words were spoken. Georgiana, looking pale and red-eyed, ignored me completely. Darcy looked distracted, Lizzie gave me a strained smile and the Hon. Theo gave me a sly wink.

I had left the note on the night table in my room, dear reader, so you can imagine my consternation at the events which transpired during the meal. After a warming game soup, I toyed with a fricassee of pheasant. The conversation was stilted at best.

"You are looking particularly lovely tonight, my dear." The Hon. Theo bestowed a patronising smile on his fiancée. She sniffed loudly and dropped her fork to the floor. In the ensuing scuffle Georgiana appeared to be fumbling with something in her reticule.

230

When everyone straightened up and resumed eating she produced her *coup de feu*. Waving my note from Theodore at the assembled family she shrieked,

"See how I am betrayed by that low vixen you harbour in this house!" This was addressed to her brother specifically, and to everyone else generally. We all regarded her in stunned silence and then Darcy, the Hon. Theo and I made a simultaneous lunge for the note.

Georgiana evaded our clutching hands, jumped up and ran around the table screaming hysterically until restrained by her brother and fiancé. Lizzie called for *sal volatile* and brandy while I wondered who had betrayed me yet again. I knew it could not be Adelaide so I assumed that Georgiana had sent one of her servants to investigate my room while it was empty. The servant had found the note and endeavoured to pass it to her mistress at some point before or during the meal. This was the outside of enough. There must be something malignant in the very air of this place that brings nothing but misfortune to the innocent.

When Georgiana's sobs and moans had subsided a little I stood up and declared loudly, "I will not be traduced in this manner." Glaring at my brother-in-law and the Hon. Theo in turn I continued, "I have never sought this man's attentions. They are unwanted and unsolicited. The notion that there is anything untoward between us is pure piffle-poffle and I will not be blamed for it." I sat down amid complete silence except for Georgiana's moans. I waved my hand at the Hon. Theo. "Tell them the truth," I commanded. "If you do not, you are no gentleman." All eyes swivelled towards him but he remained the epitome of effrontery, as cool as iced lemonade.

Darcy stared at Theo and spoke in a low, dangerously calm voice.

"What do you have to say, sir? If you do not have a satisfactory explanation I shall be obliged to call you out. My sister's reputation is precious to me." Theo shrugged and looked quite relaxed.

"I know nothing of this. The note is obviously a forgery — an unfortunate prank by someone in this house." Everyone turned to stare at me at this point and I almost exploded with rage. My reputation had been tarnished but this was of no interest to anyone. Georgiana's reputation was, naturally, extremely precious. Fiddlesticks! Georgiana was a tawdry slut who ran off with Wickham when she was scarcely out of the schoolroom. Of course, I did the same thing, but at least we were later married. Miss Darcy was damaged goods and now a duel would be fought over her.

I was so furious that I uttered a scream of rage and fled to my room where I remained until the following afternoon when my brother-in-law appeared in my chamber waving a letter.

"I have received confirmation from a Mrs Letitia Makepeace of Widcombe House in the city of Bath that she will engage you as her companion forthwith. She is a most respectable widowed lady of good standing in the community. You are fortunate to have this opportunity, madam, and I trust you will benefit from it."

232

I tried to engage my voice with some difficulty. "But . . ."

"But me no buts, Lydia. You are a viper in the collective bosom of this family and the sooner you leave the better it will be for all." With that he turned on his heel, closed the door loudly and I collapsed in a flood of tears.

"There, there, madam," soothed Adelaide. "Don't take on so. I'll go below stairs and get the whole story." She left me alone to face my tragic destiny — an old lady's companion — in Bath!

CHAPTER
TWENTY

Bath, Winter 1816

I am not usually given to utter despair, dear reader, but Mr Darcy's news sounded like the knell of doom . . . doom to all my dreams for a golden future — or indeed any future at all. I could hear in my head the surly, sullen, midnight bell described in Mr Lathom's Gothic novel. This time it was tolling for me, for all my hopes and plans.

Even Adelaide could not raise my spirits. She will accompany me but the prospect of the long journey south filled her with gloom. I knew that she was prepared to part with her pet footman for Paris but Bath was a poor substitute. It was time to plead with my sister.

"There is nothing I can do, Lydia. My husband's mind is made up and I cannot but agree with him. This scandalous behaviour cannot continue." Lizzie turned away from me and looked out of the window onto the vast acres of Pemberley. We were standing in my room while Adelaide packed my belongings nearby.

As I began to sob noisily Lizzie rushed over to embrace me. "Oh, Lydie, don't take on so. I do not wish you to be unhappy. We simply want to save you from yourself." I hiccupped and almost snarled through my tears.

"Happiness . . . you talk of happiness while I am to be immured with an old trout in dismal Bath for the rest of my days?"

"It will not be forever," said my sister briskly. "Old ladies do not live so long and Mr Darcy and I may be able to find you a suitable husband — if you refrain from outraging propriety for a while."

"I suppose you mean some impecunious, terminally boring curate such as you yourself refused to wed, if I recall." My sister looked pained but could not deny the accuracy of my taunt. Adelaide was so fascinated by our conversation that she remained frozen on her knees holding one shoe aloft. I warmed to my subject hearing my voice rising into shrill invective. I hoped that my brother-in-law was nearby to hear my tirade.

"I do not give a fig for respectability!" I shrieked. "I will not be shackled to someone I despise. I will not be poor for the rest of my life. How can you, Lizzie, having achieved so much wealth and status, wish this for me? Ah, I know . . . you are more deserving than I."

I stopped for breath and saw my sister's eyes fill with tears. She made to seize my hand for a moment then rushed from the room. I collapsed onto the bed snuffling and weeping, feeling sick and wicked, while Adelaide quietly rustled tissue paper.

As soon as I could I fled from the room out into the parkland of Pemberley. I rushed down to the lake and stood staring into its depths, my whole body trembling with rage and sorrow. The lake was like black glass, unmoving. I knew that under its surface, life was teeming — fish were rushing hither and thither as fish tended to do, and vegetation of all kinds flourished. On the surface, under the lowering clouds on a dark afternoon the water was still and sinister — not even a gentle susurration stirred at my feet. In this lake of darkness I could bury my own dark thoughts, my fears and my enemies, real and imaginary. It was not surprising, in the circumstances, that the spectral figure of my brother-in-law rose from the black water gnashing his teeth at me in a malignant manner. I hurled a stone into the lake in a pointless fashion, and returned reluctantly to the house.

Adelaide was waiting for me with the laudanum bottle she had acquired from the cook. I have never been in the habit of taking laudanum but, as my maid measured out the drops, I decided that my life had reached such a low point — a positive nadir — that it was justified. I lay on my bed and drifted into an uneasy sleep.

Naturally, my outburst with Lizzie achieved nothing and within the next twenty-four hours, after the briefest of farewells to the assembled family, we were embarked on the coach en route for Bath once again. There was no sign of the Hon. Theo.

My brother-in-law was determined to heap every possible indignity upon me. To this end he instructed his steward to escort us for the entire journey, arranging accommodation at numerous inns, fussing over seats and generally ensuring that I did not attempt to take flight and disgrace the family once more.

In London, where we awaited the coach for Bath, I was carefully observed at every moment in public. However, Watkins the steward reckoned without female ingenuity. In the privacy of my room I had written a note to Selena and Miles giving them details of my whereabouts and instructing them to inform the Count.

When I appeared in the courtyard to await the mail coach, Watkins noticed that Adelaide was absent. I informed him that she had been unwell during the night and would emerge at the last possible moment.

"She is sickly this morning and I instructed her to wait inside the inn. We do not want to have her spewing over everyone in the coach." I smiled warmly at him and he shuddered saying that he would travel on top with the coachman. In fact, my maid was entrusting the letter to a messenger, paying him well to ensure a swift delivery.

The coach swept out of the yard and I bade a fond farewell to the capital, not knowing when I would see it again. I trusted in my friends' loyalty. Surely they would come to free me from my servitude.

Words cannot describe the agony of coach travel from one end of England to another. It should never be undertaken unless one is in a deceased condition. My bones ached and I dismounted at the Bear Inn feeling at least one hundred years old. Adelaide was almost bent over with cramp and even Watkins looked exhausted. I took pleasure in knowing that he would have to return with all haste to Derbyshire. After we had fortified ourselves with hot drinks he ordered a chair for me and I was conveyed to Widcombe House on the lower slopes of Widcombe Down overlooking the city. Adelaide followed on foot with our luggage in a handcart.

It was an elegant building, not large, but with a pleasant aspect. At the time views of the city did little to comfort me. I was shown into a room decorated in pale grey and primrose yellow where an elderly lady sat on a chaise longue toying with an overweight pug dog. My new employer wore a voluminous purple bombazine gown in the fashion of the last century. Her absurd headdress consisted of many starched white frills perched uneasily on sparse yellow curls. The purple gown contrasted ill with the primrose silk upholstery. It gave me a queasy feeling in my stomach.

I gave a brief curtsey as the footman announced my name. The old lady, Mrs Letitia Makepeace, looked at me carefully through her lorgnette and invited me to sit down.

"Ah, there you are, my dear. Take off your bonnet and join me in a glass of sherry. Coach travel is the very devil is it not? Were there any handsome men to enliven your journey?"

Rendered speechless by these remarks, I smiled weakly and drank down a large glass of sherry very quickly. I noticed that Mrs Makepeace had already finished her own drink. She immediately poured two more large glasses and we drank them with equal speed. It was ten thirty in the morning. The room became pleasantly hazy at this point but I noticed that the old lady poured sherry into a saucer which the pug drank enthusiastically. Very little conversation ensued. We were both quite sleepy (from the drink on her part and general weariness on mine).

"I am sure we will get along very well, my dear," said Mrs Makepeace, slurring her words a little. "Tell the servants to show you to your room. No doubt you need to rest." At this point she fell asleep while the pug collapsed across her lap snoring loudly. I tottered from the room and followed a maid upstairs, feeling the need to hold quite tightly to the balustrade. I collapsed on the bed and fell asleep immediately.

Adelaide came to rouse me for a late luncheon telling me that the situation below stairs was tolerable if not full of fascination. She was obviously suffering from the loss of her footman. I looked around my room with interest. It was not large but it was decorated in excellent taste. The walls and the ceiling had been painted in a delicate celadon green with a design of birds and fluffy white clouds painted in vertical columns. The furniture was upholstered in the same pale shades and the whole effect was delightful. I was still sufficiently tired and muzzle-headed to wish to hide behind the bed curtains for another hour or two, but duty called me downstairs. I descended slowly, regretting the large amount of sherry taken earlier.

Mrs Makepeace greeted me warmly once again. I noticed that she had already poured a generous glass of wine for herself and one for me. I was in danger of passing my entire employment at this house in an alcoholic daze, but perhaps that would be no bad thing. After a surprisingly good meal we returned to the salon where I was invited to look among the books piled on a table.

"Select one and read something to me, my dear. I am a devotee of the Gothic. *The Necromancer of the Black Forest* is a particular favourite, or *The Midnight Bell*." My spirits lifted a little. At least my employer and I shared an enthusiasm for hair-raising literature, if nothing else. I read until I was almost hoarse and I realised that Mrs Makepeace had once again fallen asleep.

As the days passed I read my way through the entire library and drank far more than was good for me. No message came from Selena and Miles and I feared that they had removed from Portman Square and were now lost to me. If I was to escape from this place it would be by my own efforts. At that moment I was at a loss as to how to proceed.

Mrs Makepeace confided in me quite freely. She told me that she found the society of Bath intolerably dull. Her late husband had left her well provided for but isolated.

"The poor man disliked company and by the time he died I had lost contact with any agreeable society. I take solace in novels and my deceased spouse's excellent wine cellar."

She had lost the urge to venture into the centre of Bath. An occasional perambulation on the downs provided some exercise, but the staff attended to her daily needs. For this reason I was sometimes sent into the city on various errands — to borrow library books or to obtain gloves and lace on Milsom Street.

My employer was not unduly troubled by religious scruples and rarely attended church on Sundays. I convinced her that I needed to attend services at the abbey for the good of my soul. This gave me ample opportunity to survey the congregation, noting any interesting newcomers, although I had no means of meeting any of them. I became lost in a reverie, gazing at the beautiful ceiling of the abbey with its carved palm trees. I am not sure that Mrs Makepeace believed my protestations of virtue. She was quite shrewd underneath her absurd eighteenth-century mannerisms. The alcoholic mists frequently parted to reveal a mind sharp enough to detect hypocrisy and dissimulation.

"Tell me more about your life before you were widowed, my dear, and pray make it sensational," she urged. I would try to oblige by describing my early married life, embroidering when necessary. I endeavoured to convey the boredom of life in army quarters with a husband whose diversions seldom included the company of his wife. Mrs Makepeace understood perfectly.

"I feel for you, my dear. I know what it is like to be shackled to a boring and dissolute spouse although my Hereward, poor love, was merely boring, not having the wit or the energy to be dissolute."

When I described the ball on the eve of Waterloo she was entranced. "How I would have loved to attend such an historic event. Did I ever tell you of the ball I attended at Versailles in the old king's day? I mean Louis XVII of course." I was amazed to hear that this old lady, wedded to her chaise longue and the sherry bottle, had such an interesting past — and in Paris, too. My envy must have communicated itself to her.

"Yes, I was in Paris with my parents — this was during the *ancien regime*, of course. Before that wretch Napoleon came along and ruined everything."

I pointed out that there had been a revolution before Napoleon came along.

"Yes, yes, it all went wrong so quickly. I was presented to poor Marie Antoinette, you know. She was charming — so gracious. I cannot describe the clothes, the luxurious display on that occasion."

"Please try," I begged. Mrs Makepeace drew a deep breath and closed her eyes.

"The queen wore a magnificent gown of gold tissue overlaid with cream organza swags and covered with embroidery — sequins, beading and jewels. She wore fine diamonds and a towering headdress of white feathers." My employer sighed, recalling these past glories.

"And what did you wear for such an event?" I asked. "Your gown must have been very special."

"Oh, it was raspberry pink silk taffeta, if I recall, with fine pleating and tulle flowers. I had heard that pink was the queen's favourite colour and, indeed, she complimented me on it. Me! An obscure little English girl! The fashions were so wonderful then, not like these skimpy Grecian-style gowns you young things are wearing. What was good enough for the ancient Greeks is definitely not good enough for us! The event was marred only by my introduction to my future husband. My parents thought him very suitable, but my preference was for a French Vicomte. If I had married him I suppose our heads would now be in a basket. I often wonder what happened to the poor fellow."

"I would give anything to see Paris," I sighed. But my employer was eager for more revelations.

"Why has your prominent family cast you off?" she asked. "Oh, yes, I can read between the lines. Your brother is a very wealthy man, is he not? Yet here you are — a lady's companion. What heinous crime have you committed, Mrs Wickham? Come, tell me everything."

I flushed indignantly. "Mr Darcy is not my brother, merely my sister's husband. My own family is far from wealthy and I was accused of bringing disgrace on my relatives. I own that I can be impetuous on occasions, but I could have removed myself permanently from this country had not my brother-in-law intervened. He has no affection for me."

For a long time I resisted telling her about the Count and our ill-starred relationship but she wheedled it out of me. Her appetite for scandal was insatiable.

"I can only live vicariously, my dear. Tell me more." She was impressed by my description of the Count. I think she would have pursued him herself if she could have dragged her body from the couch. "I would give you leave to run off and find the man, my dear, but I find I cannot manage without you."

CHAPTER
TWENTY-ONE

Her words echoed mournfully around my head as I dragged the odious Wellington across the downs on his velvet leash. I had rashly remarked that the dog would suffer an apoplexy if it did not take some exercise and this was my reward, a daily walk in all weathers. Perhaps I should not traduce the unfortunate animal too much: after all, he was the reason that I met Vincente that chill and otherwise dreary morning.

Wellington had slipped his leash and had skittered across the grass, only to skid to a halt almost in the jaws of a low-slung beast with a truculent expression.

"Turk! Turk!" cried the beast's companion, an unusually tall man with striking looks wearing a dark green frock coat and a buff-coloured waistcoat. I noticed these things only in passing because I was mesmerised by a pair of large, dark eyes, glittering with *joie de vivre*.

The man bent down and seized his dog's collar. Wellington was crouched down in an imploring manner silently begging to be rescued.

"I am extremely sorry, madam," the stranger said. "My Turk is a faithful dog but none too fond of other canines." His voice had a foreign lilt.

"You are not a native of this city, sir?" I ventured. He swept me a low bow — not easy when restraining a fierce dog.

"I am from Rome, madam, but this fair city has been my home for many years." I resisted an urge to commiserate with him. "My name is Vincente Randaccio." I introduced myself, smiled brightly and explained my role as Wellington's escort. "I cannot imagine why we have not met before, madam. I'm sure I would have remembered so *vivacious* a lady." The dark eyes glittered at me as he smiled and offered his arm. I found myself walking across the heath with the Italian stranger, the dogs dragging behind us.

I discovered that Vincente was one of the most famous singers in Europe and, as I later found out, the most sought after music teacher. He had settled in Bath in order to become musical director of the Assembly Rooms.

"I am also a castrato," he glittered at me again. "So you are quite safe with me, my dear!"

I stopped in my tracks, struck dumb for a moment. Vincente turned and gave me a cynical, amused smile. I had heard of castrati but I scarcely believed such creatures existed. Then I recalled how my father had described hearing the exquisite voice of Farinelli while on his continental travels. My late husband had once made a ribald reference to the procedure involved in making someone a castrato. He had been drunk at the time.

I shuddered and my companion laughed aloud showing remarkably good teeth. "Do not pity me, my

245

dear. Life has been good to me. My parents were poor and my life would have been a hard one — and probably short. Instead, I have had a wondrous career. I have sung for kings and popes — and I have not been short of female admirers!" Again, I recalled papa saying that Farinelli had hordes of female followers.

It was impossible not to smile in Vincente's company. By the time we had arrived back at Widcombe House, where he raised his hat and bade me farewell, my heart felt considerably lighter. He expressed the hope that we would meet again soon and I found I was blushing like a sixteen-year-old.

I lost no time in telling Mrs Makepeace of my adventure but she was less impressed than I expected. She had heard of Signor Randaccio. But she was not a great music lover and seldom went to concerts.

"If you are so taken with him, my dear, we must invite him to call upon us. She was as good as her word and Vincente duly visited and charmed us both.

Naturally, I continued the daily walks with Wellington with some enthusiasm. I knew that Vincente would exercise Turk on a regular basis and that our paths would cross. My acquaintance with him over a few months was a joyous interlude in an unhappy period of my life. I spent hours walking and talking with him while he spun incredible stories and described his fascinating life. Although he was now in his fifties there was a strange allure about him which I can scarcely describe. I had never met anyone like him.

He described to me how he had been summoned to the eccentric, Gothic masterpiece called Fonthill Abbey

246

by its equally eccentric owner, William Beckford, the richest man in England.

"Nobody visits him," Vincente explained. "His alleged sexual perversions have made him a social outcast. However, he is a man of great taste. I was invited to sing for him for a very generous fee. As I am by way of being an involuntary sexual perversion myself, I felt quite at ease. The centrepiece of the abbey is a vast staircase that winds in several directions. Beckford's evil smelling dwarf stood at the bottom of the staircase as I sang, perched on a higher level." I explained that I had read and enjoyed Beckford's novel, *Vathek*. Vincente laughed again. "It is full of excesses and cruelties, is it not? Just like my own life." Then he told me how the "change" had come about.

"I was twelve years old when my parents sold me for a castrato. I was taken to the barber surgeon, drugged and placed in a hot bath while the deed was done. When I was healed I went to sing in the choir of the Sistine Chapel."

I lost count of the hours I spent listening to Vincente's stories during those long months in Bath. We wandered many times near the great estate of Prior Park with the dogs, or visited the abbey churchyard, he in his green coat and me in my country mouse grey. He could transport me to another place with a few sentences. Especially, he could conjure up Italy.

"One day you will see my country for yourself, my dear. You will appreciate its beauty." At that moment I saw little prospect of ever reaching London again, let alone journeying to the continent. Where were my friends . . . why had I heard nothing?

To add to my aggravations Adelaide had taken a violent dislike to one of Mrs Makepeace's housemaids. The theft of a box of ribbons was mentioned and violence ensued. I returned from a walk with Vincente one morning to discover the two women fighting at the back door, wielding mops.

After I had separated them Adelaide was in such a gumbustion that she was purple and almost speechless. When she recovered a little she remained venomous.

"The very teeth in your head are not safe in Bath if you sleep with your mouth open!"

Vincente's company inspired me to try again to coax Mrs Makepeace out of her lethargy. If only I could persuade my employer to leave the house on a regular basis for some light exercise. Who knew where that might lead? I needed to reignite her lust for life and for going into society. She would make an ideal chaperone for me, although my family would assume that I was escorting her. With a sigh I slipped back into the house, noting yet again that there was no mail for me.

"Is that you, dear?" Mrs Makepeace called from the music room. "Do come and read a portion of the *Times* to me." She no longer asked me to play something for her. My attempts were too painful for both of us, even on occasion causing the dog to howl in derision. I brushed the mud from my hem, handed the muddier dog to the footman, and entered the music room. My employer was again seated on the primrose sofa wearing another of her plum coloured ensembles.

248

"Pray read only the more entertaining extracts," Mrs Makepeace directed, as if there was anything entertaining in that publication. She meant, of course, read only the social and court news varied with details of the occasional homicide. This time my eye was attracted to a short piece quoting the king's own physician, no less.

The man responsible for attending to our poor, mad sovereign announced that his majesty's condition had greatly improved by following a strict regime of daily exercise in the fresh air, cold baths, simple food and the occasional glass of red wine. His melancholia had lessened and his faculties were less distracted.

I wondered whether I could persuade my employer to adopt a version of this regime. She was not, of course, insane, and I feared that the cold baths and lack of alcohol would be rejected out of hand, but if I could approach her in the right way . . . The dog was returned to the room suitably freshened up and an idea struck.

"Wellington's constitution is much improved by the exercise and fresh air," I told her. "We occasionally meet other dogs en route and he enjoys some canine socialising."

"Excellent, I am delighted," replied Mrs Makepeace gazing out of the window in an abstracted manner.

"I cannot help but think that a similar activity would be beneficial to you, madam." I refrained from adding that the action of lifting a glass to her lips could not be counted as exercise. Mrs Makepeace remained staring out of the window. "I know I should make an effort, my dear," she said, wistfully, "but I fear I have lost the will."

"Nonsense, madam," I replied briskly, "You will feel much happier and more alive if you go into society again. Just like poor little Wellington," I added for good measure. Indeed the porcine pug was attempting to climb on to a couch at that very moment, something he would not have contemplated before his exercises began.

"The society of Bath is seldom worth an effort," she continued. "Even the theatre here can be tedious. I believe they are giving another of Mr Loder's dreary subscription concerts this week."

"Signor Randaccio is acquainted with Mrs Sarah Siddons, the celebrated actress. She lives in retirement in the Paragon. Perhaps we could call on her?" I suggested hopefully. My employer shook her head sadly. "That would not be proper, my dear. Actresses, even if famous and in retirement, are not accepted in polite society." I recollected that the Prince Regent and the Count had no qualms in that direction.

I could hear the devil whispering in my ear. I would not be buried alive any longer. I would not continue playing tedious games of whist or accompanying a dog for walks. I launched into a vivid description of my visit to Drury Lane and the delights of the *Beggar's Opera*. Naturally, I omitted all reference to Jerry and Mr Getheridge and the outcome of that evening.

This was the first of my storytelling episodes in which I endeavoured to entice my employer back into the world. I fancied myself as Scheherazade in *One*

Thousand and One Nights, telling stories to save my life. For if I could not escape from this house I might as well be dead. I enlisted Vincente's help and he agreed to call frequently to regale us with his stories of musical and theatrical life on the continent.

Little by little I drew Mrs Makepeace out of the house, leading her across the downs recounting Gothic tales and dragging Wellington in the rear. I had read so many of these stories that I was able to embroider my own versions. Sometimes I would recount my adventures in London and elsewhere, carefully adding and subtracting incidents where necessary, and sometimes Vincente would accompany us both at my request.

I talked, walked and read aloud until I was hoarse and weary. My employer continued to ply me with far more alcohol than decency dictated.

I succeeded better than I knew. Within another month I had convinced her to leave Bath. One morning as we drank our chocolate Mrs Makepeace declared that she never did anything half-heartedly.

"If I am to go from complete seclusion to giddy gadabout, let us go the whole hog and take a tour to the continent, my dear!" I stared at her in amazement. The walls of the morning room began to close in upon me and I felt a little faint. "The continent, madam . . . did you say the continent?"

"Yes, yes of course. We shall see Paris and Rome . . . and Venice. I have always had a longing to see the Water City." Venice, the present home of my hero Lord Byron! Was it possible that our paths might cross finally?

For many days we discussed travelling clothes, itineraries, the effects of travel upon Mrs Makepeace's digestion and the welfare of the dog. Vincente called frequently to advise us on all matters Italian. She herself declared that she was *au fait* with every detail of Parisian life. I returned to my French studies with renewed vigour.

My employer was a most amiable woman and we had become quite close in a short space of time. I regarded her as a more sensible version of my own mother. My spirits began to rise a little. I would finally get to Paris, but before that we would be in London where I could attempt once again to contact my friends and discover the whereabouts of the Count. No doubt he had already departed for Paris. I had a great deal to write in my journal which suddenly lost its melancholic note and became full of the joys of life.

In preparation for our great adventure to the continent I decided to shed some excess weight. I was not in any way portly, dear reader, but I coveted a more sylph-like frame. For one week I subsisted entirely on soda water and Dr Oliver's biscuits, varied with a little Cheddar cheese. This had the desired effect and I would be able to try on my new wardrobe with some satisfaction. I had heard that Lord Byron followed a similar regime to preserve his own slender figure.

We journeyed to London in Mrs Makepeace's carriage with everything necessary for her comfort which included half the household contents and several servants — all of whom would accompany us across

Europe. Vincente had waved us off assuring us that we would be fascinated by continental life.

"You will love my beautiful Italy," he promised us. I vowed to write to him regularly while we were away. I had grown very fond of him and I hoped to meet him again in more favourable circumstances. By that, dear reader, I meant a change from my lowly position as a companion.

In London we lodged at a hotel for a few days while fittings were arranged for suitable gowns. My employer was most generous in these matters. Putting aside the sober outfits I had brought from Pemberley I acquired more colourful pelisses and paler evening gowns which were the high kick of fashion. My bonnets were somewhat more outrageous than before. I was embarked on a new life and I was confident that I would not remain a companion for very much longer.

Adelaide complained about the dangers of foreign food and perilous sea crossings. She could not appreciate that we were about to enter the acme of culture and fashion.

"But they're all Frenchies, madam!" she wailed. "We was at war with them a year or so ago."

"And now they are conquered and perfectly agreeable. You should be grateful I am taking you along," I scolded. "Would you rather remain in dismal Derbyshire or boring Bath?" Adelaide's eyes filled with tears. I had forgotten her footman. Never mind; she will find plenty more in France. I bequeathed two of my old Pemberley gowns to her as a consolation. She will do very well with them.

Before we left for Dover I made a last attempt to find my friends. I dragged an unwilling Adelaide from the hotel just before dawn, planning to be back before we were missed by Mrs Makepeace. We travelled by cab to Portman Square only to find the house empty and desolate. A bailiff's notice fluttered disconsolately around the porch indicating that my friends had made a hurried departure.

I peered through the window into the forlorn, dust-sheeted salon. Why had my friends not waited out the six months offered to them? Their financial affairs must have taken a turn for the worse. What I would have given at that moment to hear Miles calling for porter or Selena's voice upbraiding us for our shortcomings. How long had it been since I had played cards seriously or filled my purse with hard won gold? Even the splendours of Paris faded into the background momentarily.

I sat despondently on the cold stone steps and shed a few tears. Adelaide advised me that I was making a show of myself for the neighbours, as if any would be abroad at that hour. Morning had broken with ominous vermilion waves in the sky and grey cumuli scudding in from the west. The first trades people were entering the square calling their wares, milk panniers were clattering and the coalman with sacks on his back was shouting the need for small coals.

Life was returning, but the whereabouts of Selena and Miles remained a mystery. Had they searched for me at all — and where was the Count? He must have been established in Paris for many weeks. I would have

254

to locate the Austro-Hungarian embassy as soon as I reached the city. I dried my eyes and collected myself. With a loud sniff I gathered my cloak about me and returned to the cab.

"Never mind," I announced to the world. "I am bound for Paris and a new life."

CHAPTER
TWENTY-TWO

Paris, Summer 1817

My employer, who loved her creature comforts, had arranged through her legal advisor to hire a private yacht for the channel crossing. We were not too discomposed but Wellington was violently sick for most of the journey and Mrs Makepeace required constant reassurance that we were not about to sink. Adelaide was prostrate for the entire time and in order to avoid being worn out with demands I too pleaded *mal de mer* and retired to my berth for the rest of the eighteen hour journey.

It was not possible to disembark from our yacht at Calais pier. All ships must anchor offshore and the passengers transfer to small boats in order to reach the shore. Even then, the boat could not come right up to the shore and we suffered the indignity of being unceremoniously piggy-backed to the pier on the backs of insalubrious Frenchmen of the seafaring class, who rolled their eyes and muttered French oaths as they transported us. The men carrying portly Mrs Makepeace, in particular, did a great deal of oath muttering.

Adelaide, suddenly recovered from her sea sickness, found the whole episode hilarious. While I hung on grimly to my porter, the giddy creature shrieked with laughter and urged on her bearer in distinctly salacious terms, clasping him around the neck so tightly that the fellow could scarcely breathe.

Once we had arrived on dry land we were soon able to embark on the travelling coach that my employer had purchased from a member of the aristocracy who was returning home. This large, lumbering equipage was fitted with every conceivable device for comfortable travel but the appalling French roads made any progress slow and disagreeable. Nevertheless, Mrs Makepeace was so pleased to be on terra firma that she declared she could easily become addicted to genteel vagabondising.

Our journey overland to Paris was otherwise uneventful. I was consumed with excitement at the thought of seeing *la belle Paris* at last, but we arrived at night and I saw nothing. We retired to bed in the Hotel Meurice and I slept soundly.

As soon as I woke I rushed to the window and drew back the draperies. The rue de l'Echiquier lay before me, full of elegant mansions, many of them occupied by the nobility. When I joined Mrs Makepeace she was enjoying chocolate and croissants and accosting the staff in shrill, heavily accented French. I could not wait to be out and about in the city but my employer announced that we should first pay our respects at the British Embassy on the Faubourg St Honoré where we might be presented to the rat catcher himself — I mean the Duke of Wellington.

I wondered if the duke's former mistress, Harriette Wilson, was in residence on the rue de la Paix. Such a woman of the world might be acquainted with the Count or know something of his whereabouts. All I needed was some time away from Mrs Makepeace. Wild thoughts rushed through my mind. Would she give me the use of her carriage so that I could make my enquiries? Would an excess of French brandy render her sufficiently somnolent for a few hours so that I would not be missed?

As we passed No. 48 rue de L'Echiqier my employer told me that it had once been a pavilion where dances were held. "All gone," she sighed, "all gone."

Although the duke was not at home during our visit we were entertained splendidly by one of his aides, Captain Marshfield, who poured out a veritable treasure trove of gossip and information about Parisian life. Mrs Makepeace nodded amiably and addressed herself to the Burgundy while I listened all agog.

"You will have noticed dear ladies that the streets of this city are very narrow and dark, except for the grand boulevards. They are even worse than London and equally dangerous. Do not venture out alone and on foot at any time." I nodded eagerly waiting for something more pertinent, such as a hint about fashionable society and where to find it. The captain continued in his own way.

"The city is still full of occupying troops from various countries. They all hate each other, everyone hates the Prussians and the French hate us all. They insult us on the streets and constantly challenge us to duels. Napoleonic riff-raff! Duelling is the principal mode of exercise in this city." I was concerned to hear this. Duelling inevitably led to fatalities, which would shrink the numbers of eligible men.

"Gambling," continued the captain, "is an obsession with both sexes here. At the Salon des Étrangers in the Palais Royal vast fortunes are wagered and lost." I perked up at this point, as he added that rouge et noir and roulette were the games of choice. Paris was definitely to be my home from home.

"I have heard that the Palais Royal is the centre of fashionable life here," I remarked.

"All the great ladies and the not-so-great take their mocha and ices at the café Tortoni. The opera is also madly fashionable. Gambling, dancing and the pursuit of women — these are the universal preoccupations."

Mrs Makepeace appeared to be quite comfortable if not comatose at this point, so I agreed to accompany the captain on a tour of the beautiful house while he continued to advise me on matters Parisian.

"The minuet, gavroche and monaco are the popular dances. You must obtain an invitation from the Princess Beauvau. She gives elegant dances in her hotel on the Faubourg St Germain."

As we drove back to the hotel I gaily informed my employer of this social gossip but she remained unimpressed saying that things were altogether finer in the old days.

"Paris has sadly deteriorated," she sniffed, then to my horror she muttered something about not staying long. "I think it would be far more enjoyable in Venice." She continued in this vein for some time — everything was better in the old days and the world was going to the dogs.

I almost choked with impotent rage. All my efforts in prising the old lady off her Bath sofa in order to reach the city of my dreams — wasted! Still trying to relive her youth, she naturally found that things were not the same. As a mere employee I was powerless to do anything but agree. How I silently cursed my brother-in-law for putting me in this position. If my curses find their mark his fine teeth and hair will drop out overnight.

Mrs Makepeace detected that I was much cast down by her remarks and had the grace to apologise.

"Forgive me, my dear, I am simply a catastrophising grumbletonian." I was not sure of her meaning but my spirits rose a little when she commanded the coachman to drive us about the city from the Bois de Boulogne to the Tuileries Gardens and along the boulevards. However, the views were spoiled for me by the knowledge that we would be leaving so soon. On arrival at the hotel I was obliged to read aloud passages from *La Nouvelle Heloise* while I choked back tears of mortification.

My disappointment was scarcely alleviated when Adelaide reported that fine jewellery could be obtained far more cheaply in Paris than in London. Now I would never have the opportunity to find out for myself.

260

Adelaide did not believe that my employer was serious about departing for Italy.

"The lady hates travelling too much for that," she declared.

"You are wrong, her mind is made up."

"My eye in a bandbox!" she retorted. I was not always sure of her meaning.

CHAPTER
TWENTY-THREE

I remained aghast at Mrs Makepeace's announcement: truly she was a veritable flippetygibbet, a weathercock in petticoats. I was occasionally able to take advantage of our circumstances by using the carriage when my employer was resting. Accompanied by Adelaide and occasionally escorted by Captain Marshfield, who made himself very agreeable to our household, we glimpsed more of Paris.

The city was full of the English as well as crowds of foreign soldiery. In the Palais Royal the captain eyed his assembled countrymen. "John Bull gadding about," he said sardonically. "I wish they would all go home or depart for Florence, that other home from home for our people."

It was noticeable that the prostitutes in the Palais were doing great business and many of them sported jewellery of enormous value bequeathed by their patrons. As these ladies occupied rooms conveniently sited next to the gaming salons, the attractions were obvious.

There could never be enough time to enjoy this great city. The captain agreed to escort me to the casinos, saying that he was amused by my daring behaviour. I had occasion for some good fortune at the roulette table — followed by an even greater streak of bad luck on another — but I saw no sign of dear Count Ferenc. I hoped to do so before we left the city. If only Selena and Miles could have joined me. How they would have loved everything.

On several occasions I went with the captain to some places in the Palais Royal known as restaurants. These institutions were unknown in England and scarcely existed outside Paris. Members of the public paid to eat a meal together in one room which was prepared and served by strangers. In one of the most popular of these places — patronised by Wellington and his officers — we partook of soup and *bifteck aux pommes frites*. On another occasion I ate for the first time *pieds de mouton gras double sur le gril*. I could not imagine eating pig's trotters in England but in the French style they were delicious. Indeed, everything seemed improved in the French language.

My employer refused to eat in public but she delighted in ordering meals to be delivered to her rooms in a heated box. A *garçon* would appear with soup, a main course and a pudding. He would lay the table and serve the food — and all for a few francs. A bottle of wine was added for another franc or two. Restaurants were not respectable places, she declared, but she did not object when I visited them.

I loved the Palais Royal above all. It was the only place in Paris that was well-lighted. I dared not walk alone in the dark and dangerous side streets and I could only walk in the Palais Royal when Captain

Marshfield agreed to escort me. This was so tiresome, I would have given anything to be with the dear Count — or Miles and Selena. Nevertheless, all was dazzle and gaiety in that wondrous place. Everyone paraded in their finest clothes and jewels — great ladies, actresses, officers and ladies of the night together.

The jewellers' shops, cafés and casinos shone with light and warmth. Drinking and gaming were all around us. The captain complimented me on the Prince Regent's necklace which I wore with my best gown when we visited the place. I had an uncomfortable idea that he knew or guessed how I had acquired it.

Seven p.m. was the optimum hour to be in the Palais Royal. The captain pointed out the King of Prussia, and any number of dukes and princes among the strollers at that hour. They mingled casually with ordinary folk of all nations. If only my Count had been among them. Instead, I ogled Count Hunyady, excessively handsome and a notorious gambler, always dressed in the high kick of fashion. He was the talk of the town.

"He will end badly," the captain remarked. "Gamblers always do."

As we strolled among this sparkling throng I passed several very tall ladies endowed like Greek goddesses, their height enhanced with ostrich plumes and lofty headgear. I have always been somewhat petite and I suddenly felt overshadowed, inadequate and quite unattractive, although I am not usually lacking in self-confidence.

I tried to walk taller and I reminded myself that I had danced with the Prince of Orange and shared the

Regent's bed, although that particular prince was not known for his discrimination.

"You are looking pensive, Mrs Wickham," my companion remarked. "Time for a little wine and refreshment, I think."

"And then let us try our luck again at rouge et noir," I insisted.

My excursions into this heaven were all too rare. It was all very well for Mrs Makepeace. She knew Paris intimately, as she never tired of reminding everyone. She scorned the new king, ineffectual little Louis XVIII, remembering the glories of Versailles in the past. Neither was she impressed by the number of uniformed officers present, having lost all taste for anything other than ices and Napoleon brandy.

"In my day," she declared, "one needed more than a few pairs of kid gloves and a foppish manner to enter the highest Parisian society. The city is full of mountebanks and officers without a penny to their names." It appeared that I would not wear my new white gauze gown with its pink satin underskirt on this occasion, after all.

In fact, I had the opportunity to attend one *soirée* in the house of one of the nobility. I recall the white and gold panelled rooms and the creaking wooden floors. Once again accompanied by Captain Marshfield, wearing my white gauze and a soupcon of rouge, I was introduced to an elderly Duke who passed me on to a younger partner. We essayed a waltz and I was amused to see that the Parisian fashion was to dance on the balls of the feet while keeping one arm aloft. This made the dance so difficult that I was in danger of falling over many times. I was also disconcerted when my partner executed a pirouette or two; not a sight that would be seen in London. My journal, faithfully kept, grew more cosmopolitan by the day.

When we returned to the hotel my employer said, "There, my dear, you have had your taste of Paris." Fortunately, the captain came to my assistance by warning her of the excessive cost of travelling through France and Italy. "Around eight guineas per day, I believe." He enlarged upon the filthy inns, the appalling roads and the lack of decent food. "Travellers of my acquaintance have been forced to subsist on tea." Mrs Makepeace, who seldom drank anything but alcohol, was not greatly disturbed by this last remark, but the captain's words cast some doubts in her mind and we continued our stay while she thought the matter over. She went as far as employing a Parisian laundry woman and instructing the staff to unpack her mountains of luggage.

When the time finally came to leave I gave vent to some sighs and tears as we repacked the household goods and chattels and set off on a journey of five weeks or more through the entire length of France and over the Alps into Italy. Eventually we would reach the Brenta canal, the traditional gateway to Venice.

As we trundled out of Paris I took comfort in the letter hidden in my reticule. I received it only yesterday from an Austrian acquaintance made at the gaming tables and it informed me that the Count had been recalled to Vienna. Was Vienna anywhere near Venice? I wondered. If only I had listened more attentively when papa taught us the use of the globes. I enquired of my employer who waved a hand vaguely in the direction of Calais and said it was "quite near." This and the presence of Lord Byron in Venice offered me a few crumbs of comfort.

I will not trouble you, dear reader, with a description of our travels save to say that they were the stuff of nightmare. Captain Marshfield, on orders from the embassy, kindly escorted us to the Swiss border with two outriders. France remained an extremely danger-ous country for travellers with remnants of Napoleon's defeated army marauding everywhere. Indeed, the captain had been so solicitous that I began to wonder if he was attracted to me. Surely he was not interested in my employer? She remained largely oblivious to the discomforts, being pickled in brandy most of the time.

When we reached the Alps we found the Swiss to be a dull and surly people surprisingly unwilling to help us across their mountains despite the good living they made from this enterprise. Captain Marshfield told me they lived mainly on cheese and chocolate which must affect their disposition. The awful and terrifying ordeal of crossing the Alps resulted in the loss of many household items and of the coach itself which literally disintegrated like matchwood.

I cannot imagine how the ancient general Hannibal conveyed elephants across these mountains. I remember papa telling us the story. Perhaps the Swiss were more obliging in those days. As soon as we were able to procure another vehicle we travelled on to the Brenta canal where we transferred to a horse drawn barge which was surprisingly comfortable and luxurious. The local people call them burchiellos.

We drifted along the canal past glorious Palladian villas belonging to Venetian nobles. It was most soothing after our ordeals. Finally, the magical city appeared through a light haze and, as we made our way through the basin of St Mark's, the sky was pale pink tinged with gold and the spires and domes pierced the sky as in a fairytale.

CHAPTER
TWENTY-FOUR

Venice, Winter 1817

The Hotel Europa on the Grand Canal was our designated abode. Mrs Makepeace was in ecstasies with the place and even Adelaide thought this city worthy of note although she has complained of foreigners and their ways right across Europe.

The morning after our arrival I was in the lobby of the hotel gazing out across the water, lost in thought, when the proprietor, Signore Grazzielli, approached me in an overly familiar manner. Speaking in excellent English he pointed out some of the magnificent buildings across the canal, San Giorgio Maggiore with its tall tower and the church they call Zitelle, which means "the spinsters".

"There was a convent there which took in destitute females." He showed me the colourful facade of the Palazzo Dario and mentioned its sinister reputation, adding in a more conspiratorial fashion, "Welcome to Gehenna by the sea, signora!" He was leering at me in an unsettling continental manner. "This city is given over entirely to sinfulness and pleasure, every vice is indulged here."

"Really?" I replied, "and you have such beautiful surroundings for it." The man eyed me warmly. "You and your mistress will be very satisfied in Venice. The English especially appreciate what we have to offer." I disliked his inference.

"Are you by any chance referring to Lord Byron?" The man leered again,

"Indeed, signora, the English milord is famous here. He appreciates our women, our culture, our indulgences." He moved away as Mrs Makepeace appeared demanding to know whether any mail had arrived from England.

When my employer had finished fussing and fuming the proprietor advised us to take chocolate or an aperitif at Florian's in the Piazza San Marco. He procured a gondolier for our exclusive use while we were in the city, whistling up a gondola rowed by a burly and quite handsome fellow called Tito Salieri who sang constantly and quite charmingly in the Venetian manner.

He did not seem too happy to have Wellington in his vessel. I fancy he muttered something uncomplimentary about the English as we set off across the Grand Canal. I had already observed that the city must be a sad shadow of its former self. I knew it was once a great and splendid republic but it has been ruled by the Austrians for several years and their soldiers were very noticeable in the throng around the Piazza San Marco. There was no longer a doge, their maritime empire had vanished, the canals were weed-choked, and the exquisite buildings were crumbling and scarred with leprous patches of plaster. But the lagoon glittered in

270

the sun and the lambent quality of the light continued to delight artists and lovers.

When we arrived in the Piazza San Marco we were overwhelmed by the huge number of people of all kinds and nationalities who were thronging the place. The piazza was a vast square. Napoleon called it the drawing room of Europe because you may in due course meet everyone you know.

As we sat in Florian's sipping prosecco, a delightful sparkling wine, I was surprised to see Captain Marshfield entering the café. He had left us before we crossed the Alps to return to Paris, as I thought. He acknowledged us nonchalantly and asked permission to join us. Mrs Makepeace scarcely seemed to remember him.

"This is Captain Marshfield from the embassy in Paris," I reminded her. I looked keenly at him but he affected not to notice.

"What a coincidence that we all arrived in Venice at the same time. You made no mention of coming to Italy when we parted in France, captain."

"Indeed, madam, I was unexpectedly given a mission to Venice which I hope to execute in the next few days. I shall then be free to enjoy a short holiday in this glorious city. I am sure our paths will cross; of course if I can be of any assistance . . ."

"Charming! Charming!" Mrs Makepeace interrupted. "How delightful to see you dear boy. Where are you staying?"

"At the consul's house on the Grand Canal."

"We are at the Europa," I remarked, "although I am sure you already know that." He refused to meet my eyes which confirmed my suspicions. The man was following us — but why? Either my employer had committed grand larceny of which I was unaware, or the man was in thrall to my attractions. I was flattered of course, but not greatly complimented. The captain was nondescript in every way. He had one of those instantly forgettable faces, was of average height and bearing, and appeared to have no fortune worth noting. I have had my fill of penniless officers, even if they had the ear of Wellington himself. I fear he will be tiresome if he insists on escorting us to social events.

As if he had read my thoughts the captain said, "Most of the nobility in this city are virtual paupers. They squander their money in casinos and at theatres and endless balls. Their poverty does not seem to be a hindrance to their enjoyment."

"Why not? We are a long time in the grave, sir."

"Indeed," my employer added with feeling. "I am well-acquainted with the truth of that, for am I not one of the living dead?" We looked at her in horror. "I did not mean literally, my dears, only that I have been a recluse for so long." I smiled and patted her hand.

"Do not fret, madam, now you are in Venice, the carnival of Europe."

The captain asked if we would be staying for the carnival. This event began on the day after Christmas in Venice, and, as it was still early November I doubted that Mrs Makepeace would stay the course. She surprised me by declaring her intention of remaining.

272

The captain turned to me, bent on furthering my education.

"Did you know, Mrs Wickham, that this city was built on stilts? Huge wooden piles were sunk into the lagoon and this wondrous place — this city of decadence — was erected on top of them." He sipped his wine thoughtfully, watching the *melee* around us. Gehenna by the sea, Signore Grazzielli had called it. So it was decadence on stilts — an alarming and provoking image. The captain's eye was on me again and I strove to change the subject,

"They say Lord Byron often comes to Florian's. I hope to have a sight of him."

Marshfield snorted and waved a hand at the crowds thronging the piazza, Greeks, Turks, Arabs, Europeans and Austrian officers in the fanciest of uniforms. Orientals were puffing on pipes called shiskas and a goodly number of Venice's thousands of whores were parading their wares. Hawkers, street people and musicians milled around. It was a veritable maelstrom of humanity. "Would you recognise an English aristocrat in this crowd — or anyone else for that matter?"

Nevertheless I felt I should know the poet's noble features anywhere.

The captain eventually took his leave assuring us that he would make enquiries about renting an apartment on our behalf. No-one of consequence stayed in a hotel for any length of time, he assured us. I thought the man was impertinent. We had not asked for his assistance and the Europa was perfectly comfortable.

We remained to be ogled and clucked over by passers by and men in the café. A Turkish gentleman approached us and courteously asked if I would consent to become his fifty-fourth concubine. The man was obviously a person of note but I was not impressed. He claimed to have been overcome by my fair English looks. There were noticeably few of our countrymen and women in evidence. Mrs Makepeace rapped him with her reticule and told him to be off. He departed evidently overcome with grief. Incarceration in a seraglio was not part of my plans although it would certainly have solved some of my problems.

I came back to earth when my employer decided to return to the hotel. Adelaide was instructed to accompany me to the Venice *poste restante* to retrieve the mail. Pulling my cloak around me I took possession of the passports and weaved my way through the crowds followed by Adelaide. Once again I remarked how few English people were in evidence. Florence and Rome were their favoured cities and they seldom stayed more than a day or two in Venice, but my employer was an incurable romantic and the water city bolstered her fantasies.

As we returned to the hotel through tiny side streets bordering sluggish green canals the marine melancholy of the place became more apparent, adding to my own barely suppressed sorrows. I handed a small parcel to Mrs Makepeace containing a copy of Lady Caroline Lamb's scandalous novel *Glenarvon* which she received with joy. I declared firmly that I would not read a book that slandered Lord Byron. In the excitement my employer almost forgot to show me the invitations she had received. I was to accompany her to a conversazione at Countess d'Albrizzi's palace and to a luncheon with the British consul.

During the following weeks Mrs Makepeace seemed to shed ten years while I felt myself ageing imperceptibly although I was barely twenty-one. The dampness made my bones ache and I found the food disagreeable. There was too much of rice and liver for my taste, although the fish was plentiful and fresh.

Because we were unable to speak the language our opportunities for conversation were limited. Wherever we went Captain Marshfield would materialise in the vicinity. Even when Tito rowed us out into the lagoon, the captain would endeavour to draw alongside in his own gondola. He offered to escort us to the theatres for which Venice was famous and Mrs Makepeace was delighted with his attentions. The captain spoke French and Italian fluently. He was a diplomat, after all.

He negotiated the rental of an elegant apartment in a palazzo on the Zattere, thus ensuring a long stay on our part. Mrs Makepeace was very satisfied with the move. The apartment, like so many in the city, was full of frescoes and faded grandeur and remarkably short of furniture. She did not consider that the man had become our virtual shadow. I, however, spent many hours in my room pondering the matter. I was convinced that I was the focus of his interest — although I could not fathom why.

"Perhaps he's sweet on you, madam," Adelaide said, but I could not agree. The man did not behave like a lover. I found I was unable to sleep at night. Often in the small hours I would gaze out of my window at the stupendous view, watching a cold moon rising from the sea and silvering the lagoon. I hated having to linger in this damp place redolent of lost hopes and dreams.

Was Marshfield following a long trail from the Prince Regent and Von Mecks, even from poor Mr Getheridge? My highwayman had said that the Von Mecks affair was not yet concluded. I shed a few tears. Everything in my life had turned to ashes. I had lost love, prospects and friends. I was an exile from my country and, worst of all, I was a lowly companion to a mad old woman who was reliving her youth while I festered on the sidelines. And it was all my own fault. I had encouraged her in this madness.

The one consolation I might have derived — a sight of Lord Byron — had eluded me. Wherever we went he had been there, often only minutes before, but he remained elusive, invisible. Sighing, I returned to my bed where my dreams were haunted by ghostly gondolas on misty canals on which I floated alone, searching for something that was always out of reach.

"You look fairly like an antique remnant, madam," was Adelaide's verdict the next morning.

CHAPTER
TWENTY-FIVE

The consul was a dullish but kindly man called Hoppner. My employer and I attended a luncheon party at his beautiful house on the Grand Canal. Captain Marshfield, inevitably, was in attendance waving tickets for the Benedetto theatre under our noses and insisting on accompanying us there. The consul remarked that he had entertained Lord Byron only a few days past. The events of my daily life had become set in stone; the captain would always be at my heels and Byron will have just left wherever I arrived.

The solution lay in acquiring a cloak and mask such as the Venetians wore during Carnival. The alleyways and humpbacked bridges of the city were thronged with these mysterious revellers disguised by the masks of the *commedia del'arte* — hideous long-nosed men, white faced clowns, quaint feline creatures and even a death's head. Surely this last would discourage the captain's attentions.

I asked Signore Grazzielli at the Hotel Europa to obtain a costume for me and sometimes I slipped away into the crowds while Mrs Makepeace enjoyed a siesta. I was determined to throw off these bouts of melancholia brought on by my position in society — or

277

lack of it. I confided to my journal my failure to meet up with the Count, Lord Byron or indeed, anyone other than Captain Marshfield.

During one of my own masked wanderings I came upon Adelaide who had been disappearing into the back streets of the Castello district during her off duty hours. I was curious about her activities and as we wandered around she confessed everything. She had struck up a relationship with a relative of our gondolier, Tito Salieri.

"Tito introduced me to his cousin Vittorio who is a baker in the Castello district. We sort of got to know each other better. He was lonely because his wife has taken up with that Lord Byron."

"Byron! Are you sure about that?"

She shrugged. "Everyone in Venice knows about it. The woman is very beautiful and spends most of her time at the Palazzo." I swallowed my indignation and surprise. Why did my hero prefer Italian women to his own womenfolk?

"What does the baker think about this situation?" I asked. Adelaide grinned.

"He don't mind too much. You know how these Venetians are. He just wants a bit of company." Adelaides's only problem was the fearsome temper and jealousy of La Fornarina, the baker's wife. She feared crossing the path of this virago.

"If she found out I was a-dallying with 'er other 'alf I'd be mincemeat, madam," she assured me. "That female 'as a fearsome temper and she always carries a

278

knife." Adelaide rolled her eyes indicating her amazement at the strange ways of foreigners.

"It is the Italian character," I told her.

"They say she is like a wild cat," my maid continued with a nervous giggle.

"The women of Brighton are pussycats beside her."

I left her to return to her baker reflecting that my trusty maidservant had a determination to make the most of every opportunity and to seize the day that was in tune with my own desires. We were very compatible. I feared this relationship of Adelaide's was the closest I would get to Lord Byron.

Despite her fear of the baker's wife Adelaide continued to spend her free afternoons with Vittorio, returning to our apartment with a toothsome collection of Venetian pastries and breads. The consul's wife had told me that Venetians made terrible servants, intent only on robbing their employers.

"This is such a corrupt city," she had said. "Deception is in the very air, even Lord Byron takes care to have English servants. Venetians are good only as lovers!"

Vittorio was certainly good for Adelaide. She positively glowed and bounced as she went about her duties. I was glad that she had recovered from her passion for the footman in England. A distracted, lovelorn retainer would have been of little use to me. Adelaide was my eyes and ears and I needed her in peak condition.

The affair, however, came to a sudden and painful end. I met Adelaide as she tried to board the traghetto, the communal gondola used by the common people to cross the Grand Canal. Several people can be accommodated in a standing position on payment of a few coins. My maid was in an agitated condition and in danger of overturning the vessel. A small riot seemed imminent. Still clad in my carnival costume, I was forced to pluck her from the hostile crowd and deposit her on a seat by the canal. After snivelling for a few minutes she confessed the latest developments in her romantic saga between loud sobs.

"His lordship 'as thrown over that woman, the baker's wife."

"What happened?"

"I suppose 'e got tired of all the temper tantrums. But that's not the worst of it, madam." I sighed, there was always trouble following us like a stray dog sensing leftovers.

"Tell me everything," I urged. More sobs ensued.

"The baker's wife rushed out of the palazzo and threw 'erself in the Grand Canal."

"Is she drowned?"

"No, they fished her out and sent her back to the baker. I managed to slip out of the back door before she saw me, but . . . she knows about me, madam. Someone must 'ave told 'er, and she 'as sworn to kill me."

"Nonsense! You are with me and she would not dare attack you in my presence. You must not go out alone. Always go with Tito, he will protect you."

I wondered if there was now a vacancy at the palazzo but my maid assured me that it had already been filled — by another Italian.

Naturally, all Venice was agog with this latest development, as Captain Marshfield hurried to remind me. A few days later we were walking near the little church called the Miracoli when he turned to me and said,

"Your hero has added another notch to his bedpost. I do not know why he is so successful with women. They say he is no great lover — it is merely his title and his reputation that attracts them."

"And possibly his looks and his poetry," I added. "Quite a formidable collection of advantages, would you not agree?" The captain's upper lip contorted in imitation of the humpbacked bridge on which we were standing. I enjoyed watching his discomfort. When we returned to the apartment I informed him that Mrs Makepeace could not receive him that morning. "She is having a little conflict with the rheumatics. The dampness of this city is a trial to us all." He gave me a speculative look.

"Do you think she will wish to move on soon?" I shrugged. "She sometimes mentions Rome and Florence, but nothing more. I fear she is overcome with Venetian indolence." Marshfield nodded,

"I do not know how these people became a great trading nation. Nowadays they cannot rouse themselves to do anything. First Napoleon had them by the throat and now the Austrians."

I could see he was getting into his stride for a long, political speech. I made an excuse that I needed to collect letters from the *poste restante*. Adelaide would accompany me. The captain looked nonplussed and finally left us.

As we walked along Adelaide cast nervous glances over her shoulder.

"Are you sad about the baker?" I asked. She sighed.

"There's no use in wanting someone you can't 'ave." Perhaps this girl had more sense than her mistress.

"Have you had many romantic entanglements, Adelaide?" I was curious about my maid's past in Cheapside. She looked coy and hesitated for a moment.

"Well, I did 'ave a beau when I lived at 'ome. He was my pa's apprentice and his name was Jack Perry. I called him Jacko or Jackie. We might 'ave tied the knot and lived 'appily ever after, but pa didn't approve. You see, Jacko was a foundling. My parents took 'im in. They thought I could do better for myself."

"What happened?"

"In the end Jacko left and joined the army. I went into service. I couldn't bear to stay at 'ome. I don't go back often."

"And what about the footman?" She gave me a reproachful look.

"There was no future there either, what with us moving about so much. Leastways, I'm a-gettin' to see the world."

We were threading our way through the myriad arcades of the Frezzeria as we spoke. I recollected that I also could not wait to leave my home and I had had much leisure in which to repent my decision. We stopped to admire the famous doll in a shop window, the *Poupée de France* who was always dressed in the

282

latest Paris fashion. Venetian ladies were able to follow the trends by copying *la poupée*'s ensembles.

All kinds of materials were on display, brocaded fabrics with gold thread, striped satins and Pekin silk. We feasted our eyes before returning to the apartment where Mrs Makepeace complained of the lack of visitors. I was obliged to read another chapter of *Glenarvon* to her greatly against my inclinations.

Mrs Makepeace had been invited to a masked ball at one of the palazzos and I accompanied her. Gaming was always a feature of these events and this would be an opportunity to replenish my personal coffers. I could not hope to become an independent woman on the meagre allowance I received from Mr Darcy and the modest one from my employer. I was surprised that my brother-in-law had not reduced the amount now that I was employed. No doubt I owed that to Lizzie's intervention.

Now that carnival was under way there were balls and entertainments every night. In truth this differed little from normal life. It appeared to be carnival every day here. The Venetians coped with their loss of status in the world by throwing one long continuous rout which ceased only during Lent. Indeed, poor Getheridge should have set up his business here where his banking methods would not have been considered unusual.

As we were preparing for the ball a surprising thing happened. When I had dressed in a new silver gauze gown trimmed with red roses I presented myself to my employer who produced a velvet covered box which I had never seen before. I was familiar with her everyday jewellery — unremarkable pieces in heavy, old-fashioned settings — but when she opened the box I was astonished to discover it contained several rows of lustrous, milk white pearls of the finest quality and a necklace of diamond and sapphire links with matching earrings. I exclaimed over these beauties while my employer nodded approvingly.

"These are my finest pieces. I seldom have occasion to wear them now. The pearls were my mother's and the sapphires were a gift from my husband."

Along with the bountiful wine cellar, of course. Then Mrs Makepeace produced an exquisite letter M in diamonds attached to a black velvet ribbon. "It was given to me by the queen — M for Marie Antoinette. She singled me out, as you know. I have always treasured it." She wiped away a tear and replaced it in the box. "Tonight I shall wear the sapphires. It is fitting that I should wear them once more before I die."

Adelaide and I exchanged glances. Mrs Makepeace was given to making these mordant comments of late although her health and spirits had improved greatly since we left England, except for the rheumatics. Her maid dressed her in a gown of grey silk and velvet, added the sapphires and a blonde wig, a cape and a clown mask, and we set off. She had offered to loan me some of the pearls for the night but I had decided to wear the prince's necklace again. It would not cause comment in this city. The Venetians cared nothing for the niceties of English society.

The night air was chilly but full of magic as we glided along the Grand Canal. The windows of the palaces were ablaze with candlelight that gilded the black waters beneath and picked out the bobbing red lanterns in the gondolas of the ladies of pleasure which flickered like dozens of fireflies. Tito joined other gondoliers in song as mandolins played in the distance.

The palazzo was vast and after I had deposited my employer on a seat where she could watch the dancing, I went in search of the gaming tables. When I settled myself at a table I saw Captain Marshfield sitting nearby with a plate of delicacies at his side. By this time I would have been surprised if he had been absent.

After a prolonged game of bassetto, a Venetian version of faro, I had made few gains and I decided to stop before my luck ran out completely. I noticed that the captain had been losing steadily. Evidently his sleuthing skills were superior to his gaming abilities. Nevertheless he carried on regardless with a glittering, manic expression in his eyes that I had seen many times before when people were losing at the tables. Wickham often wore such a look.

Marshfield was offering his possessions as surety — a ring and a gold watch chain. I began to be alarmed for him. Although the man was a confounded nuisance I felt a degree of responsibility for him. After all, he was *my* personal shadow. I walked around the table and stood behind him seizing his wrist as he made to take another card.

"No, captain, I cannot let you ruin yourself in this manner," I declaimed in my most dramatic manner.

"You are not a Venetian, you are a servant of His Majesty's Government." He looked up at me, bewildered, and the manic light left his eyes. For a moment I had a glimpse of the small boy he must once have been. He allowed me to lead him away, helping himself to a champagne cup as a consolation. This concoction, mixed with the rum punch habitually served here at their *soirées* rather than the barley water we were accustomed to in England, can be lethal. Slurring his words slightly, Marshfield produced a pack of cards and challenged me to another game.

"What are the stakes, sir?" I asked, trying to humour him.

"I am the prize, madam." He staggered a little. "If I lose I become your liege lord of life and limb. Do with me what you will!"

"And if I lose?"

"Then I will be your consolation prize!" I surveyed him with alarm. The captain was undergoing a personality change before my eyes.

"A widow in want of a fortune has no need of a penniless officer even if he comes free with a wager."

He bowed, swaying dangerously. "I take your point, madam. I could not have put it more elegantly myself. Nevertheless I am yours if you will have me." He found this statement so amusing that he scattered the cards on the floor at my feet, sniggering uncontrollably.

When I attempted to lead him away to a nearby seat he seized me around the waist breathing rum fumes into my face. "I find myself attracted to you like a moth to a flame, Mrs Wickham. May I call you Lydia? You have a delightful *farouche* quality, fey and fiery at the same time." I pushed him away indignantly. I was not sure what the word *farouche* meant — I have neglected my French studies of late — and I did not trust the captain's interpretation.

"You forget yourself, sir! Is this the reason why you have stalked me across the continent?"

"No, indeed, there is quite another reason for that, but I try to combine business with pleasure — a subsidiary dissipation, as it were." He was growing more familiar by the minute but I felt no amorous darts entering my bosom. As he seized me about the waist a second time he attempted to whisper in my ear but missed his way and nuzzled my neck instead. "Are you a good kisser, Lydia?" he enquired. "Venetian women are very good kissers."

I was saved from this embarrassing situation by Mrs Makepeace who had sent a servant to find me. Evidently she had imbibed too much rum punch and needed to return to the hotel. I tore myself from the captain's clutches just as I might have discovered something important. I found my employer prostrate on a chaise longue.

"I am unwell, Lydia," she moaned, "help me into the gondola." Indeed her face was livid and beads of perspiration covered her forehead. As we tossed gently on the waters she was forced to lean over the side and void the contents of her stomach while I attempted to prevent her from falling overboard. Back at the palazzo I found Adelaide in a fury. The dog Wellington had procured a titbit that violently disagreed with him. Like his mistress he had been very ill and had managed to bite Adelaide when she was forced to attend to him.

My employer remained indisposed for several days, unable to take nourishment. I wondered if she had caught the fever that besets this unhealthy spot. The consul sent a doctor who prescribed purgatives and presented a large bill. Mrs Makepeace refused his advice. It was well known that Italian doctors were the worst in all Europe.

She grew querulous as she recovered demanding that I write to London for supplies of red tooth powder and other necessities of life unobtainable here. I was scarcely able to leave the apartment for several days except to collect mail from England. Among the letters I was overjoyed to find one addressed to me in a familiar hand. It was from Selena. How had she discovered my whereabouts?

I paused in the covered archways of the Frezzeria to tear open the letter, unable to wait until I reached the palazzo. It was dated several weeks earlier.

Dearest Lydia,
News has reached us that you are in Paris and I am therefore sending this, poste restante, to that city. I do not have your present address but doubtless it will reach you in due course.

The letter went on at great length to describe how they were forced to leave Portman Square to escape their creditors. Not even rent free accommodation could prevent financial catastrophe. I wondered if Miles

288

had been buying more etchings. Selena had written to me at Pemberley several times but had received no replies.

I deduced that your family, particularly your disagreeable brother-in-law, must have been withholding them.. It followed that he had discovered your plans to leave with the Count. We were concerned for your welfare, dear Lydia — with visions of incarceration and worse. It was a long time before Miles discovered through his military connections that you had been seen in Paris. Does this mean that you are reunited with the Count?

For some time we have been staying in the country with a cousin of mine — a dull, dreary existence you may be sure. But here is our exciting news. We have decided to move to the continent, "as all paupers do" (Miles). We will leave very soon and we hope to see you again in Paris, dear Lydia. I trust that you are in good health. We are well, if a little chastened by recent events. We will leave our new address, poste restante, in due course.

Your affectionate friend,
Selena Caruthers

CHAPTER
TWENTY-SIX

I positively skipped along the Zattere with a spring in my step, although there was little evidence of springtime around me. Venice in winter was cold, often grey, with a penetrating dampness.

As I burst into the palazzo I found Captain Marshfield waiting patiently in an anteroom where Adelaide was plying him with grappa and coffee. We had not met since the evening at the ball when he made his absurd declaration. I regarded him uneasily. This time he appeared clear-eyed, polished of boot and generally spruce. No mention was made of our previous encounter. He greeted me with the words,

"Catalani is singing tonight, Mrs Wickham. I am determined that you should hear her." He produced the tickets to clinch the matter.

"I cannot leave Mrs Makepeace unattended. She is unwell and I am in her employ, you know."

"Do not worry on that account. I will explain the situation to her."

In vain I protested that Mrs Makepeace was not receiving visitors. Of course, she was delighted to see him and readily gave permission for me to visit the theatre. Indeed, my employer has always been kindness itself and I am greatly indebted to her, but on this occasion I wished for her to be firmer and more ill-natured. I was not greatly enamoured of opera and still less inclined for the captain's company.

"I will accompany you only on condition that you remain sober and make no advances to me," I managed to hiss as he took his leave.

"I'm sure I do not know what you mean, madam." The man's effrontery knew no bounds. "Nobody remains sober for long in Venice," he continued. "It is a floating gin palace, as your poet friend could testify."

"Have you had sight of his lordship lately?" I asked, ever hopeful. "If you could introduce me to him I would be eternally grateful."

The captain's eyes lit up. "How grateful?" He shrugged and turned away when I glared at him. "I cannot think why you have not stumbled across him before now. Where the ladies are concerned he puts it about quite freely."

"You are coarse and soulless, captain!" I shrieked. "Take yourself out of my presence before I lose control." He smiled roguishly and whistled for the gondolier, promising to call for me at eight in the evening.

My employer was much improved in spirits. She enjoyed a good lunch and declared her intention of going out onto the lagoon tomorrow. I was told to inform Tito. I feared the weather was totally unsuitable for a recovering invalid but she insisted.

Angelica Catalani was the greatest soprano of the age. Her voice covered three octaves while her long face and Roman nose gave her the appearance of a friendly antelope. She was singing the role of Susanna in the *Marriage of Figaro* and the Fenice Theatre was agog. Lord Byron was not present, I was told he did not care for opera.

During the intermission I contrived to ask the captain once again why he had followed me across the continent, but he refused to answer. He said only that it would be useful if I could persuade Mrs Makepeace to return to Paris.

"What do you mean by 'useful'?"

"Only that we have need of you there, Mrs Wickham." I was rendered speechless by this statement, but the captain would not elaborate. As I opened my mouth to protest he hushed me saying that Catalani was about to sing another aria.

When he escorted me back to the apartment I took advantage of our intimate situation — seated side by side in the felze, the little cabin on the gondola, to press him for information again.

"I will do nothing for anyone — including king and country — unless you tell me why Von Mecks was murdered." This sudden remark caused the Captain to start in surprise. I said, "The emeralds were recovered, the man had played his part successfully . . . so why was he killed?" Marshfield gave me an enigmatic look.

"Your friend Getheridge could answer that."

"The man is sadly deceased. You must tell me." My companion heaved a sigh.

"It was a bungled business, most unfortunate. We believe that he was mistaken for Getheridge by the hired thugs who were ordered to murder the banker. They went to the apartment owned by Getheridge, found Von Mecks there and killed him, probably before he could say a word." I had deduced all of that for myself but one mystery remained.

"Why was Von Mecks in the apartment?"

"He was waiting to see Getheridge — perhaps with a message from the royal household. He did not know that you were occupying the place — and neither did the hired assassins, fortunately." I shuddered at the remembrance of that event.

"Why was Getheridge targeted — and by whom?"

The Captain laughed. "He was up to his neck in all kinds of fraud and financial devilry. There must have been a number of people waiting to have their revenge. We do not know their names in this instance."

I remained silent for the rest of the journey listening to the splash of the gondolier's pole and the far off sound of bells coming from the lagoon. Everything rested on that terrible trip to Brighton. The events of those few days were now determining my fate. I closed my eyes as I recalled the scene with the Prince Regent, the body of poor Jerry lying in the forest, Mrs Fitzherbert's remarks.

Suddenly, a thought struck me with great force. "How did Von Mecks get into the apartment without a key?"

Marshfield shrugged. "Someone must have let him in. Was your maid there at the time?"

"Yes, but Adelaide would not have let a stranger into the place. Certainly, she would have told me if she had. She is most reliable." He shrugged again.

"Then you should question her, if you are concerned." Of course I was concerned. The murder might not have happened if he had not gained entry.

The evening had passed well enough but I stayed awake in my bed long into the night worrying about the meaning of the captain's words. My first task on waking would be to reply to Selena's letter, before suggesting to my employer that we should return to Paris. My aim was to meet my friends once more — I was less concerned about obliging the captain and his masters. I noted Marshfield's explanation in my journal for future reference. Then I needed to question Adelaide.

Anxiety about Mrs Makepeace's health would be the best approach, I decided. In truth, if we remained until the spring we risked catching the fevers that swept the city regularly. Yes, a concern for her health, and my own, was the answer. The final card I held would be concern for the wretched Wellington. Venice was no place to keep a dog. A servant was forced to spend hours every day transporting the animal to the Lido for exercise — something loathed by Tito, the servant and the dog. I closed my eyes and drifted away.

The following morning started well enough: the weather was milder than of late and Tito appeared promptly with the gondola. Mrs Makepeace was well-wrapped and shielded from the elements in the vessel's small cabin.

After an hour on the lagoon we were re-entering the Grand Canal passing the great white dome of the Salute church when I spied a man swimming across the water about ten yards ahead of our gondola. Lord

Byron had taken a lease on the Palazzo Mocenigo nearby and his swimming exploits were legendary. I leaned further out and saw a dark head bobbing in the water.

"Yes, it is the English milord," Tito assured us. At last! Frantically, I called out to him but he appeared not to hear. In my excitement I leaned very far out over the gondola's side and the next moment I found myself submerged in the freezing, odiferous waters of the canal. I sank and rose and sank and rose, waving my arms in the air and swallowing a great deal of filthy salt water before I managed to scream. I heard answering screams from the gondola and the startled swimmer turned his head in my direction.

As I was hooked on board by Tito's pole I thought I heard his lordship cry out, "Bring the poor woman to my palace, let her stay." Later, Adelaide maintained that his actual words were, "Get that infernal woman out of my way." She has a cruel tongue sometimes.

As I collapsed in a shivering, sodden heap behind the curtains of the little cabin I became aware that the wretched Wellington had disappeared and that Mrs Makepeace was lying very still on her cushions.

"I think the old girl's dead," Adelaide remarked.

I gulped and shivered volcanically. "Where is Wellington?"

She shrugged. I looked at Tito who also shrugged.

"I think 'e fall in the water, signora."

He must have been dislodged when I fell in — or was he pushed? Adelaide disliked the animal intensely and Tito had been nipped on the ankles more than once.

He could easily have used the pole to keep the dog under water while attention was focused on me. Mrs Makepeace's cries were probably for her pet rather than for her companion. I examined her more closely, dripping water over her velvet hat. She had indeed expired, from shock, no doubt, at losing her canine companion. And once again it was all my fault. I looked around distraught. Astonishingly, Captain Marshfield was nowhere to be seen.

"By the body of Diana!" Tito swore his favourite gondolier's oath. "Now I think we go back 'ome," he added. Where was Lord Byron when one needed him?

CHAPTER
TWENTY-SEVEN

Thus ended my sojourn in Venice, dear reader — in chaos and death. I was left with the responsibility for conveying my late employer's corpse and her belongings back to England, hampered by several hysterical servants, a severe chill caused by my dip in the Grand Canal and a total lack of experience in such matters.

I took to my bed after Adelaide had provided me with a mustard bath, and a message was sent to the British consul forthwith. I was mortified that Lord Byron had not seen fit to enquire after my health when I had almost drowned in front of his eyes. Captain Marshfield was soon on hand, however, reminding me that one's heroes usually had feet of clay. He assured me that the poet always greased his body from top to toe before swimming in the winter and he advised me to do the same. He also added, with a snigger, "I have heard on good authority that your hero is not well-endowed in the pleasure department. He would not have wanted to appear before you in a sodden condition, if you take my meaning." I was not greatly diverted.

In truth, I had reason to be grateful to the captain and to Mr Hoppner, the consul, who came to my rescue, attending to everything and leaving me with little to do except pack, which chore I delegated to the servants. In the circumstances it was decided that Mrs Makepeace should be buried on the cemetery island of San Michele. She had no close relatives and it would have been extremely difficult to arrange transference of her body to England.

It was a mournful procession which set off on a singularly beautiful Venetian morning. The domes of the city's thirty-two churches were aflame in the early morning light and mist curled around the landing stages in an appropriately sinister manner. How my employer would have enjoyed this spectacle. She had loved all things Venetian while I could think only of the slime-coated walls of the side canals with limp washing strung across them, the dark, unlit buildings and the tiny, claustrophobic alleyways that ended in the black waters of an unseen canal. Those who were abroad at this hour were saying their morning prayers at the little shrines adorning the walls, or laying a few pathetic blooms as an offering.

"This is a city of the dead," the captain remarked cheerfully as we followed the black and gold funeral barge in Tito's gondola. "There is nowhere else in Europe that speaks so eloquently of decay, don't you agree, Mrs Wickham?"

I sniffled and wept a few tears thinking his remarks curiously insensitive. As we crossed the lagoon Marshfield explained that the cemetery island had been created a few years before on the orders of Napoleon. The city had run out of places to bury the dead.

"The Venetians would have done nothing about it, naturally," the captain continued. "They would probably have chucked the corpses in the canals."

"Oh, really!" I growled and he had the decency to keep quiet for the rest of the journey.

Many trees had been planted on San Michele and in fifty years' time when they had fully grown the island would look very beautiful, but as yet it appeared a bleak spot. The corner reserved for non-Catholics was even bleaker. Mrs Makepeace was interred while the consul's chaplain said the words of the Anglican burial service, the six servants looked on indifferently and the few Venetians present stood aside to avoid Protestant contamination. The consul had promised to arrange for a headstone and with that we all returned to the palazzo for a welcome lunch.

Before we set off for England I had one last meeting with the captain at Florian's. He ate a hearty dish of polenta smothered with onions and anchovies and washed down with grappa. I toyed with my glass of prosecco and peach juice. The captain would accompany us as far as Paris to ensure our safety. I had told him that I intended to meet my friends there before returning to England.

"You must come to the embassy when we reach Paris," he told me as he speared an anchovy. "Then we will explain the service we would like you to render to your country."

"Does it have anything to do with the death of Von Mecks and the affair of the Cambridge emeralds, by chance?" He raised his eyebrows.

"Of course, what else? You are involved in grave affairs whether you realise it or not." I suddenly felt lightheaded and called for more wine. The tone of his voice indicated that I had no choice in the matter. My late husband had given me little in the way of useful advice but I recalled his favourite saying about keeping one's options open.

I was determined to return to the casino before we left Venice. My previous visit had been taken up with the Captain and I had not been able to replenish my store of money. I was intrigued by the croupiers in their little booths, all dressed in an androgynous way in tight breeches and ridiculous codpieces, eighteenth-century style. Their faces were covered in white paste and their lips were rouged. I knew that some of them were women — or rather, young girls, spreading the cards, rolling dice and fleecing the customers. The stakes were always loaded against the gamblers. Sometimes the croupiers withheld important cards or allowed patrons to take one away.

The Venetians did not care: they were the custodians of the world's greatest plaything, the city of Venice itself. They were utterly familiar with winners and losers, paupers, millionaires and the desperate. As the custodians of this city of pleasure they regard the whole world as ripe for picking.

But I had also served an apprenticeship in these matters, although in less striking costumes and in less exotic surroundings. When it came to fizzing, cogging and sleeving the cards I could hold my own. My teacher, Mr Wickham, had at least done me that service.

I dragged Adelaide along with me promising her a generous tip from my winnings. She looked unconvinced as we set off in the gondola with Tito. I wore black in deference to my late employer, together with Mrs Makepeace's pearls. She had, after all, offered to loan them to me. I carefully placed my personal pack of marked cards in my reticule.

I seized the opportunity to question my maid about the Brighton Affair, as I had named it. She admitted opening the door to Von Mecks and allowing him to come in.

"He was so handsome and so well-dressed, madam! I could not turn him away. I thought he must be one of your admirers," she added, in an attempt to flatter me. When I chided her for this she scowled and remarked that he was much more attractive than "that Sartain fellow". Adelaide knows how to wound me.

When I asked her why she had not admitted all of this at the time she said that she was afraid of losing her place, or even of being arrested. I understood that and, in truth, I could scarcely blame her.

"We will say no more about it," I agreed.

At the casino I offered a coin at one of the booths and the youth fanned out the cards. I gave him a bewitching smile and took one. It was the eight of clubs.

As I refreshed myself with a glass of wine and watched the other players a gentleman in an elaborate military costume gave me a low bow and introduced himself as the Marques de Monte Vittoria. He was from Portugal and his accent and form of English were very strange to me. Only foreigners and visitors were allowed into that casino. The Venetians must go elsewhere for their gambling.

After complimenting me on my appearance he launched into a conversation, apropos nothing, to which I listened in some bewilderment.

"In England you are very fond of the wild life, are you not?"

"There is an appreciation of horses and domestic animals," I replied politely.

"But you are fond of the monkeys, no?" I assured him that I had never seen one in the flesh as they were not native to my country.

"In Portugal I kept a marmoset for a short time," he continued. "It is a kind of monkey which was sent to me from our lands in Brazil. They are quite good to eat, you know." I looked at him in horror. "Do you mean that you ate the monkey, sir?

"Yes," he smiled broadly, "I craunched the marmoset."

"Crunched," I said automatically, "not *craunched*, crunched." As the full meaning of his words dawned on me I stepped back with a yelp of horror. Adelaide obliged me by grabbing my arm and calling loudly, "Come madam, you are wanted urgently." We beat a

302

hasty retreat into another salon where I restored my equilibrium by winning a little money at bassetto.

When we returned to the apartment for the last time as dawn was breaking, the buildings on the Grand Canal appeared to be suspended between earth and sky, the light slanting off them as in a Canaletto painting.

Once again we embarked on the long journey back over the Alps and through France with everyone in the party moaning and complaining incessantly. My second sight of Paris inspired feelings in my breast comparable to those pilgrims reaching the Holy City of Jerusalem for the first time.

As soon as we had recovered from the journey I rushed off to find Selena and Miles who were overjoyed to see me.

"We thought we had lost you, dear thing!" Miles wiped his eye while Selena enveloped me in a carnation-scented embrace. It was agreed that they would accompany me back to England. Miles would remain in London while Selena and I would travel on to Bath to deal with Mrs Makepeace's household matters. I explained that I needed to visit the embassy before leaving. They assumed this was on my former employer's account and asked no questions.

When I presented myself I was ushered into a room where I was greeted by Captain Marshfield and another gentleman who did not vouchsafe his name. The captain had left our party suddenly on the outskirts of Paris and rode ahead of us "on urgent business". I was told that my part in aiding the Prince Regent (the two men exchanged brief glances at this point), had involved me willy-nilly in an affair of the utmost delicacy and secrecy.

"You are referring to the Cambridge emeralds and the death of Von Mecks, I assume? You know I had nothing to do with the death of that man!" I cried, thus giving the game away very neatly. The captain twinkled at me. "We know that, but the man's boots were discovered in your apartment, madam. Can you explain that?"

"How did you —?" He quickly interrupted. "Your apartment was searched in your absence. What did you do with those boots, by the way?"

The other man took up the interrogation at this point. "Your involvement with the affairs of a notorious executed banker was unfortunate, madam."

If only they knew.

"I was not involved with the banker, except inadvertently," I lied.

The two men smiled at each other.

"Perhaps we should ask Mrs Wickham who arranged for her to stay in that apartment."

"My friends and I rendered a great service to the Prince Regent," I squeaked, still terrified. "Surely that counts for something?"

"Indeed," they chorused, "and now you can render another. You see, dear lady, the emeralds were in the possession of Princess Caroline and she is estranged from her husband, as I am sure you are aware." As if all England was not aware of that situation.

"The princess's activities on the continent have caused great dismay and embarrassment to His Royal Highness." I could not imagine anything embarrassing our portly prince but I held my tongue. "I understand that you plan to return to the continent soon, Mrs Wickham. There is a service you can perform for the crown. It is connected with Count Ferenc Esterhazy. You are acquainted with him, are you not?" Captain Marshfield tried to hide a smirk behind his hand as he observed my startled expression.

"What . . . what has the Count to do with this?"

"He is a diplomat, a servant of the Hapsburgs, and he has had several meetings with Princess Caroline. We fear she will be used by the Austrians to inflict further indignities on the British Crown." This was ridiculous: the crown was already in disrepute owing to the antics of the Regent himself. The people sympathised with Princess Caroline. Many politicians sided with her plight for their own ends.

The second man peered at me through owlish spectacles as if trying to determine my level of determination and cunning. "When you are reunited with the Count you will be well placed to obtain certain information which you must pass on to us. You are a true patriot, madam."

I felt this was meant to be a rhetorical question. Papa had once explained the meaning to me. An alarming prospect danced before my eyes. I jumped to my feet.

"Do you want me to spy on the Count for you?" I said in anguished tones. "My feelings for him would not permit it."

305

The nameless man looked impatient. "Come, come madam, think of England. It is your duty. You will of course receive a renumeration for your efforts. The government is not ungrateful in these matters."

Captain Marshfield chimed in again. "Did not your husband fight and die at Waterloo? Can you truly refuse our request with honour?" I wondered if they knew how Mr Wickham had met his end. I had a feeling that between them these two knew more about me than I knew myself. I sat down suddenly and the captain poured me a glass of sherry.

"Our prime minister, Lord Liverpool, wishes to set up a committee to investigate the princess's behaviour. For that we need evidence. You will be uniquely placed to provide that." The unnamed man sat down and crossed his legs in a sententious manner before continuing. "You are not in a position to refuse, madam. The consequences would be, shall we say, unfortunate for you — and possibly for the Count. You would not wish that, I am sure."

Alarming thoughts scurried through my head. What would happen if I failed in this mission? Would the prince demand the return of my necklace — or my head?

The prospect of a monetary reward was an inducement. Certainly my finances needed a boost now that I was no longer employed. The unknown man spelled out the tasks I would be required to perform.

"The Count is in Vienna but he will return to Paris shortly. We will make arrangements for you to meet him."

306

It was agreed that I needed to spend a few weeks in England attending to my late employer's affairs and my own. The fee payable on successful completion of my task would be three hundred and fifty pounds — and expenses. It was a *fait accompli*. I now fully realised that I had not been given the option of refusing. As I left a darker thought struck me.

"What if I am discovered. I would be in danger, would I not? The unnamed man shrugged and bowed. "Your country would be in your debt, madam."

I shrugged. What would have happened if I had refused to come to the embassy? Marshfield would have discovered me. He was indefatigable. I was not greatly diverted by the prospect.

"Think of the money," said Marshfield.

CHAPTER
TWENTY-EIGHT

Pemberley, England

After we arrived in London, Selena and I pressed on almost immediately to Bath. As we travelled I regretted that I could not tell her about my commission from the embassy but I had been sworn to secrecy on pain of I knew not what — incarceration in the Tower, probably.

Mrs Makepeace's legal advisor was waiting to receive us. He instructed me to pay off the servants and to close up the house.

"Before you leave, Mrs Wickham, please be good enough to attend me in my office on George Street. There are some matters I need to discuss with you."

When I presented myself he informed me of the contents of my late employer's will. Her house and the bulk of her fortune had been left to a distant cousin, but to my astonishment I had been left a legacy of three thousand pounds and Mrs Makepeace's fabulous pearls. As I sat dumbstruck at this good fortune, Mr Whittier handed me a small box containing a folded notelet. The note read:

For Lydia in recognition of the companionship and pleasure she gave me in my last days, Letitia Amelia Makepeace.

308

Under the note was Marie Antoinette's brooch.

Tears trickled down my cheeks while Mr Whittier pretended not to notice. I tottered out of the office to meet Selena who was waiting outside. Only then did the full import of his words penetrate my brain. I became so agitated and tarradiddled that my friend was obliged to walk me as far as Duffield's library in Milsom Street where I sat for a while trying to compose myself. It was only after we had continued across the bridge to revive ourselves with tea at Christopher's Hotel that I was able to impart the good news. My friend was duly amazed.

"You are an independent woman at last, Lydia. What will you do now?"

"I intend to return to Paris as soon as possible, but before that I must visit Pemberley. A little revenge would be in order, I think."

There had been no communication from any member of my family in recent months, although I had informed them that I was travelling to the continent with my employer. Obviously, I was still in disgrace.

Selena chuckled as I described my plan of action. "You are a wicked creature, Lydia, but I would do the same in your place." We agreed that she would rejoin Miles in London and I would meet them in Paris in due course. Adelaide and I prepared to make our way north. I had done nothing but travel for weeks and my bones ached. Only the thought of the scores I would settle kept my spirits high. I had sent a letter on ahead indicating my imminent arrival, writing eloquently about my forlorn situation following the loss of my employer. I had made no mention of the startling change in my circumstances as I had no idea of it at the time.

It only remained for me to visit Vincente for the last time. I found him far from well and low in spirits. He was delighted to see me and rallied a little after I told him of my adventures. I bade him a fond farewell, fearing that I should never see him again.

During the interminable journey north I pondered on the extraordinary discussion that had taken place at the embassy. How long ago it seemed, that affair in Brighton. Poor Getheridge and my lost highwayman, not to mention my night with the prince. The coach shook and rumbled as we entered Derbyshire and I became aware of the noxious breath of the hag sitting opposite me. If I did nothing else I would acquire my own carriage with my new found wealth.

When I presented myself on the steps of Pemberley dressed demurely in midnight blue wool crepe, accompanied by Adelaide and numerous items of luggage, I was received with surprise and pleasure by my sister and something akin to incredulity by Mr Darcy.

"We understood you were still travelling abroad," were his welcoming words. He was pretending that my letter had not arrived. I could detect his devious mind at work. *And I am happy to see you too*, I declared silently. Composing my features into something resembling gravitas I explained that the death of Mrs Makepeace had forced my sudden return.

310

My brother-in-law regarded me through narrowed eyes. "Upon my word, madam, you are remarkably accident prone." Even Lizzie was shocked by this heartless statement. She reproached her husband for his unkindness and he turned on his heel and left us.

I was soon deposited in my former room. Fortunately, the ghastly Georgiana had already married and departed with her husband. I settled down to enjoy the comforts of a large country estate for a while. I was anxious to return to the continent but I could spare some time in which to stir the dark waters of family life and to see what queer fish emerged.

After a few days of country walks with Lizzie and little Charles Fitzwilliam and much taking of tea and macaroons, the inevitable happened. I knew that Mr Darcy would not waste time. At dinner one evening he announced that he and Lizzie were expecting a party of guests for a few days. I smiled, murmuring, "How delightful." But enjoyment was not uppermost in my brother-in-law's mind. He came straight to the point.

"One of the guests will be a Mr Seton Arbuthnot who has just taken holy orders. The parish of St Nicholas Chantry in this county is within my gift. I have a mind to appoint him to it."

"How interesting," I replied, glancing at Lizzie who smiled nervously. Darcy leaned forward and fixed me with a penetrating look. "A newly appointed minister is always in need of a wife. You, Lydia, are in need of a husband. I suggest you make yourself agreeable to the gentleman. This could be the solution to your aimless existence."

I had been expecting an announcement of this sort although I confess I anticipated another employer. "So I am destined for the church after all," I smiled brightly at him, while he urged me to take the proposition seriously. He turned to his wife. "The Reverend Arbuthnot would be a highly suitable match, do you not agree, dearest?" Lizzie paused for a second then smiled apologetically at me.

"Surely such an arrangement is preferable to a life as a lady's companion, Lydia dear." She could not know that Mrs Makepeace had been a far more generous and entertaining companion than any clergyman was likely to be. Remembering my plan, I smiled sweetly and said I would be most interested to meet the gentleman. Lizzie looked relieved and Mr Darcy attacked his roast beef with renewed vigour. I stared dreamily at my plate picturing his reaction if he had known of the events of the last few weeks.

When the party arrived on Friday afternoon, the first guests to appear were the Vicomte du Pin de Lisle and his English wife Henrietta. The Vicomte had arrived in England after the French Revolution in a penniless condition. He had managed to marry a local heiress and the gratitude he felt at evading the guillotine and complete penury rendered him virtually speechless. His wife compensated by scarcely drawing breath.

The next guest to arrive, Lady Albany Boulter, was a well-preserved matron of some forty-odd years with a fine quantity of auburn curls, most of them her own. She spent a great deal of time bemoaning the fact that her husband's poor health prevented her from going about in society as much as she wished. Sir James Boulter's indisposition was a mysterious affair possibly linked to his vanishing finances.

"It is, of course, imperative that I introduce my darling daughter Sapphire into Society," she declared, as if their presence at Pemberley required an excuse. Sapphire Boulter was unremarkable in every way, but pleasant and self-effacing in her manner. She was only seventeen and painfully shy. I realised that I felt many years her senior although only a few years separated us.

The Reverend Seton Arbuthnot was a suitably serious clergyman of about thirty with a receding hairline and a forthcoming manner whenever Sapphire was in the offing. I recognised immediately that they were attracted to each other and I pitied them. Sapphire was not destined for a humble man of the cloth even if his uncle was a baronet.

Her mother had other plans. Her sights were set on Mr William de Lawrence, the final guest to arrive, who had lately come to England from the West Indies where he had vast estates. Lizzie whispered to me that the man was reputed to be as rich as Croesus although his grandfather had been a humble cobbler in Chester. The ridiculous affectation of adding a "de" in front of his name fooled no-one. I wondered why my brother-in-law had not suggested I throw myself at de Lawrence instead of a clergyman. Families were supposed to stick together.

Lady Boulter was prepared to overlook the lack of blue blood in return for unlimited wealth. She was a veritable Lady Arabella Drystick with her worn out pedigree and ridiculous airs. I once surprised her in the library furtively scanning the Baronetage. She hurriedly put it away and enquired after my health. Her ladyship was prepared to overlook a number of things. Mr de Lawrence was fully forty-five years old and appeared older due to the ravages of a tropical climate. His conversation was limited to discussions about land and its value and his taste in cravats was deplorable. I could not see poor Sapphire taking kindly to life on a plantation in Barbados with that saturnine slave owner. She was made for the soft light of an English spring day.

Her ladyship was condescension itself when I surprised her in the library. She complimented me on my gown — a pleated lilac silk which I had acquired in Venice.

"Upon my word, Mrs Wickham, you have an excellent wardrobe for a widow in straightened circumstances. You were a lady's companion, were you not?" I ground my teeth silently and nodded pleasantly.

"Indeed, my family is far from wealthy but I am economical by nature. My late employer was most generous and with the help of my maid, who is a veritable treasure, I manage very well." From that moment milady did her utmost to prise Adelaide from my employ. I was vexed at this and at my maid's willingness to change her place, but I knew she disliked foreign travel and I could not in conscience stand in her way. I would have to find another maid.

I decided to give her a glowing testimonial. "Adelaide is a perfect mistress of Mantua making,

314

getting up small linen and hairdressing," I assured her ladyship.

"But will her character bear the strictest investigation?" she enquired.

"As my own," I assured her.

When the time came Adelaide refused to leave me after all saying that the Boulters were no fun and she would stick with me even if it meant, perforce, living in foreign parts. Apart from these distractions my main concern during those few days was how I could convince Mr Darcy that I was doing my best to snare the clergyman, while pursuing my own ends.

Only that morning after breakfast he had whispered to me as we left the room, "Have you had any success as yet?" Arranging my features into an insincere smile I replied, "Oh yes, I need little encouragement to attach myself to anyone." In truth I had already had a few conversations with the Reverend Arbuthnot which had proved most interesting. He tended to say very little but managed to convey a great deal unspoken. I realised that he regretted his choice of vocation, that he was in awe of Darcy and that he worshipped Sapphire Boulter.

As we strolled across the expanse of emerald lawn I acquainted him with my brother-in-law's intentions and described how they could be thwarted for our own ends. He protested weakly about the deceit involved but his protests lacked conviction. I assured him that no blame would attach to him for my indiscretions and when I was off the scene he would be free to pursue Sapphire. I did not tell him that his chances were non-existent, I had not the heart. I feared for the man;

he had little obvious leaning to religion and no skill at all where the machinations of the heart were concerned. I could feel Darcy's eyes watching us approvingly from a window.

"Why did you choose the church?" I asked. "Forgive me, but you appear to be an unlikely clergyman." He gave a mournful sigh.

"I intended to join the navy and serve my country on distant seas. My uncle obtained a commission for me but I resigned after my first voyage."

"Why?"

"I was acutely seasick."

I burst out laughing but the expression on his face was so wretched that I apologised immediately. "What happened after that?"

"I had studied theology at Cambridge so I took holy orders. What else could I do?" His face assumed the expression of a lugubrious spaniel. "It appears that I cannot serve either God or my country satisfactorily, but if I had the help and comfort of Miss Boulter by my side I am sure I could acquit myself well enough."

"Do you plan to elope with Sapphire?" He looked horrified.

"I thought not. You must know that her mother intends her for Mr de Lawrence. He is very wealthy and you are not." My partner in crime looked even more dejected but insisted, "I am sure I can convince Lady Boulter to accept me." The poor man was deranged but his problems were his own. I needed only his co-operation for a few days.

Sapphire was informed of our plans and was only too willing to assist. She met with her admirer in secluded places whenever I could distract Lady Boulter and at other times she suffered de Lawrence's attentions meekly. Seton was in agony whenever his beloved was with "that man".

"That creature is not to be trusted, despite his wealth, ill-gotten no doubt. He looks like a veritable slip-gibbet to me." Having uttered these un-Christian sentiments he returned to the matter in hand.

CHAPTER
TWENTY-NINE

That evening, after Sapphire had entertained us with a spirited rendition of Koczwara's "The Battle of Prague" on the pianoforte and Lizzie and I had managed to sing a few verses of a melody by Handel, I prepared myself for battle. I had already instructed Adelaide to pack our belongings and to be ready to leave when I signalled. Before that, I needed to confront my brother-in-law for the last time — or at least for a long time to come.

Late that evening when most of the guests had retired I tip-toed after my brother-in-law into the orangery and had the satisfaction of seeing him jump in the air when I spoke. His startled look quickly turned to a frown.

"Lydia, is there something you wish to discuss with me?" I nodded,

"Indeed, sir."

"Can it not wait until morning?" When I looked serious and shook my head he beckoned me further into the orangery. In the soft golden light from the candelabra Darcy held aloft, the exotic fronds and ferns appeared to wave slightly in a faint breeze and the vivid, tropical plants bent over us in a manner almost sensuous. The perfume from the orchids made me feel languid, even nauseous, but I collected my wits and addressed Darcy firmly. "I believe, dear brother, that you have been withholding some things from me while I have been away — and indeed before I left."

"Things, what things?" There was a note of unease in his voice.

"To be precise, my letters. Letters from my friends and from Count Esterhazy. I trust you have not destroyed them. That would be disgusting as I am sure you are aware. I will not leave this house until you return them to me." My brother-in-law regained his composure and declared that he had done what was necessary. "You should be grateful to me that you are at last about to make a respectable alliance. I saved you from yourself!"

"And indeed I am saved, but I need to show perfect candour to Mr Arbuthnot in the circumstances. I intend to show him the letters." I felt this was a stroke of genius on my part. I could see that Darcy was nonplussed. He placed the candelabra down on a shelf and retreated into the gathering gloom.

"I am not sure that would be wise."

I pretended surprise. "Do you not advocate honesty between spouses?"

"Of course, of course, but in your case I'm not sure . . ."

"I am sure," I interrupted. "I will not consider embarking on matrimony under any other circumstances."

This threat was sufficient; he led me away to his private study and unlocked a drawer in his desk. He handed me a bundle of unopened letters without a word while wearing his most acidulated expression. I turned on my heel and walked away to my room.

I spent half of that long night reading letters from Selena and Miles and two reproachful missives from the Count wondering why I was maintaining total silence. Finally, he decided that I had changed my mind and that he would depart forthwith for Paris. Included in this small package was an undated love letter from the Count. As I read my heart pained me a good deal. I had never received such a tender note, dear reader. Mr Wickham had not thought it necessary to woo me in such a manner, and Jerry had been cast from the same mould.

> *I had felt such a strong attraction to you when we first met, but since our parting and your cruel silence that attraction has grown into despairing adoration. Now that you have left me my world has become a desert. Wherever you are, my dearest one, send me a sign that you have not forsaken me. This separation is unbearable to me. Come and join me and let us be happy while we may.*

I wept a few bitter tears over my misfortunes in love, but surely all that was about to end. I was a woman of means and I could pursue my own life, once the little matter of the task for my country was accomplished.

Any satisfaction I felt at recovering my property was countered the following morning by the realisation that

Rev. Seton was intent on making a regular humblebroth of our joint scheme. I was summoned to Lady Boulter's room before breakfast where I found her ladyship with her face steeped in mud and vinegar to banish wrinkles and her mouth working hard. Did I realise that Sapphire and Rev. Arbuthnot had formed a liaison?

"Do not deny it, madam, I know that you have aided and abetted them!"

"I have done nothing shameful, Lady Boulter. I am as shocked as you are by these revelations. It seems I am to be blamed for everything that goes awry in this house. Of course I shall have to reconsider my own position with regard to the Rev. Arbuthnot." I left the dowager grinding her teeth as far as that was possible when one's face is covered with hardened mud.

Lady Boulter decided that discretion was the best course. My threat regarding the Reverend must have struck home. Was it not possible that I might also inform Mr de Lawrence of his intended's behaviour? After privately threatening the two lovers in the strongest terms she omitted to inform her host and hostess of anything amiss and dinner that evening passed without drama. The Reverend and Sapphire were suitably subdued and I concentrated on my final preparations, reviewing my escape plans in my head while Darcy and de Lawrence monopolised the conversation.

After dinner we all settled down in the small salon for a hand of loo while Lady Boulter twittered anxiously about the size of the communal pot. To my annoyance, Mr Darcy assured her that we would play

321

for pennies only. My fingers itched with frustration as I was dealt my three cards. Here were two excessively wealthy men at the same table, willing to play for — pennies! What a lost opportunity. In the event, I was dealt a poor hand and when Lizzie led with an eight of hearts I could not follow.

I discarded my lowest card, a three of spades, and I would have rapidly lost interest in the game had I not noticed that Lady Boulter was cheating. This amused me greatly. I am sufficiently adept in the art of deception in gaming to recognise another cheat, however well they disguise their methods. Lady Boulter was not particularly adept at disguise. Mr de Lawrence shot a few sharp glances in her direction and I realised that he was also aware of the situation. Our West Indian nabob was a self made man. I wondered how he had made his fortune. Perhaps the Reverend was right after all.

By this time one of the cards in the trump suit had been played and her ladyship, having produced the highest trump, took the trick. Her glee at winning a handful of pennies was pathetic to behold. Her cheeks were flushed and her manner became arch.

"I am enjoying such good fortune, Mr Darcy," she simpered. "Perhaps we might play for higher stakes?" My brother-in-law looked at the small pile of pennies with a puzzled expression. At that moment Sapphire stood up abruptly, pleaded a headache and left the table. The Reverend and de Lawrence almost fought each other to escort her to the door. I guessed she knew of her mother's ruse and despised it. We continued to play and my lacklustre cards produced no tricks at all. I was finally "looed" to the obvious delight of Lady Boulter. I placed three pennies in the pot.

In the following double pool rounds I had better luck, eventually winning all of five pence. Lady Boulter continued to win most trumps, concealing her own cards in the folds of her flowing shawl which she wore due to her "extreme susceptibility" to the cold. Only Mr de Lawrence and I appeared to notice the deception.

Late that night, in my own rooms, I took the bold step of preparing for my flight by taking a bath. I hoped it would not have a weakening effect on my constitution. I bathed in my chemise with a sachet of almonds, pine nuts, linseed, marshmallow root and lily bulb-something the French call a *bain de modestie*. Afterwards, I recovered lying on my bed having dabbed tuberose essence liberally on my person.

Adelaide laid out a walking dress of lilac blue edged with Pomona green. One cannot be too well dressed when planning a Great Escape. I had decided that this was the moment when I would sever relations with my family, at least for some time. I was now a person of means and I intended to sink or swim by myself — with a little help from my friends. I held my destiny in my own hands as if it were a new born babe and I the midwife. In particular I shall sever all ties with Pemberley and my odious brother-in-law.

As the night wore on Adelaide and I sat around in my chamber, ill at ease, with our belongings packed at our feet. Pausing to light another candle, Adelaide smothered a cry when a large spider emerged from under a rug like a calling card from the underworld. I did not voice this gothic thought aloud for fear of unsettling my maid even more.

At a little after midnight the house seemed quiet enough. We stole through the corridors with all that we could carry. A large portmanteau had been deposited in a summerhouse on a remote part of the estate the day before. The Rev. Arbuthnot had been charged with recovering it and placing it in the chaise which he had ordered at my request. I paused for a moment to slip a letter under the door of Darcy's study. I had taken the utmost care over its composition.

My Dear Brother-in-Law,
You will receive this letter when I have left this house, I hope for the last time. I have been hated and despised while under its roof — an object of scorn to all. Now I am able to shake off the dust of Pemberley from my shoes. Thanks to a generous legacy from my late employer I am now a woman of independent means. You must know that I never had any intention of marrying the Reverend Arbuthnot but I derived great pleasure in convincing you otherwise. I am returning to the Continent to resume the life of my choice. We will be well rid of each other, I believe.
Your servant,
Lydia Wickham

As an afterthought I added my fondest love to Lizzie.

Adelaide had been able to copy a key obtained from her favourite footman and we unlocked one of the large windows opening onto the terrace. We moved swiftly down the drive to where the chaise was waiting accompanied by the Reverend who was shivering with apprehension. The man had no stomach at all for dissimulation and treachery. Lady Boulter would eat him alive. He was glad to bid us adieu. I instructed him to deny all knowledge of my flight, but I fear Darcy will easily prise the truth from him.

We were thankful to reach an inn in the nearest town where we sat up all night waiting for the early morning coach at first light. No effort was made to apprehend us on the long journey to London. I fancy that Darcy was indeed glad to be rid of me.

And so, dear reader, I took flight from these English shores once more like a wayward bird that follows its own path rather than join its fellows. As we journeyed to Paris I wondered whether I would ever have a house or even a city I could call mine. Would I be forever in transit like a ghostly portmanteau? Adelaide obviously shared my fears.

"We won't never settle, will we, madam?" I stared out of the window seeing my pale face reflected. "I truly hope we shall," I replied, but I did not convince either of us.

CHAPTER
THIRTY

Paris again

We lodged with Selena and Miles in their apartment on the charming rue St Sulpice. It was a somewhat cramped lodging for all of us but I knew I would not be staying long. I had informed the embassy of my arrival but I was sure they already knew. I did not have long to wait; within a few days while Selena and I were enjoying coffee and ices at Tortoni's, I was presented with a letter carried by my demonic shadow, Captain Marshfield. It contained my instructions. After the briefest of conversations the captain departed and I hastily scanned the note. I told Selena that it was a message from the Count who was anxious to be re-united with me.

"He asks me to leave immediately," I told her. It was almost true. The letter informed me that the Count had returned to Paris and I was to make myself known to him as soon as possible. My joy at the prospect of seeing him once more was mixed with the trepidation I felt at the task before me. Selena was aghast at the news.

"You have scarcely had time to see the sights of the city — or visit the milliners, not to mention attending a *soirée* or two."

326

"It is for the best," I assured her. "My future lies with the Count." I crossed my fingers firmly as I said this. Selena gave a cynical sniff. "You are full of moonshine, Lydia. How can your future lie with this man? You scarcely know him, and he may be married. He is also an aristocrat and a foreigner. You will be nothing but a plaything for him."

"One thing can lead to another," I replied, spooning the last of the ice-cream into my mouth while looking around the crowded café for I knew not what. The place was awash with well-dressed women and officers in uniforms of every hue. The babble of voices was so loud that Selena and I were reduced to lip reading.

"I will write to you from Vienna," I promised. "They say it is a charming city."

But we did not go to Vienna. My reunion with the Count was a rapturous one, sealed in his lodgings by an afternoon of love and the presentation of a sapphire necklace similar to the ones adorning the necks of the ladies of the night in the Palais Royal.

Selena was right, as always. I was the Count's plaything, but he was kind and attentive and generous and my task was to deceive him. In short, my family's view of me was correct. I was a dissolute woman who could be bought and sold. Even my country had purchased me for its own purposes. Once again I heard Wickham's voice in my head.

"Ten thousand pounds to make an honest woman of you."

Perhaps if Wickham had really loved me. If he had lived. I pushed these thoughts from my mind as I changed for dinner that evening — *poulet marengo* at the Café des Colonnes followed by the Paris Opera. Women have so few choices in this life and mine had been blighted by lack of money and a false husband. Yes, I admit I am rash and often foolish but I have a determination to succeed in securing the things I crave. Despite my dalliance with the Count I have not despaired of making a good marriage one day. In the meantime I would enjoy my life. If only awkward incidents would not intrude on my plans. Sighing, I followed the Count out to the carriage.

He held my hand as we lurched over the Parisian potholes, kissing my fingers and admiring my delicate oval nails.

"I cannot wait to see Vienna," I prattled, "the Hofburg and the Schonbrunn palaces, the Vienna Woods and the music. I hear that Schubert's melodies are divine." I had been reading all I could on the subject. The Count released my hand.

"We are not going to Vienna immediately. I have an invitation to visit the Princess of Wales in Italy, at her villa in Pesaro. You may accompany me if you will."

"Italy?" I had a vision of the mildewed canals of Venice. "I hear it is very unhealthy in the summer."

"Nonsense!" he chuckled. "The Villa Caprile is perched on a hill overlooking the gulf. I believe it is a most healthful spot. It is a great honour; as an Englishwoman I thought you would be overwhelmed." I gulped, thinking of my instructions from the embassy.

"Yes, yes, of course," I replied hastily, "although the princess is not highly regarded in England . . . but the people love her." I thought this statement covered all eventualities.

The carriage drew up at the opera house and I fantasised briefly about my own carriage. It would be lacquered jet black with my monogram in gold, upholstered in aubergine leather with cushions of matching silk. Perhaps the Count could be persuaded to pay for it.

The embassy would be delighted to know that I was to visit the Princess of Wales, but of course they already knew and I soon received another note detailing how I was to send dispatches back from Pesaro. A local man who supplied the villa with eggs would be my courier.

The Count arranged for me to replenish my wardrobe before we left for Italy. Selena fulfilled her desire to drag me around the milliners of the city. The modistes of Paris were on a level far above their English counterparts. I chose a lilac pelisse worn with dove grey kid gloves and grey satin slippers, a black lace parasol, a straw bonnet trimmed with cherries and leaves, a gown all of palest grey lace over silver, and yards and yards of muslin which is worn everywhere here, often over a scarlet silk underskirt. I had my monogram embroidered on parasols, gloves and reticules in gold thread and raised white threadwork. The Count never questioned the cost of all this finery and I repaid him in the time-honoured way.

"I must have a fur muff," I told my friend, "what shall it be — seal or chinchilla?" It was now spring officially, but I satisfied my lust for fur with a large chinchilla creation. I liked it above everything.

In between bouts of shopping Selena and I ate dainty coloured macaroons and sipped *café au lait* in the Palais Royal while discussing our futures. Earlier I had introduced the Count to my friends and he had been courtesy itself. He had discussed Waterloo and the fate of Napoleon with Miles. The two men agreed that the little corporal had fared very well.

"He should have been shot," declared the Count.

"Yes," agreed Miles, "the Russians would have shot him."

It was only when the Count casually mentioned the number of duels he had fought in Paris that Miles looked somewhat disturbed. When the Count had departed Miles gave his opinion. "The fellow must have rats in the garret. Four duels! He is a mad man . . . damme if he ain't!"

Selena advised her husband to avoid any situation where he might be challenged. "What would become of me with Lydia gone away and you dead in the Bois de Boulogne?"

Miles promised to do his best but duelling continued to be the main pastime of the men in Paris. The remnants of Napoleon's army continued to challenge everyone at the slightest opportunity, especially English officers.

In the meantime my wardrobe continued to expand and I familiarised myself with the Count's well-muscled body with its fine silky hairs. He was an athletic and considerate lover but given to petulance when fully dressed. I observed that he disliked sudden changes to his daily routine. His manservant suffered the brunt of this but I took care not to give him grounds for complaint.

We embarked on the journey to Italy, splendidly attired on my part, but with a sense of foreboding curdling my stomach. Over confidence in my abilities as a spy alternated with moments of sheer terror. After all, I told myself, the Prince Regent had not been difficult to manage and his estranged wife was said to be terminally stupid. It would surely be possible to obtain some information to send back to the embassy. On the other hand, the Count was another bowl of schnitzel entirely — or whatever they ate in Vienna.

CHAPTER
THIRTY-ONE

Pesaro, Italy

The journey to Pesaro passed well enough. I was surprised that the springs of the coach were not etched on my rear, I had made so many journeys across the continent in the past year.

The Villa Caprile was a delightfully elegant house on the San Bartolo hill above Pesaro. It had three tiers of terraces adorned with box hedging and fruit trees, a grand frescoed salon which stretched the entire length of the house and two tiers of apartments surmounted by a cupola. Little pathways led from the house across the surrounding hills linking it to nearby villas. The whole aspect was charmingly Mediterranean and as satisfyingly different from England as could be.

The princess greeted the Count effusively and as I sank into a deep curtsey she assured me in her fractured English that she was delighted to welcome me to her home. I doubt she would have welcomed me had she known that I had slept with her husband.

I soon discovered that I was one of only two representatives of Britannia at the villa. Most of the princess's English staff had departed due to a combination of despair and frustration. As they were responsible for providing evidence of her bad behaviour to furnish the Prince Regent with divorce proceedings, this was an unfortunate situation. I was now the only person able to provide the information because her English secretary, Joseph Hownam, refused out of loyalty to say anything detrimental about his employer.

The household presently consisted of low class Italians led by the man called Pergami who served as chamberlain, bodyguard and lover to Princess Caroline. Various members of his family attended to the cooking, the laundry and the buying of provisions. The princess herself was a small, dumpy, Germanic woman with very little education or polish, although she played the pianoforte very well. I christened her the musical dumpling.

We had barely settled ourselves into the guest apartment when we saw evidence of the princess's eccentric behaviour. After having disgraced herself in Milan and Rome where she had thrown wild parties and brought a donkey to the dinner table crowned with roses, she had resolved to lead a more bucolic lifestyle. Her new passion was for amateur theatricals using the small, open air theatre in the grounds of the villa.

"You must meet the neighbours, my dears," she declared. "The area is a paradise of poets and artists. We shall give delightful performances in our little theatre. There will be parts for all of you."

The Count looked most uneasy at this announcement. He was trying to come to terms with the presence of Pergami at the dinner table. The princess had given him the title of Barone. The Count decided to ignore the man and instructed me to do likewise.

"I think the Count could only be relied on for military parts," I assured our hostess. "He is uncomfortable out of uniform." This was said jokingly but the princess did not grasp this.

"Oh dear, I intend to give extracts from French plays, starting with Racine's *Phèdre*." I wondered if she saw the Count as an oversized Cupid with his blond hair and blue eyes.

"You will come down to bathe with me in the morning?" Princess Caroline addressed me directly. I was not sure whether this was an invitation or a command.

"I would be delighted, your highness," I murmured, although I dislike immersing myself in salt water, so bad for the skin. At least the princess's hygiene habits had improved in recent years.

When we left for the bay early on the following morning I spied the Count riding off in the direction of the cardinal's villa. Cardinal Albani was the princess's most important neighbour. I wondered if the Count intended to compare notes with him.

As we basked on the deck of the little boat the princess suddenly turned to me. "The Prince of Wales is a very poor lover." My eyes were closed and I was caught off guard. "I know," I replied languidly then added, "that is, I have heard rumours to that effect."

She nodded. "He is a disgrace as a husband, a lover and a prince, but when my daughter is queen I shall return to England in triumph."

334

"In the meantime," I ventured, "your life here is a very pleasant one. Could you bear to leave it?" The princess looked astounded,

"I am the Princess of Wales and I shall be the mother of a queen. What could be greater than that?" Did the poor woman not realise that Prinny intended to divorce her as soon as he had sufficient ammunition? Mindful of this I tried to turn the conversation to Pergami. The princess sang his praises like a lark. He was the most faithful retainer and bodyguard. He could take over all duties if necessary but at the moment Captain Olivieri was her equerry and her Italian secretary.

"Captain Olivieri?" I enquired. "I do not believe I have met him."

"He is away in Milan on a commission for me but he will return in a few days. He is most dashing and handsome." She leaned forward confidentially. "Tell me my dear, is the Count a good lover?" I found my mouth opening and shutting like a fish in astonishment. One did not expect such coarseness from a princess. Seeing my expression she shrieked with laughter, "Come, come, you are no blushing virgin. You may confide in me."

I smiled weakly, suddenly feeling very warm although I was only partly clothed. I was supposed to extract this type of information from her, not volunteer it. I made an evasive reply but she had moved on to another topic.

"On our wedding night the prince was very drunk on brandy and spent the entire night collapsed in the fireplace. It was not what I had been led to expect." I could picture the scene in my mind's eye only too clearly. Mr Wickham had often returned from carousing with his fellow officers too drunk to discharge his marital duties.

Later, I asked Adelaide about Pergami. She had already acquired a smattering of Italian and she was able to listen in to the kitchen talk.

"Of course he's her lover; Pergami's mother boasts of it. It's the only remark she ever makes. I wouldn't be surprised if that Captain Olivieri obliges her as well. They say she's insatiable."

I lost no time in approaching Hownam again. The egg man courier was due at the villa in a few days and I would be expected to deliver a report. The quiet naval officer was as usual writing letters to England on behalf of his mistress. He twisted his hands and looked miserable when I asked him directly about Pergami.

"You must decide for yourself. I cannot betray her . . . I owe everything to her generosity. I am the son of a footman, did you know that? The princess paid for my education and obtained a commission for me." I felt for the unfortunate man. We were both in a wretched position and the cause of it all was lack of money, the curse of humanity.

"I have been tasked with sending information to England," I confessed.

He shrugged. "Everyone in this place is spying for someone." He also confessed that he was dying of boredom and was unlikely to stay more than a few months at the villa. "I have no life here at all and I must return to England, but I will not give evidence against her, do with me what they will." I had to admire his loyalty, however misplaced. The musical dumpling was not a figure to inspire devotion or so it seemed to me, but I was not in her debt.

It occurred to me that Hownam might know something about the mystery surrounding Von Mecks and the Cambridge emeralds. When I taxed him with this he admitted that he had been in the princess's service when Von Mecks arrived.

"He was a plausible fellow, handsome, aristocratic and continental — just the type guaranteed to appeal to the Princess of Wales. However, he acted in a low and underhand manner. I was powerless to prevent the loss of the emeralds. He went off with them like a thief in the night."

"Surely it was all above board?" I remarked. "The Prince Regent had a right to ask for them. They were to be given to the Princess Charlotte, were they not?" Hownam nodded in disgust. He appeared to be taking the whole matter personally.

"The princess was perfectly agreeable to hand over the jewels, especially after Von Mecks had buttered her up and flattered her to death, but that was not good enough."

"Yes?" I enquired. Hownam snorted.

"What did he do? He stole the jewels from the princess's chamber and made off in the night. Obviously, he had confederates and fast horses waiting across the Continent. The whole affair was arranged by the British Government in a disgraceful manner."

None of this, however, explained the murder.

"You know how Von Mecks met his death?" I asked. Hownam shuddered and turned away.

"I know nothing of these sordid affairs. I simply serve the princess." I reflected that he could hardly be as innocent as he pretended.

"Does the name of Getheridge mean anything to you?" He shook his head, made an excuse and left the room.

Visions of Captain Marshfield arriving at the villa to interrogate me filled me with dread. I tried to persuade the Count to take me to visit the cardinal but he was shocked, saying that I was not a Catholic and one could not introduce one's mistress to a cardinal. I refrained from commenting on this. I knew that many cardinals in Italy kept mistresses of their own, although probably not Protestant ones.

I retreated to the library and attempted to write my report. After some thought, I began my task, resolving to fill up the pages with news of the amateur dramatics. Let Marshfield make what he could of that.

The egg man's name was Enrico. I watched him wending his way up the drive with his donkey and panniers filled with new laid offerings. I slipped out to meet him and handed over the document. I soon realised, after a few minutes of conversation and polite chitchat (enquiries after my health and the health of the villa's inhabitants, and so forth) that he already knew everything that went on in the royal household and could have written a much better report than I, had he been able to write. He handed me the box of eggs after outlining the situation as he saw it.

"So you are telling me that Captain Olivieri is spying for the cardinal?" I asked.

"Si, signora, the cardinal pay him well, so he tell me. He pay *mooch* better than the *Eenglish*." A note of reproach entered his voice which I ignored.

"But why would the cardinal want to spy on the Princess of Wales?" I continued. Enrico gave an expansive Italian shrug.

"I done know, maybe the cardinal do it for the Pope."

"For the Pope?" I spluttered. "That is ridiculous. What has the Princess of Wales to do with the Pope?" He gave me a pitying look as he loaded up his donkey with the empty panniers. "She ees in Italy; anyway the Vatican done need no excuse. It like to spy on everyone."

I stood in a patch of brilliant sunlight carefully balancing the eggs in both hands conscious of the ridiculous figure I must present as I digested this information. Enrico, despairing of prising any more money from the British government through me, prepared to take his leave. He patted his leather-clad chest to ensure that my letter was safe and moved off with the donkey.

"Wait!" I called in a low voice. "Are you sure there is no-one else in the villa spying for anyone?" Enrico stopped and stroked his bristly chin, "*We-ell*, I am reporting on the villa to the chief of police in Pesaro. He also pay me better than the *Eenglish*."

"You are a double agent!" I cried. "That is despicable." He shrugged again. "It ees the same information. I am just, how you say, passing it around.

The chief wants to know what goes on in his area and I have six children to feed."

After he had gone I sat on a low stone wall still clutching the eggs. I felt almost sorry for the princess, spied on by her husband's minions, the Austrians, the police and the Catholic Church. If only she knew. But I conjectured that she would care little. The musical dumpling went her own way, regardless. I wondered what the Pope and the Austrian Emperor would make of the donkey at the dinner table and the vision of an ageing princess wearing short skirts and pink ostrich feathers. Perhaps Louise Demont, the princess's Swiss maid, was spying for the Russians just to complete the circle.

At that moment Pergami's brother, Luigi, emerged from the kitchen and silently removed the eggs from my hands. In the distance the sound of pistol shots disturbed the peace and little puffs of white smoke rose into the azure sky. Pergami and his cronies were hunting again.

I watched as the princess's carriage rattled down the drive. She leaned from the window waving a bag of gold in each hand to be scattered among the undeserving poor of the district at the British taxpayers' expense.

CHAPTER
THIRTY-TWO

When the princess returned for lunch she was accompanied by a military man whose headdress sported improbable black cock-feathers. He bent over my hand with much flim-flammery in the Italian manner. This man was Captain Olivieri, the Italian equerry described as handsome and dashing by his employer. In truth he was flashing-eyed and handsome enough in a Latin way but I preferred the Count's blond, northern restraint.

The musical dumpling was determined to make her lovers jealous. With a sideways smirk at the scowling Pergami she announced that Olivieri would play the part of Hippolytus, Phèdre's stepson and the object of her incestuous passion. ("Because he is so young and handsome," she explained.) Pergami was struck dumb by this which was fortunate as he generally gabbled while he gobbled.

I dreaded to think what the Count would say about his starring role. In fact, he resolutely declined to play Theseus and lapsed into a fit of the sullens until the part was given to the local poet. The Count was in disgrace for a few hours until he mollified the dumpling with sweetmeats.

We were coaxed, bullied and chivied into playing scenes from this horrid and violent tragedy. Indeed, the ancient Greeks appeared to be a thoroughly nasty and unnatural people, which is probably why they have not survived to the present day. Various people from the surrounding villas had been persuaded to watch, including the chief of police and the Cardinal.

Unfortunately the princess, with her small, dumpy figure, was not convincing as a Greek tragedienne. It was difficult to keep a straight face as she emoted among the box hedges.

"Look at me. See a woman in frenzy! I am in love," she shrilled in heavily accented French. Her encounters with Captain Olivieri as Hippolytus caused him to start backwards in genuine shock as she moaned about the flame hidden in her veins. We all recited our parts in French overlaid with German, Italian and English accents. My father and Lizzie would have been appalled. I noticed Adelaide doubled up with mirth behind a bush, even though she could not understand a word.

Princess Caroline threw herself about the stage so violently at the end of the scene that several servants rushed to pick her up, which created something of an anticlimax. Later, as we drank champagne in the salon, she exclaimed, "I have never enjoyed myself so much!" The cardinal remarked that it had been one of the most original versions of Racine he had ever watched.

The theatricals were the high point of our stay in Pesaro. Otherwise I had very little to report to my masters. Once it was established that Pergami shared the princess's bed and the prevalence of spies at the villa, it was simply a round of swimming, dinner parties and walking in the grounds. Sometimes I was asked to read to our hostess in English so that she could improve her eccentric grasp of the language.

The Count became increasingly sullen in his demeanour as the summer wore on. One afternoon when we had been taking our afternoon rest, matters came to a head. Usually, this interlude led to a great deal of amorous dalliance, but of late the Count preferred to rest on a chaise longue with his limbs splayed out in an attitude of irritated affectation.

His English nightgown of cream flannel was marked to give an imitation of ermine. This, together with cream linen Cossack pantaloons, topped with his matching hair, gave him the appearance of a very large Persian cat — an irritated Persian cat.

"Your ardour has cooled somewhat of late. I realise that I am merely a plaything to you but in that event a little more play would not come amiss." I adjusted my white lace tea gown in a manner I hoped was languorous and inviting.

"Englishwomen talk too much," was the rejoinder. "In my country women know when to remain silent."

"Like the Princess Caroline, I suppose."

"Royalty does not have to follow the rules of etiquette," he snapped. Indeed not, especially if they were German, I thought. He swore a Germanic oath and laid flat once more with a discontented sigh.

My own discontent bubbled to the surface and I returned to the attack.

"Why do you chide me, sir? You are not my mother and of late you have not been my lover. I wish only to know where I am placed in your life — and in this household." The Count sighed again and looked at me for a moment.

"You know your position in this household, Lydia. We are all here to entertain the princess. She seems to be greatly taken with you."

"And my position with you?" There was another lengthy pause.

"Perhaps we should not be under the same roof. Love and attraction have nothing to do with living together." I answered in a shriller tone this time, bitterness creeping in to my voice.

"I had not thought that love had anything to do with our arrangement. You no longer covet what is easily obtained, I see. The thrill is in the chase, is it not?"

He shrugged. "Men are made that way, my dear."

After he left me I attempted to restore my spirits by painting my toenails gold — a trick I had learned in Paris. I knew this was extremely fast behaviour but the effect was delightful. Later, I exhibited my gilded extremities to the princess as we sipped orange pekoe. She was entranced and insisted on having her own toes similarly adorned. Her maid, Louise, obliged, throwing me evil looks and muttering that only women of a certain kind did such things, and it was not fitting for a royal lady. This made the princess hoot with laughter.

By early July the Count was spending more and more time away from me and I had somehow fallen into the role of companion/entertainer/lady in waiting to the princess. He made frequent trips on horseback to the cardinal and other officials in the area on what he said were "Austrian matters" and nothing to do with me.

His attitude to me remained indifferent although he was polite at all times. He was completely out of patience with the Italians at the villa, but the princess found no fault in him. She herself was in high spirits: her daughter Princess Charlotte was with child and Princess Caroline eagerly anticipated being a grandmother.

My reports to Captain Marshfield and the embassy were merely gossip about our social activities but messages sent to me via the egg courier indicated that they were satisfactory.

The Count had been hinting for some days that we would be leaving Pesaro shortly. He needed to return to Vienna and I wished to go back to Paris. I did not anticipate any objections from my lukewarm lover. However, the end of our sojourn at the Villa Caprile came about in rather unfortunate circumstances.

"Pray entertain me!" commanded our royal hostess after dinner one evening. She was bored with music and charades and wished for something new. With the impetuosity for which I am noted I immediately offered to teach everyone a game called bullet pudding which we often played at home.

"You must have a large dish filled with a floury pudding," I explained. "The pudding is made up into a peak and a bullet placed on top. Each person cuts a slice and whoever is cutting when the bullet falls must poke about with their nose and chin until they find it. Hands cannot be used. Of course, everyone becomes covered in flour, unable to speak for fear of choking. It is most uproarious."

The Count and the Italians appeared mystified by my account but the princess shrieked with laughter and entered the game with gusto. We were soon covered with flour and howling like banshees while the princess uttered a great many profanities. People started to choke which she found hilarious. I was also carried away with merriment and we both enjoyed ourselves thoroughly. It was only after we had spruced up and returned to the salon that I realised the atmosphere had become somewhat frigid. The Count took me aside and said my behaviour was eccentric and disgraceful. I almost wept with frustration. He had positively *praised* my high spirits when we first met.

At dinner that evening the Count made an announcement. "We must return to Vienna forthwith, your highness. I hope you will give us leave to say goodbye."

"Could not Mrs Wickham remain with me for a while?" she replied. "Her company is so jolly for me." I was stunned to hear the Count say quite sharply that this was impossible.

"She is needed in Vienna." This was so obviously untrue that a long moment of silence followed, until Princess Caroline shrugged and said something in German that I did not understand. She often spoke with the Count in that language. It might have been more effective if a German speaker had been sent to spy on her.

346

"I *will* return to Paris!" I said furiously when we were alone in our chamber. "I wish to see my friends and you are completely indifferent to my presence." To my astonishment the Count became very contrite and begged me to accompany him, paying me more attention during the next twenty-four hours than I had received in weeks.

White roses were laid on the steps of the coach as we left and Prince Caroline waved from her balcony. I would never see the musical dumpling again. Like so many others she came and went in my life in a short time, but I regretted being forced to spy on her. She had so much in common with her husband that I cannot understand why they were not suited.

The princess was aware of her popularity in England claiming that the people loved her because she supplied them with gin and gingerbread on festive occasions. I was saddened to hear later in that year of the death of Princess Charlotte in childbirth. Now her mother would never have a grandchild and she would never be queen.

As the coach trundled across Italy once more the Count gave me a number of reasons why I should stay with him.

"You know we could not remain at the villa indefinitely. The summer is almost over and I have duties to attend to." I was not convinced.

"I am aware of that," I replied, "but I cannot see why you need my presence in view of your earlier remarks. It would be better if we parted as soon as possible." Impulsively, I leaned forward and placed my hand on his immaculate knee. "If we are no longer content with each other why prolong the agony, my dear? We will part and remember happier times — unless you plan to make an honest woman of me by proposing marriage?" I threw in this remark in an arch manner, just for the pleasure of seeing his reaction. It was not quite what I expected.

He removed my hand with an impatient gesture. "That would not be possible. I have a wife already."

I gasped and flushed with fury. Such deceit! Men are deceivers all.

When I had controlled myself a little I remarked in a low voice, "It is strange that you have never mentioned this before, sir. I had taken you for a gentleman." It was the Count's turn to appear flushed and furious.

"If you were a man I would call you out for that remark, my dear."

"If I were a man I would accept the challenge gladly. Now, kindly set me down in the next town. Our association is at an end." The Count ignored my request.

"It is essential that you return with me, at least for a while. I will explain my reasons in due course." I regarded him through narrowed eyes as a thought struck me.

"Are your reasons anything to do with a certain Captain Marshfield?" His expression did not change but he adopted a guarded tone.

"Marshfield . . . what do you know of Marshfield?"

More than you think, I told myself. "We have met socially on occasion," I said.

348

"I do not know this Marshfield," the Count said staring fixedly out of the window. As it was obvious that we were both lying, I gave up and attempted to read. I do not know why men bother with deceit when women are wise to the smallest signs.

Miles had once told me that all the countries of Europe spied on each other and sometimes exchanged information. It seemed very schoolboyish behaviour to me.

At this point my companion decided to tell me the truth. It appeared that we were not bound for Vienna at all.

"You lied to the Princess of Wales," I reminded him.

He shrugged. "It could not be helped. I have an important mission here in Italy that concerns you directly." My stomach churned with rage and apprehension. Would there ever be an end to these assignments? I returned to the fray.

"Do my wishes mean nothing to you, sir? I *need* to return to my friends in Paris."

The Count would not hear of this. His conscience appeared to be making him uncomfortable. With a sudden change of mood he smiled insincerely. "I wish to be of real service to you, my dear. I can arrange a situation for you that will advance your standing considerably."

A situation . . . what could he mean, surely not a position as companion to a broken down Italian dowager instead of a Bathonian? No, that would not advance my standing in any way. Did he intend to pass me on to a fellow aristocrat? Such things were not

349

unknown. Filled with curiosity and foreboding I listened reluctantly as he continued, my mind set on writing to Miles and Selena.

I would return to Paris with or without the Count's permission.

I became aware that he had managed to open a bottle of champagne that he was endeavouring to spill into two glasses as the coach lurched along.

"I owe you an apology, dear Lydia. I am distraught that our association has become, shall we say, detached. I invited you to join me and I must in some way repay you." His distress did not seem at all apparent to me.

"What can you mean? I do not require you to offer me money," I said stiffly, although I am never averse to such suggestions. I accepted the glass of champagne.

"I am offering you a new life, my dear — in royal circles." My eyes widened.

"Royal circles?" I echoed, remembering my previous forays in such places.

"The Emperor's daughter, Archduchess Leopoldina, is to be married to the heir to the Portuguese throne, Dom Pedro. She has already left Vienna and is now waiting in Genoa with her entourage, ready to embark on a Portuguese ship. She requires an English speaking lady-in-waiting. I have recommended you. You will be presented to her in a few days. I am sure she will find you satisfactory."

I felt quite dizzy at this news and quaffed another glass of champagne. "You are suggesting, then, that I leave for Portugal?"

The Count fidgeted a little and looked embarrassed. "Wait until you have met the Archduchess and then decide. It would be a golden opportunity for you to move in the highest circles and you will certainly escape the tedium of my company." He gave a strained smile and gazed out of the window.

I was utterly discombobulated by this, as Adelaide would say. My mind was disarrayed — did I want to enter royal circles officially? My previous encounters with both the Prince Regent and his wife had been eccentric and unofficial to say the least. Perhaps the Count was right and this could be a golden opportunity for me. How I would enjoy informing my relatives of my new status. On the other hand, the Count may have some nefarious purpose in mind. One cannot trust anyone, least of all men.

I mused on this as we travelled on to Genoa where I was deposited in an apartment in another crumbling palazzo. The Count would call for me when I was summoned to see the Archduchess. Hastily, I considered my wardrobe and my toilette. In order to look my best I instructed Adelaide to wash and anoint my hair. First of all she applied the whisked up whites of six eggs and I sat patiently until the concoction had dried. Then she removed the egg white and washed my locks in rum and rosewater so that my chestnut curls appeared glossy and sweet smelling.

Then there was the question of what I should wear. What would be suitable in the circumstances? I decided on pale grey silk edged with grey velvet and a black straw bonnet. I would dearly have loved to take the chinchilla muff but it did not seem appropriate. I wore Getheridge's little gold watch for luck.

As we drove to the palace I was so nervous I clasped my gloved hands tightly to prevent them from shaking. Clutching my best parasol with the ivory handle I followed the Count to the princess's apartments. As I curtsied to her the Count made a long introduction in German. If only I could understand what was being said.

Dona Leopoldina, as she will be known, was fair, composed, intelligent and gracious. She addressed me in perfect English with great warmth, inviting me to sit. We talked about England, my home county and my family. She commiserated with me over my husband's death at Waterloo.

"How proud you must be."

"Indeed ma'am!" I replied with feeling.

"I think we will deal very well together, Mrs Wickham, do you not agree? Will you accompany me? It will be for two years, after that you may reconsider your position." I found that I was grinning foolishly and agreeing enthusiastically. What larks!

"I have always wanted to see Portugal," I remarked gaily. The princess looked puzzled and turned to the Count. "Does she not know?" The Count flushed and began to fidget.

"I may not have been completely explicit in the matter, Your Highness." Seeing my startled expression Dona Leopoldina explained. "We will not be going to Portugal. The Portuguese court removed to Brazil in its entirety ten years ago. It has remained there ever since."

She smiled at me. "It will be a great adventure for us all."

I can scarcely recall how I left the royal presence: a wave of giddiness swept over me as I toppled into a curtsey. The Count held me in an iron grip and half carried me out of the chamber. I recovered my senses in the carriage. "You traitor," I snarled, "you have sold me into service on the far side of the world!"

He started to splutter excuses but everything was becoming clear to me. I was the victim of a conspiracy between Captain Marshfield and the Count and who knew what else? I was an embarrassment, I knew too much — about Von Mecks, the emeralds, the Prince Regent and his wife, the Count, the price of fish . . .

I gasped for air and began to bawl uncontrollably, arriving at the apartment red faced and raw of throat. Adelaide attended to me as the Count drove away with my curses ringing in his ears. She waved burnt feathers under my nose and administered eau de cologne to my forehead.

"I am being sent to Brazil!" I cried. "Stay with me, Adelaide, I have no-one else."

"Where's Brazil?" she asked, "is it near Australia?" I nodded wildly.

"How long will we be at sea?"

"About three months." We both collapsed onto a sofa and sobbed.

CHAPTER
THIRTY-THREE

It was ever so, dear reader. Whenever my future appeared rosier than usual a black cloud would appear to cast its shadow over my life. In this instance the black cloud was larger than I could ever have imagined. I, poor little Lydia Marianne Bennet Wickham, who had never ventured farther than the shores of the Mediterranean, was to be cast adrift on the other side of the world. It was by no means certain that I would survive the journey to Brazil, let alone return in two years.

Of course, this sad state of affairs was due to the perfidious nature of the man . . . men with whom I had become involved. It did not seem possible that a good man would ever cross my path. I should have remembered the story of *Vancenza, Or the Dangers of Credulity*, which I read some time ago. The plight of a royal mistress in that tale should have taught me something. Perhaps I should have settled for a boring curate after all, but I had no doubt that even that arrangement would have ended in disaster.

It was a wet, cold Monday morning in my heart. Even after we collected ourselves and Adelaide urged me to look on the bright side I could not lift the weight

354

from my spirits. Details of the journey were sent to me from the palace. I needed to bring adequate clothing and other provisions for a three month journey at least, in which fresh water would be scarce and very rough weather could be expected. The ever practical Adelaide urged me to "make a run for it" to Paris but I could not in all conscience do such a thing, having given my word to a royal princess. In addition I would run straight into Captain Marshfield who would find me even if I had ventured into darkest Africa.

Of course, he knew my whereabouts exactly and I was not unduly surprised to find a messenger from the British Embassy at my door a few days later. I was more surprised when I read the letter which assured me that the fee due to me for my efforts in Italy would be held in trust for me until I returned to Europe. I tore the letter up in a fury. So they had decided to pay what was owed to me but in such a manner that I might never be able to claim it. Such perfidy. After all I had done for the Regent (in various ways). This was how patriotism was repaid by the British government.

It was more than likely that I would never return from Brazil. Apart from the immense journey there were surely all manner of dangers awaiting me in that country. The wildlife was probably beyond imagination. I recalled the strange Portuguese lord and his monkey. I was in such a fury that I could have craunched a marmoset myself at that moment. Instead, I contented myself with tearing up the Count's love letter and flinging the pieces into the gutter.

Reluctantly, we began to make preparations. I changed my small fortune from Mrs Makepiece into gold pieces for transportation in a stout chest with iron locks. I wondered if it would vanish overboard in a storm taking my security with it — or whether it would be stolen by pirates and savages.

Dona Leopoldina summoned me for another discussion about Brazil. She had read a great deal about the country and described its great beauty, its vast forests and exotic flora and fauna. The country swarmed with primitive peoples and millions of African slaves. Diamonds were to be found as easily as eggs in an English farmyard. This news comforted me a little.

"The climate is fierce and may be difficult to contend with, but we will become accustomed to it," she assured me. So far I have heard little that encourages me, except for the diamonds.

Adelaide compiled a huge laundry list. I required dozens of chemises, petticoats, stockings and other items of intimate wear, as well as yards and yards of muslin and other flimsy materials. There will apparently be little opportunity for washing clothes on the voyage, or for washing ourselves, I fear. I dared not contemplate how our basic needs would be met on board ship. In addition, Adelaide had it on good authority that Portuguese women are not acquainted with the use of tooth brushes. Their company at close quarters will be most unpleasant.

As I watched Adelaide pack supplies of Gardner's Alternative Pills against worms of all sorts, and a liberal supply of Floris's orange blossom toilet water to disguise bodily odours, my heart sank further into my boots. When would I ever wear my chinchilla muff again? It had been put into storage with many of my heavier items of clothing. My journal entries were once again lapsing into melancholia.

I was told that ginger was a sovereign remedy against sea sickness. My maid procured as much as she was able but it was barely enough to see us out of European waters. The entire ginger supply in the city had been commandeered by the Imperial party. During those last few days my only pleasure was in writing to Pemberley and Longbourn with news of my elevation into royal circles. I hoped that it would cause my brother-in-law to choke on his pheasant at the very least.

On the day before we left the city I was required to attend a service at the cathedral to bring blessings on the affianced couple. Dona Leopoldina has, naturally, never seen her future husband. Perhaps that was wisest for all concerned. Propinquity guarantees nothing. When the carriages rolled out of the palace courtyard I caught sight of the Count waving adieu with a sheepish smile on his face.

His parting gift to me was a handsome mahogany medicine chest with silver topped bottles. In the circumstances his choice showed the greatest effrontery. He obviously believed that I would not survive the journey or, at the very least, I would need all the concoctions therein as a matter of necessity: so much for erstwhile lovers.

I noted that the chest had been obtained from Savory and Moore of Bond Street, London. Adelaide and I wept when we saw the label. Oh, dear departed home! I turned away and contemplated my new duties. I was to speak only in English at all times to Dona Leopoldina. As I did not speak German I could not communicate with the other ladies in waiting. All of them were aristocrats who treated me as someone beneath their notice.

We had been obliged to wait some time in Genoa for the arrival of the Portuguese escort ships. They had been delayed by extremely bad weather at sea and rumours of an uprising in Brazil which did nothing to raise my spirits. My royal employer, however, was relentlessly optimistic, urging us all to study our Portuguese grammar books. She showed me a miniature of her bridegroom Dom Pedro. He was only eighteen and she was twenty. His appearance was certainly not handsome but she declared it "interesting". The miniature was surrounded by diamonds the size of large buttons.

When we finally boarded *Dom Joao VI*, a huge ship weighed down with many passengers and animals kept below decks, I feared it might sink in the first storm. Adelaide and I watched as the vessel pulled slowly away from Italy, heading first for Lisbon and then the New World. I was wearing a suitably funereal black damask gown with long tight sleeves of white lace with a white frill at the neck.

I had obtained a supply of new notebooks in which to record my Brazilian adventures and to while away the long voyage. I imagined this flimsy and pathetic record bobbing on the high seas after our disastrous shipwreck. Perhaps it would one day reach England where I would be remembered as a heroine by future generations. After all, I had rendered a service to my country, even if it did not compare with Wellington's. He, however, was not being banished to the other side of the world.

"Did you remember to pack the laudanum?" I asked Adelaide.

My maid had caught a glimpse of the luxurious royal suite. "Gold plate and a grand piano . . . lots of red and gold silk."

"And what of our accommodation?" I asked.

"Small," she replied.

I feel a sense of impending doom.

I gazed at the horizon wondering if I would ever see England again — or even Europe. Had I done something so terrible, so offensive to the Count that he needed to banish me to the ends of the earth — or did he genuinely believe that he was advancing my position? With such friends I had no need of enemies. If only I had not found the body of Von Mecks. All my misfortunes sprang from that event.

Adelaide rallied me as she always did. "It will be another great adventure, madam." I essayed a smile and thought of those large diamonds as the breeze ruffled my hair. It might be true, after all, but at that moment I was not greatly diverted.

After a while I sent Adelaide below to our cabin. Her cheeks were beginning to acquire a green tinge. I continued to stand at the ship's rail with the wind ruffling my skirts, staring out at the ocean and thinking melancholy thoughts. A crew member touched my shoulder and urged me to retire to my cabin.

"You will be more comfortable there, madam." I turned to face him — and found myself staring at Jerry Sartain! He was looking aggressively nautical.

"What are you doing here?" I gasped. He gave me the familiar grin.

"I am bound for Brazil, as a crew member, madam. I am sure our paths will cross frequently!"

My knees began to buckle just as the ship listed to one side and Jerry caught me in a firm grip. There was too much drama in my life and the shocks were affecting my normally placid disposition, as my readers will appreciate.

I gaped at him. "You cannot possibly be here." I may have repeated myself several times. Jerry looked disappointed.

"I had hoped for a warmer reception from you, my love. You have so often told me of your affection for me."

Various scenes passed before my mind's eye in rapid succession. My hopefully rosy, royal future grew decidedly overcast. If my association with a humble crew member/outlaw became known . . . well, it must be avoided. But how, in the close confines of the ship? Conscious of possible prying eyes, I threw off Jerry's restraining arm.

"It is imperative that you do not recognise or speak to me in public," I whispered, urgently. I am a lady-in-waiting to Princess Leopoldina. All will be lost if you persist."

Jerry picked up a coiled rope lying conveniently nearby and resumed his nautical persona.

"You have done well for yourself, my love. I can see that my presence is unwelcome to you. So much for the constancy of the heart." He gave me a speaking look and turned away.

This man could play upon my heartstrings like a consummate harpist.

"I did not mean to be harsh," I pleaded. "My feelings for you are unchanged, but it will not advance either of us if we are discovered." Another thought occurred to me. "How were you able to join this ship's crew? You have no nautical skills — have you?" Jerry's face darkened. He returned the coiled rope to the deck and kicked it.

"I am not here by choice, I assure you. Those rogues on the Yankee ship played me false."

I raised my eyebrows as he hurriedly described his adventures. Unable to restrain his criminal urges, Jerry had inveigled the crew of the *Pride of Boston* into card games, and was discovered cheating. The enraged crew set him ashore at the last port before they crossed the Atlantic. "I was stranded in the Azores and forced to sign on to any ship that was passing. I had to offer a sea captain those splendid Hessian boots of yours in order to be taken to Lisbon. There I was offered a place on this vessel. At least it is heading for the New World, even if further south than I anticipated."

"What will you do in Brazil?" He grinned.

"Jump ship! Perhaps you can find me a position in the royal household? Of course, I plan to reach New York eventually." My heart sank as I explained that I was bound to my post for two years. Jerry did not seem at all downcast. "What adventures we may have, my love." He picked up the rope again and walked off with a jaunty step. It was just as well that he did not know of the diamond situation in Brazil.

I was quite sure that Jerry would inveigle himself into the Portuguese royal household. After all, he was able to say truthfully that he had served the Prince of Wales. It would be months before any checks could be made, and what havoc he might cause in that time . . . What part would I be forced to play in his schemes? If only I could control my feelings for this handsome wretch. I recalled how fit and inviting he had looked in his sailor's outfit. This led me to remember our moments in the Assembly Rooms in Bath. I was forced to grip the handrail of the ship in order to gain control of my wilder emotions.

When I had recovered myself somewhat I made my way below deck to our cramped quarters. I informed Adelaide of Jerry's presence on board but she was lying on her narrow berth groaning quietly and I do not think my words made any impact.

I straightened my gown, smoothed my hair and prepared to attend the princess. As I made my way to her stateroom I was almost thrown to the floor by the listing of the ship. Various shrieks and moans emanated from behind closed doors. I found Dona Leopoldina upright and alert.

"You and I are the only resolute passengers aboard this ship, Mrs Wickham."

I curtsied gratefully. Interesting times lay ahead.

362

Also available in ISIS Large Print:

Perdita

Joan Smith

Governess Moira Greenwood's beautiful young charge, Perdita Brodie, is a high-spirited chit. Indeed, she rebels against her stepmama's choice of mate and manages to get Moira and herself positions in a not-quite-shabby travelling acting troupe.

While Moira cooks, her lovely cousin sings, attracting the very insistent attentions of the cold, handsome rakehell Lord Stornaway — who takes the pair for lightskirts!

Although Moira explains the truth, the self-satisfied lord believes not a word; he's positive the two are ladies of ill repute. Moira finds him the most rude, uncivil of men and tells him so. Still, there is something about him she can't quite define that is not completely loathsome . . .

ISBN 978-0-7531-8294-9 (hb)
ISBN 978-0-7531-8295-6 (pb)

A Rose for Virtue

Norah Lofts

The post-Revolution years saw France in a state of flux, with the balance of power shifting back to the bourgeoisie. No-one's rise to power was more meteoric than that of the successful young general, Napoleon Bonaparte.

Hortense Beauharnais finds herself rubbing shoulders with royalty as her mother remarries to become Bonaparte's wife. As Napoleon struggles for power on the battlefields of Europe, so Hortense charts her way through the French court — a chessboard world where the motives are jealousy and greed and the prizes are thrones of conquered countries.

Despite attempts to retain her individuality, Hortense finds herself married to Napoleon's brother Louis, but her heart is with Charles de Flahaut, a gallant young officer. Unwilling to cross her stepfather, Hortense must wait and see if time will take her to her lover.

ISBN 978-0-7531-8116-4 (hb)
ISBN 978-0-7531-8117-1 (pb)

Lord Rayven's Revenge

Trisha Ashley

Alys Weston secretly writes Gothic novels, while her widowed father drinks away her tiny inheritance. After a disillusioning early morning encounter with the rakish Lord Rayven in Harrogate — in which he came off the worst — she is quite resigned to being a spinster.

Several years later she meets him again in London and he makes it clear that he has not forgotten her — indeed, he dogs her footsteps. But is it revenge, or some other reason? Is he the hero or villain of the piece?

As Alys becomes unwittingly embroiled in the dark and dangerous rites of a hell-fire club, her very life could hang on the answer . . .

ISBN 978-0-7531-8110-2 (hb)
ISBN 978-0-7531-8111-9 (pb)

Me and Mr Darcy

Alexandra Potter

Every girl is looking for their Mr Darcy . . .

Emily Albright is a hopeless romantic. The manager of a quirky bookshop in New York, she loves nothing more than curling up with a good book. And, disillusioned with modern-day love, she seeks solace by thinking about the romantic heroes in literature — particularly witty, handsome Mr Darcy.

So when she spots an ad for a specialist book tour exploring the world of Jane Austen in the English countryside, she books it on impulse. Arriving in England a few days later, she discovers her tour is full of old women, and one man. Spike is a foul-tempered journalist who's been sent by his magazine editor because of a recent poll naming Mr Darcy as the man most women would like to go on a date with.

It's every woman's fantasy. Until Emily walks into a room and finds herself face-to-face with Darcy himself. And it suddenly becomes one woman's reality . . .

ISBN 978-0-7531-7954-3 (hb)
ISBN 978-0-7531-7955-0 (pb)

Royal Escape

Georgette Heyer

Dispossessed of crown and kingdom, crushed and routed at the grim Battle of Worcester, the young Charles II is forced to flee for his life. Out of the heat of battle, the outlaw King and his tiny party must journey across Cromwell's England to a Channel port and a ship bound for France and safety.

But the King, with his love of adventure, his irrepressible humour and his unmistakeable looks, is no easy man to hide . . .

ISBN 978-0-7531-7690-0 (hb)
ISBN 978-0-7531-7691-7 (pb)

ISIS publish a wide range of books in large print, from fiction to biography. Any suggestions for books you would like to see in large print or audio are always welcome. Please send to the Editorial Department at:

ISIS Publishing Limited
7 Centremead
Osney Mead
Oxford OX2 0ES

A full list of titles is available free of charge from:

Ulverscroft Large Print Books Limited

(UK)
The Green
Bradgate Road, Anstey
Leicester LE7 7FU
Tel: (0116) 236 4325

(Australia)
P.O. Box 314
St Leonards
NSW 1590
Tel: (02) 9436 2622

(USA)
P.O. Box 1230
West Seneca
N.Y. 14224-1230
Tel: (716) 674 4270

(Canada)
P.O. Box 80038
Burlington
Ontario L7L 6B1
Tel: (905) 637 8734

(New Zealand)
P.O. Box 456
Feilding
Tel: (06) 323 6828

Details of **ISIS** complete and unabridged audio books are also available from these offices. Alternatively, contact your local library for details of their collection of **ISIS** large print and unabridged audio books.